Dear Aunt Vicki,
I hope you enjoy my book!
Love, Your Neice
Elga Wood

Crisis of Faith

Crisis of Faith

Eliza Wood

POMEGRANATE
FREE PRESS

Crisis of Faith By Eliza Wood

Library of Congress Case #1-706395231
Registration Number / Date: TXu001785603 / 2012-01-04

Kaye & Mills
8840 Wilshire Boulevard, Third Floor
Beverly Hills, CA 90211-2606

Media Inquiries:
STRATEGIES Public Relations
ATTN: PR Department
P.O. Box 178122
San Diego, CA 92177

Published by Pomegranate Free Press

First Printing October, 2012

ISBN: 978-1-938341-01-4

Cover Design: Monkey C Media
Interior Design: GKS Creative
Editor: Shelley Chung

Printed in the United States of America

POMEGRANATE
FREE PRESS

Dedication

This book is dedicated to my family,
who supported the effort from start to finish.

And to the brave readers, for considering my points,
especially to those who develop the courage
to question faith for themselves.

ACKNOWLEDGMENTS

Very special thanks to my amazing husband, David, for encouragement.

To my devoted mother, Lillian, for patience.

To my sharp Aunt Beepsie, for keen insights.

To my father, Peter, for faith.

To two of the best kids in the world.

To my business advisor, Jared Kuritz, for his magical expertise.

To my friend, Hollywood director B. C., for that Hollywood edge.

PROLOGUE

White House Press Room, Washington, D.C.

"GOOD EVENING.

"Today, our religious freedom came under attack. This morning's deadly terrorist act in lower Manhattan, at the site of a proposed mosque, was a shameful and cowardly display of intolerance by a group of religious fanatics who would call themselves Christians. Today's victims were a group of young women, some of them holding their babies, who were attending a meeting on how to organize service efforts in their community. When I took office, I asked every American to step up and perform community service, and that is what these women died doing. These were American lives lost.

"Today's acts of murder were intended to frighten our non-Christian communities, and force them into chaos and retreat. But they have failed. Our country is built on the strength of our diversity. It was a Jewish financier in Philadelphia, named Haym Salomon, who funded the completion of the Revolutionary War. He never asked for repayment from our early debt-ridden government. We are a nation of many faiths. We always have been.

"A search is underway for those who were behind this

act. I have marshalled the full resources of our agencies of intelligence and law enforcement to identify those responsible and to bring them to justice. We will make no distinction between the people who committed these crimes and those who hide or harbor them.

"From the early days of the forced conversions of the Native Americans, to the Ku Klux Klan's intent on reestablishing Protestant Christian values in America by any means possible —even citing their belief that Jesus was the first Klansman— radicals have continued to draw much support from their claims that religion justifies violence.

"Because we are a free country, we allow groups to meet. But today in our great country, something changed. Groups using religious ideology to justify violence and murder are hereby put on high alert. We've had Soldiers of God attacks against abortion clinics and doctors across the United States. The Christ Image Movement, the Christian Movement of America, the Lambs of the Lord, the Brotherhood of God, the Armed Militia of Christ or any other member organization with a violent, religious-based ideology will either change or desist.

"Tonight, I ask for your participation in the process of resecuring religious freedom. If you pray, pray for all those who have lost and who grieve, for children whose worlds have been shattered, and for a country restored to a sense of safety and security for all.

"Thank you. Good night. And God bless America."

1

White House Oval Office, Washington, D.C.

"YESTERDAY I SAID some powerful words to our country and to those listening around the world. Let me clarify what I hope, and what I expect you will do to help me reach these goals during my tenure in the White House."

The handful of attendees at this brief meeting looked at the new president with great seriousness.

"The reason I scheduled this meeting for today is that I may not be able to get back to this matter for a long time. As you know, our country is facing several extraordinary crises that require my immediate attention. Nonetheless, I want to leave a lasting impact on this great country: I want to put an end to much of the violence we as a society endure—and promote.

"If we fix the economy but fail to reach this goal, we will not be successful overall. If we crush Al-Qaeda but miss this objective, we will not be successful. Success is a long-term solution.

"So, to you, my trusted advisers and inner circle, I do not want to have to make that kind of public address again. I've grown tired of the same old excuses for why violence, injustice, and hate continue. I don't want more explanations. Don't give me reports. The problem lies in the lessons we teach. I'm told in both our schools and faith institutions that we promote violence and controversy, but that the schools are slowly changing. Therefore, I need you to establish a task force of highly qualified, diverse experts who can isolate the most problematic biblical teachings.

"Once this group isolates the problems, I need you to identify a leader to head a major movement of peaceful change in this country.

"Let me be clear. I don't want the 'what'—I know there is a problem. I don't want the 'why'; I know why. I want the fix. I want the 'how.' And I want this completed in my first term."

All in attendance stood and said in unison, "Yes, Mr. President," as he left to embark on the hardest hundred days of his life.

They would not let him down.

2

HER LIFE WAS SIMPLE, her health was good, and her faith was strong. Jane Alton was raised to work hard. From the age of fifteen, when other girls were starting to head out at night to the shopping malls or to the other hangouts with friends, Jane chipped away at a long list of chores that would take her most of the evening on the farm, and whatever she failed to find energy for at night would surely be waiting for her the next morning. Before and after school, Jane managed an eight-hour workday and rarely complained. Occasionally she took a night off to visit her friend Becky.

Jane's parents ran a third-generation dairy farm in Illinois, about an hour from Chicago. Her family enjoyed little downtime, but ate every meal together, opening the day with a Bible reading and ending the day with a prayer.

Along with her five brothers and sisters, Jane attended St. Luke's Lutheran Church through high-school graduation, and then taught Sunday school there for a mixed class of about fifteen fourth- and fifth-graders. Usually the lessons were time-tested and well scripted, and were generally the same ones—even with the same illustrations—she had seen as a child.

One Sunday, however, an uncomfortable feeling came over her as she was teaching the story of Noah's Ark.

"My dad says a boat longer than three hundred feet made of all wood would sink. That Ark was supposed to be four hundred and fifty feet long or something," Jeremy said.

"Jeremy. That is not the point. Who would like to read the verses? Katie? Genesis 6:1–8."

Katie began reading aloud:

> It happened, when men began to multiply on the surface of the ground, and daughters were born to them, that God's sons saw that men's daughters were beautiful, and they took for themselves wives of all that they chose. Yahweh said, "My Spirit will not strive with man forever, because he also is flesh; yet will his days be one hundred twenty years." The Nephilim were in the earth in those days, and also after that, when God's sons came in to men's daughters. They bore children to them. Those were the mighty men who were of old, men of renown. Yahweh saw that the wickedness of man was great in the earth, and that every imagination of the thoughts of his heart was only evil continually. Yahweh was sorry that he had made man on the earth, and it grieved him in his heart. Yahweh said, "I will destroy man whom I have created from the surface of the ground; man, along with animals, creeping things, and birds of the sky; for I am sorry that I have made them." But Noah found favor in Yahweh's eyes.

"Very nice, Katie. Thank you."

Katie looked puzzled.

"What is it, Katie?" asked Jane.

"Aren't Nephilim angels?"

"Yes, that's right."

"So, what it says here is that angels actually mated with the humans and they had children, right? And it says the angels stayed after as well, so are they still here?"

"That is what the Bible says, but listen, let's get back to the story of Noah's Ark."

"Um, why? I mean that's a pretty interesting story about the angels, right?"

"It is interesting, but today's lesson is about Noah's Ark."

Anthony cut in. "I don't like the Ark story. It's too depressing; gives me nightmares. I mean, like, I'll probably wet my bed again. God gets mad at Adam and Eve, makes their life pretty rough and all that, and the next thing you know, again with the temper, temper! Then the whole earth gets drowned, and God only saves one guy and his family—and a whole lot of smelly animals. How did they mate, anyway?"

"Well, for what it's worth, God did apologize."

"Why did God have to apologize? I thought God didn't make mistakes," Anne Marie said.

"Yes, well, it seems that in the Bible usually that is the case. But in Genesis Chapter 8:21 it says, 'The LORD smelled the pleasing aroma and said in his heart: "Never again will I curse the ground because of man, even though every inclination of his heart is evil from childhood. And never again will I destroy all living creatures, as I have done."' It just seems to be, um, a godly apology of sorts."

Not letting go, Katie continued, "Okay, now back to the angels. Are there still angels on the earth today mating with humans? Do some people have wings or special powers?"

"Sorry, guys, that's as far as we get today. Time for you to head down to Christmas Pageant practice. See you next week!" concluded Jane.

Now that she had graduated, Jane was considering getting an online degree in religion; today's lesson pointed out the need for one more than ever. She kept having this feeling that kids today are lighting-fast with information and don't buy the old stories hook, line and sinker anymore. *The stories must make sense and reflect what they know to be right,* she thought while heading to coffee hour. *What a radical thought,* she concluded as she greeted the vestry guild and nibbled on a warm currant scone.

One for the blogosphere.

What a very radical thought, indeed.

3

LISETTE COLLIERE, a perfectly put together French Catholic in her midthirties, adjusted her silk scarf and tried to bring the formidable presidential task force into focus. She considered the assignment monumental but not insurmountable. The group of experts, as diverse as she could imagine, had made steady progress toward their ambitious goal.

It was not every day that people go up against God and challenge the text of the Holy Bible itself. As days go, it was a standout Thursday, and an electrifying breakfast meeting at that. Today was also when the group would decide on a working name for their project.

Their quarterly meetings regularly assigned complex action lists, reviewed research, and facilitated discussions. Progress would be quick; there was no shortage of brainpower.

With any luck, today they would arrive at a proper name, which might be needed for publications, interviews, findings, and other yet-unforeseen reasons. Planning, storyboarding, and brainstorming had yielded these possibilities:

- Institute of Hope
- Church of All

- Exploration for a Better Humanity
- Universal Change Alliance
- Temple of Consciousness
- Hope Mission
- Project for Higher Humanity
- The Sanctuary for Grace and Hope
- Alliance for Clarity and Purpose
- Delegation for the Modification of the Word
- Instrument for Action and Peace
- The Sacred Search
- Society of Enlightenment and Change
- The Supreme Council for the Abolition of Anthropocentrism
- The Apostate Delegation of the Modern Age
- Center for Reclamation of the Word
- The Call to Abjure and Unify
- Transformation of Consciousness
- Epistemology of the Peaceful

"All good choices. We're sure about doing this project, right?" wondered Lisette.

"Did you see Jane Alton's blog this week? America is ready, definitely. That woman is like some kind of medium on the pulse of this country's religious culture—she's more accurate than Beliefnet," said someone in the group, but Lisette didn't catch whom.

"Let's review this again," said Anneke Lebner, a Russian-Jewish refugee and the preeminent art restoration resource for the National Gallery of Art in Washington, D.C. Her speciality was moisture intrusion, and she was renowned for restoring paper art with water damage and the delicate treatment of molds. Far from her beginnings in Belarus, Anneke was growing in spiritual vision and relishing her religious freedoms.

They reviewed their stated mission:

> We join in religious and cultural diversity to submit ourselves to the task of calling into question objectionable verses and possibly revising the Holy Bible, as had been previously assembled in AD 325 at the Council of Nicaea and later revised more than nineteen times.
>
> During this course, we hold close the goal of including previously lost and later found sources, reincorporating what may have been omitted, and removing those verses that are in direct contradiction with God's overarching guidance regarding human dignity.

T. Pumpkin Rowe walked with a bit of a swagger, perhaps a permanent effect of too much sailing on the southern coast of Maine. Over time, the rough, cold waters took their toll. Her white hair and leathery skin usually lent distinction. No one doubted she was one of the most influential minds of the day. Without referencing her notes and with all the others joining her, she said:

> We believe in the holy God on high.
> We believe in the sacred presence of God in us.
> We have the power to achieve our God-given potential.
> We believe in the infinite greatness of humanity.

We trust in the power of prayer to heal all wounds.
We call upon God's mercy and lean on God's grace to carry us in our lives.
We believe in the restoration of the Holy, the sanctity of worship, and the exponential change possible through combined conscious effort.
We stand together in answer to a high call to do what is right and strike from the record that which is wrong, that which is limiting, and that which is unworthy of study.
We believe in the fair treatment of all people.
We recognize that each person has purpose.
We believe in the accessibility of intelligence in God's universe.
We seek the courage to challenge and the clarity to change all that needs revision.
We require the discipline to prioritize the greater good over personal gain.
Grant that we may find your path.

Pumpkin looked around the room and added, "God on high, in whatever form you exist, vouchsafe to protect us in this, our humble undertaking. Welcome us into your holy arms if we die trying. Amen."

After reciting the creed, silence hung in the air for a while. They allowed the sober moment to linger.

Next was the Celebration of Courage. During their meetings, the members bolstered their own courage by recounting stories of real people who overcame incredible challenges in the face of real consequence—often death, imprisonment, torture, excommunication, or other atrocious results—for their actions. These stories gave them hope. These were the risks worth taking.

At each meeting, one member researched and shared a heroic story. In the life-changing, history-making moment they knew they were in, they needed all the courage they could find. And more.

Without prompting, Lisette told this story:

"There was a man, a Jew. He was from Czechoslovakia and he was called Vrba, Rudolf Vrba. After eighteen months' labor he was transferred to the death camp, Auschwitz. It was June 30, 1942. He worked sorting the luggage of arriving prisoners, who would never again see their things. He kept detailed records and since the Germans liked their records perfect, he kept doing this until June of 1943, when he was promoted and worked with another prisoner, Alfred Wetzler.

"Vrba had a photographic memory and the true desire to get the message out about the extermination of the Jews. He knew that if the world knew, they would not allow it. He and Wetzler waited and planned their escape with the help of the camp underground. Finally, after witnessing hundreds of thousands of murders, Vrba and Wetzler escaped in April 1944. They hid in a woodpile for three days and nights until the search for them was called off—they were still right under the Nazis' noses at the camp. Then they fled.

"Reaching Slovakia after fifteen days on the run, they told their story to the Jewish leaders and warned that larger facilities were being installed to kill and cremate all the Hungarian Jews. Vrba tried to reach Hungary to warn them; but in Slovakia, the Jewish leaders wouldn't believe his stories, even though he recounted with exact precision each train that had arrived, how many Jews on it were sent to work, and how many had been immediately incinerated. At that time Auschwitz could gas and burn twelve thousand each day, but they were expanding the capacity in the corpse factory for what the Nazis called the 'Hungarian Sausage' headed their way.

"Eventually Vrba persuaded them to write a report, which reached thirty-two pages and was immediately forwarded as a warning to Hungary. Sadly, the Hungarian authorities did not act on the report, since they were in negotiations with the SS. Six hundred thousand Hungarian Jews could have been saved by his heroic actions—but the authorities were too slow to act. Eventually the report was leaked to the British and Americans and found its way to the Red Cross and the *New York Times.* It prompted swift actions, and the deportation of the Jews in Hungary was halted, saving one hundred and twenty thousand lives. This was ultimately credited with stopping the war and ending the genocide. Auschwitz, the death factory, had already murdered and cremated one and a half million innocent people.

"That was Vrba, a man of courage who died in 2006 at the age of eighty-one. He was a professor of pharmacology at the University of British Columbia. This man saved more lives by a single act of heroism than almost anyone in history.

"This is a true story," said Lisette, "and we should remember his name."

The story conveyed that sense of precision, like a true north on a compass. Clearly, certainly knowing right from wrong and acting for what is right, no matter the risk.

There it was.

Vrba's name was added to the list.

In keeping with the meeting format in which each member took a turn at leading a prayer in her or his own religious tradition, Hala El Feddak, an Iraqi who had first been exiled to Morocco and later moved with her husband to New York, was going to lead the group in prayer.

First she commented, "These stories of genocide are many and they continue. In my country, we had an ongoing genocide against anyone who dared to question the government. My uncle was taken out of his home, accused of speaking against the government. He was returned the next day, dead. In a burlap sack left at the front door. We were instructed not to mourn him but to leave him there to rot. This was my uncle, my mother's only brother, and a good man.

"And so I lead a prayer from my people, the Muslim people, and a divided people at war with one another over the words given by God through our prophet, Muhammad. We also need change. This prayer is said in Pakistan in a movement for reforming society, inshallah, change will come." Bowing her head, she said, "Merciful God, you made all of the people of the world in your own image and placed before us the pathway of salvation through different preachers who claimed to have been your saints and prophets. But the contradictions in their teachings and interpretations of them have resulted in creating divisions, hatreds, and bloodshed in the world community. Millions of innocent men, women, and children have so far been brutally killed by the militants of several religions who have been committing horrifying crimes against humanity, and millions more would be butchered by them in the future, if you do not help us find ways to reunite peacefully.

"In the name of God, the compassionate, the merciful, look with compassion on the whole human family; take away the controversial teachings of arrogance, divisions, and hatreds that have badly infected our hearts; break down the walls that separate us; reunite us in bonds of love; and work through our struggle and confusion to accomplish your purposes on earth; that, in your good time, all nations and races may jointly serve you in justice, peace, and harmony."[1]

Before the meeting adjourned, the group members voted for a name. The winning name was the Sanctuary for Grace and Hope. Therefore, a sanctuary it became; or maybe already was.

The Sanctuary for Grace and Hope.

4

Boston Outskirts

JOE KLEINER HESITATED before interrupting Spiker from his morning routine. On the other side of the steel door was another kitten about to be grateful for its death. It wouldn't be granted a quick, humane, and painless death—its pain threshold would soon be maxed out, and at three weeks old it would succumb to the agony and then be destroyed. "All part of the scientific process," Spiker would say. For his part, Joe didn't care about the daily chemical-testing routine on the kittens, although after a few years it was getting old. He was a big-picture guy. He didn't worry about details. He was extremely efficient about his time, and thoughts took time, detracting from better work. Worry could suck up a whole lot of time if you let it.

Joe had grown up in the Christ Image Movement, which was closely tied to white supremacy, until the movement was later won over by the South African Boeremag, which combined Christianity with Odinism, an old German tradition. Predating Christianity, Odinism held the Paleolithic and Neolithic warlike system of ethics. Some pagan groups continued on, changing and evolving next into the Odin Brotherhood.[2]

Lately Joe had formed a joint task force with the Armed Militia of Christ, a supremacist group that equated a person's race with the person's religion. Aside from this, its ideology is similar to many white supremacist groups, in their belief that a Jewish conspiracy controls the US government, international banking, and the media.

Spiker and Joe had been highly incompatible Harvard roommates. Although Harvard had suspended its full Navy ROTC program, which had been in place from 1926 until 1971, it still allowed ROTC as an extracurricular activity. Joe was headed straight into naval flight training after commencement. Spiker was headed in a very different direction in science.

It was only after a girlfriend, who had belonged to a kind of reverse racist group, as he described it, had dumped Spiker that he began to read about the Christ Image Movement Joe spoke of from time to time. Reverse racism, Joe learned, is when a group that is discriminated against does not want outsiders to join, thereby becoming racist, too. Some of the ideas actually made sense to Spiker, and he went from a state of being dumped and outraged to a state of disbelief, but not all the way to a state of being at peace. Actually, he never got anywhere near being at peace with the situation; he just remained in an endless loop of frustration in his own thoughts, on perpetual slow boil from the rejection.

Over the years, the two had many discussions and he was convinced, as was Joe, that a racial holy war would happen, and probably soon, which would aim to eliminate both Jews and "mud races" from the planet. They were close followers of Matt Hale, founder of the World Church of the Creator, which had some ties with white supremacists and racist groups, including the skinheads. Though highly educated, neither was ready to admit that some of these groups ignored the facts at times.[3, 4]

Recruitment tactics were working nicely and on par with Al-Qaeda. Preying on mounting levels of frustration and low levels of education, the group's grassroots strategy was a winner. Access to the Internet had led to a dramatic increase in white supremacist websites, making recruiting fairly easy. The Internet was a great way to promote ideology while remaining nearly invisible.

They thought the timing of their upcoming attack was divine. Fuelled by immigration fears, the economic crisis, and the election of a mixed-race president, the number of racist and hate groups in America was increasing. The Southern Poverty Law Center documented over 900 hate groups operating in the United States—an increase of more than fifty percent since 2000.

Hate-group leaders were exploiting the difficult economic times to swell their ranks, and their anti-Semitic, violence-saturated, white supremacist propaganda provided both a target as well as an outlet for frustration and rage among a slice of the population. A neo-Nazi leader told *USA Today*, "When the economy suffers, people are looking for answers . . . we are the answer for white people."

In preparation for the meeting with Spiker that morning, Joe had reviewed his recruiting efforts for each state and country. His responsibilities included global outreach, talent acquisition, retention, and all issues of human capital. Joe was feeling optimistic. As he waited, he reviewed a newly compiled list of

California "friendlies," as he liked to think of them. As he read the list, he knew there were forty-nine other lists like it in the United States alone.[5]

Spiker did not acknowledge Joe's quiet entry. He hovered, trancelike, watching the little kitten's last responses: a faint yelp, a breath, and then nothing. Joe had long studied Spiker to see if he took any pleasure from the kittens' agony or deaths and was reasonably convinced Spiker was neutral to the outcomes. This was an important point to Joe, who was willing to take action for what he believed was right. He, however, was not someone who would cause any harm needlessly.

Noting the experiment results and then leaping to his feet in one exuberant motion, Spiker washed his hands meticulously at the sink and greeted Joe.

"Game plan?" Spiker asked.

Joe began, "The 2014 FIFA World Cup is being hosted by Brazil in seventeen separate stadiums in different cities throughout Brazil. Many games will be running concurrently. And talk about global attention: it is expected that a hundred times more people watch than those watching the Olympics. Global viewership in 2010 in South Africa proved that."

"Rationale?" asked Spiker.

"Soccer is the one sport that has overwhelming global appeal and transcends national, cultural, religious, and gender boundaries, as well as socioeconomic class. The sport's appeal continues to grow in both industrialized and developing countries.

"Because soccer is truly an international sport, we can hit hard and fast across many lines. There are over two hundred and forty *million* players worldwide. Fans top two billion, so we get an instant audience for our message with one-third of the world's population. With FIFA infiltration, execution of the plan will be easily manageable. There are more than two hundred member associations, with three hundred thousand clubs. Ducks in a barrel."[6]

After a moment of silence, Spiker reacted. "I like it. Spectacular splash onto the world stage; none of this trickle campaigning, no PR needed. Worldwide press coverage. Message delivered to all races and religions in their own languages. One swift blow. Lasting impact. Not like what those Lambs of the Lord idiots did last week in New York. This is good. Get on it."

"On it," Joe said as the heavy steel door closed behind him.

5

LISETTE SHARED THE FINDINGS about some of the controversial Bible verses with Ron Goodman. There were many topics under research by the group, including theodicy, which questions why an all-good God doesn't prevent evil. Ron, aside from being Jewish and openly gay, was masterful at research and held the esteemed title of Irene Steinberg Fellow, Senior Researcher, in the Department of Religious Studies at Yale University. Lisette wasn't exactly an academic slouch, having completed all but her dissertation in the Doctorate of Divinity program at the University of Pennsylvania. Her focus was interfaith communication. The work the group was doing was, in a sense, part of her doctoral research and might later appear in her dissertation. This was partly what attracted her to the project.

Their current assignment was flat-out depressing, but Lisette had to be cheerful for a friend's dinner party later that evening. The onerous weight of the question hung over her: What does the Bible say about genocide? Yeesh. Lisette half-laughed at the absurdity of trying to answer what someone might ask at the party about her recent work. Nope, nothing quite like the topic of genocide to kill a conversation.

Ron had no intention of starting this project from scratch. On his desk was the latest Skype speakerphone, which he often used for video calls but also used for voice-only conference calls. He dialled his childhood buddy Gilbert Schwann, who answered on the first ring.

"Hey, Gil, I am calling to find out how you are doing."

"No you're not."

"Ha! Well, I'm sure you don't mind helping me out with a tough question. Let me introduce you to Lisette Colliere, who is hot . . . I mean French. Did I say that? I mean, hot, French, single, and smart."

Lisette straightened up and threw back her hair as if Skype's video feature had been activated. On a bad day she looked better than a Chanel cover girl.

"Hello, Lisette. If you don't answer me, I'll know this is another elaborate ruse by the all-time great carrot-dangling Ron."

Thickening her native French accent for the impromptu audio demonstration, she said, "Zees ees Lisette, monsieur, and I assure you eet is ma plaisure."

"Right," Ron said, and then got straight to the point. "So, without getting all heavy so early in your relationship, what does the Bible say about genocide?"

"Well, well. Don't you two know how to have a good time? By the way, how much time do you have? Because there is quite a bit. Which pretty much stinks, and you don't hear many sermons about the topic, either—except the occasional rogue minister who says something stupid that hits YouTube in minutes. It makes me think there's some kind of secret pact among churches to tread lightly on the subject.

"Okay, you ready? By my count there are more than six hundred passages of God acting violently—and that's in the Old Testament alone. There are nearly a thousand verses where God violently punishes people. I would guesstimate one hundred instances where God commands people to be killed, and more than a few stories in which either God kills people for no reason at all or for a reason that is unclear in the story. So I would have to say that violence is the main form of action in the Old Testament, for sure. War was the main cause of death, and four of the wars would qualify as genocides. The first is in Genesis, chapters six to eight, in which God brought a flood to completely destroy all the people except Noah and his family. God later apologized for this. Personally, with all the translations out there, I like to compare them online.

"The Passover in Exodus, chapters eleven and twelve, recounts the gruesome tale when God killed all of the Egyptians' firstborns—it was applied to all people, young and old, as well as animals. Pretty harsh to kill the animals, too, I've always thought.

"Anyway, there were plenty of other examples I could point to, like the conquest of Canaan, when it appears that God told the Hebrews to exterminate the Canaanite people, including babies and the elderly. That was up there.

"Not to mention the almost total extermination of the tribe of Benjamin set off by a gang rape. That one is up there as one of the Bible's weirdest tales. In the Bible, people usually have the most trouble with these two Deuteronomy verses:

> 7:1 When Yahweh your God shall bring you into the land where you go to possess it, and shall cast out many nations before you, the Hittite, and the Girgashite, and the Amorite, and the Canaanite, and the Perizzite, and the Hivite, and the Jebusite, seven nations greater and mightier than you; and when Yahweh your God shall deliver them up before you, and you shall strike them; then you shall utterly destroy them: you shall make no covenant with them, nor show mercy to them.
> 20:17 But you shall utterly destroy them: the Hittite, and the Amorite, the Canaanite, and the Perizzite, the Hivite, and the Jebusite; as Yahweh your God has commanded you.[7, 8]

"Tell me when to stop…it turns out most modern genocides have factors in common. When we see genocide today we usually look for greed or grievance, but there were very different factors when God was calling the shots. It had more to do with anger and punishment.

"Some would say that the book of Revelation predicts another genocide ordered by God. That one we're just hanging around waiting for. I once heard that people tried to estimate the number of deaths in that one; I heard perhaps two billion people will die."

"Hard to believe, really," Lisette said.

"Why, then, was it so incomprehensible to us, the Jews, and the rest of the world that the Holocaust happened?" asked Ron.

"Like I said, it depends on how much time you have, but in a nutshell, this just keeps happening. The world's response to the Jewish Holocaust was unique and powerful considering how many times genocide has happened recently. Hey, here's a challenge: Can you guess how many genocides have taken place since 1948? That was when the UN passed its Universal Declaration of Human Rights, in effect saying, 'never again.'"

"Five?" Lisette guessed, thinking of Rwanda, Cambodia, Bosnia, Darfur, and the Kurds gassed by Saddam Hussein.

"Try fifty," answered Gil. "The second Clinton administration commissioned the navy to do a report. Why the navy I don't know, but I remember that Barbara Harff wrote it. It was called 'No Lessons Learned from the Holocaust?' and had all the facts, figures, and mind-blowing stuff such as the number of times genocides tend to happen in the same places, and the timelines and staggering death tolls. My own research is really about what the Bible *says* about genocide, but according to Article Two of the United Nations Genocide Convention of 1948, the term 'genocide' means a major action 'committed with intent to destroy, in whole or in part, a national, ethnical, racial or religious group, as such.' 'Killing members of the group' is an action that qualifies under the Convention.

"Sorry, buddy, but gays are often targets when genocides happen. So are Wiccans, for what it's worth.

"In the last century alone there were many genocides; some people are calling them 'politicides' if they were politically motivated. Regardless, large groups were still being slaughtered, in some cases due to inflexible religious ideologies. Here's the gruesome list of the killings in the past one hundred and twenty-five years:

- From 1885 until now there have been torture, rape, and murder campaigns against millions in the Congo but the numbers are unknown.
- The Armenian Christians by the Turks starting in 1915, even though the government of Turkey denies this, evidence of the genocide is clear.
- The Ukrainian famine of the 1930s, which was an artificial famine manufactured by the Russian government.
- The Holocaust, which wiped out six million Jews, millions of Catholics and other Christians, mentally ill people, political opponents, possibly millions of Poles, hundreds of thousands of Roma, and many others.
- There was a Roman Catholic fascist regime in Croatia from 1941 to 1945 that killed Catholics—many times Catholics killed Catholics—Roma, and Muslims.
- In 1943 in British-controlled Bengal, there was a great forced famine that killed perhaps four million.
- The famous Killing Fields in which the Khmer Rouge killed over a million of its educated in the mid-1970s.
- Roman Catholics were targeted in East Timor by the Muslim government of Indonesia from 1975 to 1999. Possibly a third of those Catholics were killed.
- In the 1990s Serbian Orthodox Christians in Bosnia and Herzegovina.
- There are also several ongoing genocides, mostly of non-Muslims by the Muslim government of Sudan.

- And of course Rwanda in 1994, a genocide of about eight hundred thousand Tutsis.[9]

"Wow. Don't governments have some obligation to keep their own people safe?" asked Ron.

"Yeah, 'R2P' for short," responded Gil as he shuffled some papers. "Responsibility to Protect is required under UN terms to retain sovereign status—but it's a little like the responsibility we have to take care of our own bodies. Whether or not we do a good job of it, we still have the body. No one actually comes and takes over the work."

"Yeah," Lisette heard herself numbly say as her brain left the building.

"Hey, guys, hate to cut this party short, but yours truly is the star goalie in tonight's hockey play-offs, and I need to stop home to grab my skates."

"Right," said Ron. "Hey, thanks."

"Always glad to help," said Gil. "Next time make sure to call on a Tuesday. That's when I throw in the topic of biblical violence for free—along with a complimentary gym membership. Nice to meet you, Lisette."

"Good luck tonight, Gil," she managed to say before the feeling of intense nausea overcame her.[10]

6

"SPIKER, got a minute?"

"Okay, what's up?" Spiker watched Joe carefully as they headed from the covered parking lot into their rented office space on the outskirts of Boston. The building was old and nearly vacant. It would soon be renovated into swanky art galleries and shops along a quaint cobblestone walking path. They had three months left in their lease before demolition was scheduled to begin.

"You mentioned you would need funding and a new facility."

"Pretty soon. The shoestring research has gotten us far, but you saw the spreadsheet, you know the costs."

"Yeah. About that. I'm gonna fund it."

"You? Where will you get one hundred and thirty million dollars?"

"Trust fund. When I turned thirty-five a few years back, I gained control of it."

"You what?"

"Great-grandfather was a steel tycoon."

"Man, that's pretty awesome."

"I don't think I'm headed for marriage and probably won't have kids to leave it to, so might as well put it to good use. And, I saw this property you might like in Death Valley, California. Was a private nuclear testing lab and site. Tight security, good lab design, remote location, etc."

"Very cool. When can I see it?"

7

"MS. CONIHAN, tell me about yourself." Spiker did not take his eyes off the pretty girl's resume. He did not want to be distracted by the young woman. He had no way of knowing she'd be beautiful. Since when was Harvard's science department turning out blonde bombshells?

"I'm smart, a recent Harvard grad, as you know. Chemistry and molecular biology. I'm fit; I bike thirty miles three times a week. I can do one hundred and seventy sit-ups without breaking a sweat. I work hard. Wish I could say I play hard but never had the chance. I'd like to save the world like everyone my age, but I'd settle for a good job with decent pay. Only child; when my parents divorced I lived with my dad, a great musician and attorney and a fabulous mathematician—well, he and his seagull."

"Seagull?"

"Long story. Bird tried to steal my dad's steak from the grill. Dad won. Gull lost a leg, dad felt guilty, now he has a one-legged, minimally domesticated, unrepentant, food-stealing, loud, large and messy bird as a roommate. Oh, and if you'd look at me, you'd see that I'm gorgeous."

Spiker looked up. "That, Ms. Conihan, appears to be the only thing going against you." He stood up and walked to the window.

"Mr. Williams, I can tone it down, I promise. I'll wear solid-beige everything, every day. All beige, imagine that. Two sizes too big. No makeup; just floppy hats and horn-rimmed glasses. You'll never see me in anything but running shoes. Beige running shoes."

"That won't be necessary. Look, Joe and I need a supersmart assistant. It's a start-up agro chemical company. You'd have to help me organize everything and everyone. I hate people. You would have to keep them away from me. Sometimes I sleep in my chair at my desk. I don't remember to eat sometimes. You'd have to relocate with us to California. I'm telling you, this is not an ordinary job description. It's all day, every day."

"Mark my words, Mr. Williams, you'll never find a more dedicated and talented assistant because he or she does not exist. I am entirely overqualified for this position, which means you win. Now, go shower. I'll order your sandwich for eleven thirty every day so you remember to eat every day when it gets here. And take this printout. It looks like your next meeting agenda, regarding new lab equipment, which begins in exactly fourteen minutes. Oh, never mind, just shower. I'll take that meeting for you and if I determine that they are qualified I will request a proposal for you to review. Go on. Get going."

Spiker never officially hired Courtney Conihan from Boston. It just began like that.

8

"RABBI BERNSTEIN?" Monisha asked a little more gently than her trademark bulldozer approach. She had never spoken with a rabbi, much less a Harvard rabbi, and she was a little unnerved. *Did he become a rabbi at Harvard?* she wondered. *Does Harvard make rabbis these days? Maybe he was* the *rabbi at Harvard. Surely they allow Jews at Harvard these days,* she thought.

"Yes. Well?"

"Well, now this is *not* the reason for my call, but do you mind me askin', since when do they have Jews at Harvard?" Monisha had absolutely no regret for the extremely bold, direct, and oddly placed question. She knew what she needed to know, and she was never afraid to ask.

"Certainly," he replied. "Just like African Americans, we've been here at the university for a while. Over time tensions grew, and in 1922 they kept us down to about ten percent with a quota that lasted until the sixties. Yale's restrictions were lifted closer to 1970. In 1870 we—and by that I mean Harvard—had our first African American graduate, Richard Greener. That same year we Jews had a graduate, Godfried Morse, from Boston. I think he might be the earliest Jewish graduate; I can check that for you."

"Uh, em, thank you for that bit of information, Rabbi. I was given your name by Adam Bertolski, who suggested this discussion. I thought it was a good idea."

"Right."

"I was explainin' to Adam what I was workin' on and how completely frustratin' it is to have to start from zero when all these perfectly qualified religious people, like yourself, might know some of these answers already. I'm not a person who can tolerate wastin' time."

"I see. And how can I help you?"

"I am working with this group, well, kind of a special research group, and we are having a look at the Bible, particularly some of the verses that relate to evil."

"Evil?"

"Yes, sir, evil. Genocide, sexism, slavery, all that bad stuff. Our aim is change: we need to stop teachin' those things."

"And how do you know Adam?"

"Well, sir, Adam and I both answered our calls to serve on the Board of Directors of the Civil Rights Museum in Memphis. Adam, well, of course you know why. For my part, I represented a group of outraged citizens in the Hurricane Katrina response. We fried some politicians' butts, raised a couple hundred million dollars or so to rebuild, and those two things more or less got me nominated, you see.

"Now I know you Jews had your own Holocaust, but by my way of thinkin' we had ours, too. I know it wasn't big like yours but, you see, when a government is supposed to protect its people and it's too lazy, cheap, or stupid to do that, you get to thinkin' that maybe it's just a small genocide based on complete stupidity. A small holocaust never even planned. And it seemed to me there are those to be blamed. And of course, when you take into account the slavery, discrimination, police brutality, it just started makin' for one angry black woman—and that would be me. I wanted to do somethin' other than sit around and boil.

"Not to bore you, sir, but here's a refresher about the storm. We in New Orleans were told on a Friday, and it was August 26, 2005. In fact it was at ten a.m. that Katrina had strengthened to a Category 3 storm. Later that afternoon, they told us there was a 'hurricane watch' for New Orleans for ten a.m. the next day. We had twenty hours of warning about that hurricane. They told us to leave if we wanted to, to buy bus and plane tickets to get out of town. But they knew by August 26th that there was a possibility of an epic storm. They had these fancy computer models that showed a shift in the potential path of Katrina. And they knew the possibility for disaster, as some parts of New Orleans and the surroundin' metro area are below sea level.[11]

"So they left the poor to fend for themselves—and I'm sure someone at Harvard like yourself would know that almost two thousand US citizens died in their homes or floated down the streets. The lucky ones got left in the Convention Center and the Superdome—about forty thousand people who just couldn't get out.

"So then I got to doin' some thinkin' and then doin' some math, too. Who in God's name had the money for airplane tickets—at the end of the month? New Orleans is the poorest city, full of the poorest of the poor people. The average New

Orleans family lived on sixty dollars a week. Most folks couldn't buy a bus ticket to get to work, let alone find a way out of the state. Anyway, to let you know, Rabbi, what happened to my city made me so mad that I got involved. Yes I did. And I had somethin' to do with the investigation of federal, state, and local gov'ments, which led to the FEMA director and New Orleans chief of police both quittin'."

"Ms. . . .?"

"That would be *Mrs.* Mrs. Monisha Ray, sir. And yes, there is a relation to the Reverend Montel Ray, and so you see my family, well, we're committed to nonviolence and all."

"And?"

"And so, you see, to my way of thinkin', you people, not to really say 'you people' the way some white people say that to black people, but that maybe you Jews, bein' God's ancient people and all, may have tried to do this before in your own religion—that is, tryin' to peacefully bring about change in a nonviolent way, and that might jus' be the kind of thing that could help us now. We do have two Jews in our group, but they didn't know. I suppose they are real Jews; well, maybe not Ron, on account of his bein' gay; and then, well, Anneke, 'cept for the fact that in Russia she never had a chance to learn or pray so I don't know if you could really count her authentic, either. That's why I'm callin' you, to hear it straight from the horse's mouth."

"Am I the horse?"

"Yes, sir . . . uh, no, sir."

"Well, Mrs. Ray, we did have a guy working on bringing peaceful reform within Judaism for a while. He didn't get all that far with it."

"Lordy! You see? When I'm on, I'm on. Go on, please."

"I'm not an expert."

"Rabbi, please tell me more."

"Well, it was a long time ago."

"Sir, can you maybe jus' quietly give me a name? I promise, sir, it could be confidential."

"I'm sorry. I can't. If you'll excuse me, Mrs. Ray, I have to run now."

"Sir," Monisha said, a heavy dose of *umph* entering her tone. "Would you mind at least tellin' me why you can't tell me his name?"

"He was crucified."

9

Death Valley, California

A FEDEX PACKAGE ARRIVED at 8:20 a.m., addressed to Joe Kleiner, chief operating officer, WhiteChem, Inc. WhiteChem was the newest of Spiker's project companies. Inside was a single sheet of paper with a few printed lines that got Joe's attention.

Dear Mr. Kleiner:
The Genographic Alliance is a new real-time initiative to map exactly how humankind populated the earth. Our's is a four-year research partnership between a large multinational geographic society and CBM, with support from the Lyett Family Foundation, and public participation through Family Find DNA.

We invite you and 100 of your members to submit DNA samples for analysis and have enclosed cotton swabs for saliva tests along with instructions. The process is simple; it takes less than one minute. We will arrange collection of the samples at your convenience.

As a racial purity proponent, you might be surprised and even interested to see how diverse and

yet interconnected humanity is. As a courtesy, we will keep your data as confidential as you prefer.
Sincerely,
Dr. Joanna Lyett, Founder and CEO[12]

Joe's rapid-fire morning just hit a speed bump. As he paused in the hallway and considered the big picture, he realized that if anything could stop his momentum dead in its tracks, it was this project and the general emergence of global DNA data. The United Kingdom had the largest DNA database that he knew of—but this! This he didn't know about. Did it signal the end of genetic privacy?

In the back of his mind, Joe had always known that the myth of racial purity was just that: a veil easily lifted and vulnerable to the truth. That while people imagined their ancestors neatly separated in quaint, distant villages, procreating within the same gene pool of blonds or brunettes, they were likely as sexually deviant and adulterous as people are today. He knew about recessive genes: just because people have naturally blond hair, it doesn't make them purely Caucasian. He also knew that most African Americans detested the revelation of their own Caucasian heritage. Joe wanted to make races more pure because he believed that is what God wanted.

Armenians would find out they were part Turk. Muslims would find out that somewhere along the line their ancestors included Jews.

Probably a new area of law would begin related to estate claims of ancestors, particularly more troubling in cultures where paternity demands strict provision, such as Sharia law.

What if it could be proved that Native Americans really

crossed the Bering Strait and were originally from Russia or Asia—should they still get all the reservations and casino benefits from the US government, not to mention the college funds? In a sense it could be proven they were here before other peoples, but they were not originally from the United States.

Joe was a pretty straight shooter, and some would argue he was playing for the wrong team, but he was not a liar and most certainly not a hypocrite. Of all things on earth, he hated hypocrites the most. He believed that people should stand for what they believe in; he was action oriented and all about personifying the motto "Show up or shut up."

That was the rub for Joe. Telling his hate-loving followers they were pure and at risk of contamination from other races was a fairly big stretch of the truth. He knew it. In fact, they were already likely contaminated. The idea of a pure race of any kind was actually highly unlikely—unless a plan of huge proportions got under way to correct the situation.

Which was exactly what he was trying to bring about.

His mind wandered. *God must be royally pissed off about all this mixing . . .*

Realizing the time, he had to focus again and head into a lab to review the results of a certain lethal substance. This was not the time to be distracted; this was, however, the time to listen to some of the world's leading consumer products experts discuss corn and its many derivations and uses in thousands of worldwide products.

10

LISETTE AND RON sat at a long oak table covered with various files and reference materials. Lisette looked up from the Bible she had been studying. "It seems pretty clear that in the change Jesus was bringing about, the hierarchy of men over women no longer existed. 'Galatians 3:28 There is neither Jew nor Greek, there is neither slave nor free man, there is neither male nor female; for you are all one in Christ Jesus.'"

"Yeah, but other than that, what hasn't been scrubbed out is rather ambiguous." Ron sighed. He had offered to help with equality issues although it wasn't quite his field. "There are still many fundamentalists who lean on the old 'submission' verses," he said.

"True, but there are a lot of contradictions. Some even say certain verses attributed to Paul were forged. Take Bart Ehrman, the *New York Times* bestselling author and distinguished professor of religious studies at the University of North Carolina at Chapel Hill. He published more than a few thoughts on this. Here's a guy who has moved from a fundamentalist belief system over time to an agnostic point of view."

She returned to the topic of examination, saying, "Neither the Old Testament nor the New Testament teaches that husbands ought to be owners of their wives. The New Testament states that 'Sarah obeyed Abraham, calling him lord' and there are references also in First Peter, chapter three. But, there is plenty about being submissive to your own husbands," she said. "'In the same way, wives, be in subjection to your own husbands; so that, even if any don't obey the Word, they may be won by the behavior of their wives without a word.' We know that the esteemed recognition of someone, just as in many languages there is a way to say the informal 'you,' as in 'Hey, you over there,' and a very different formal word for 'you' as in 'You, Madame, the powerful one who signs my paycheck.'"

Ron delicately cut in. "In my reasonably objective opinion, it appears there are two verses that seem to be used most often in citing the submission argument. Genesis 3:16, 'To the woman he said, "I will greatly multiply your pain in childbirth. In pain you will bear children. Your desire will be for your husband, and he will rule over you."' And First Timothy 2:13, 'For Adam was first formed, then Eve.'"

"And so the question is, Did Jesus override former gender laws and level gender in terms of power and divine promise?" asked Lisette.

"Well, I would say emphatically, yes!"

"Why's that?" she asked.

"Who do you think invested the seed money and start-up capital for Jesus? The women."

"I must say, having you on the task force was a great call—for fresh ideas alone," Lisette said.

"Well, it would be hard to tell what Jesus himself wanted because he never wrote a single word and we have to go on what is left of the writings of others, which in most cases happened decades and even centuries after his death. That would be like you writing down George Washington's intentions today based on what you had been told over the years. How accurate would you be? Would you want people dying for the veracity of your words a thousand years from now? The content of the Old Testament stayed very stable over thousands of years due to the stringent practices of the scribes—if even one letter was copied incorrectly, the Bible would immediately removed from use and buried. The New Testament is a faster-moving document entirely—it has been revised over nineteen times since AD 325. And each time it is translated, it seems to lose more of its original meaning.

"Texts, obviously, are easily edited. Look what happened to poor Junia, who for some six hundred years was written as a female apostle in Jesus's ministry, then started appearing as 'Junias,' the male. Romans 16:7 'Greet Andronicus and Junias, my relatives who have been in prison with me. They are outstanding among the apostles, and they were in Christ before I was.'

"With the addition of one letter, an *s*, someone removed an example of a woman apostle. So I think we need to review all the scrubbed, edited, and omitted sources for the Bible as well. Although they will be harder to incorporate, they will be invaluable nonetheless in presenting our case," said Ron, who was overcome with the sudden desire for a triple espresso.

"We have one powerful thing on our side: archaeology," Lisette said.

"Why archaeology?" asked Ron.

"Well, we will have to dedicate more resources to important digs because when we consider New Testament-era art, you can easily point to dozens of examples of women wearing priestly robes. Some of this art is now being found through Biblical archaeology.

"Dorothy Irvin, the legendary explorer of female roles in church leadership, has assembled numerous pictures of women in ancient mosaics, like this one from La Basilica di Santa Prassede." She slid a copy in front of him. "It is obvious, even to the nonprofessional; these were women who held some kind of religious office. She gives many examples of women in church leadership between AD 100 and 820 in the form of art, not text.

"I read some of her formal interviews and she thinks the earliest Christians, our spiritual ancestors, gathered in private homes that came to be called 'house churches.' These house churches could only accommodate up to about twenty people. The private services led by men and women went on until 313, when the Roman ruler Constantine ended the persecutions and Christians could gather in public places. Saint Paul lists in First Corinthians 9:14 the various roles that members held in these house churches. They were apostles, prophets, healers, teachers, administrators, and those with the gift of tongues.[13]

"And look at this," continued Lisette, "I came across these verses and examples myself. First, Prisca, also known as Priscilla. In Acts 18:26 we read where she shared the ministry with her husband, Aquila. So, in that verse we see a woman teaching. And if First Timothy 2 was supposed to mean women couldn't teach the gospel, then Priscilla would have violated this. Clearly, she hadn't. Also Euodia and Syntyche in Philippians 4:2 were important women in the church of Philippi, called by Saint Paul to help."

Ron nodded. "Interesting," he said. "The challenge we are presenting to the public is to consider all information we have of the time, including the many examples based on personal treatment of women by Jesus himself. We then have to ask them to use their own critical thinking skills to decide if women should be written back into the Bible on an equal level as men in all aspects of church work. I don't know how others will see it, but to me it looks like there was a campaign of wiping out women with a clear pattern over time."

"In both Christianity and Judaism, with over twenty thousand denominations under different sets of rules, it seems that each church has had to make its own progress. It is slow but you can see that change is coming. Look at this list I found.[14]

"From what I can tell, from the early 1800s beginning with the Quakers right up through the years, many Christian denominations were appointing women in leadership roles. By 1922 the Jewish Reform movement began work on ordaining women. By 1994 the first women priests in the Church of England were ordained, and by 2006 one of their women priests became a primate, or presiding bishop. The progress is broad and steady."

"Impressive. And look at this, too." Ron handed her a sheet of paper featuring a 2001 quote from Sister Joan D. Chittister:

> Obviously, discipleship is not based on sexism. It is not based on cultural norms. It is not based on private piety. On the contrary. Discipleship pits the holy against the mundane. It pits the heart of Christ against the heartlessness of an eminently male-oriented, male-defined and male-controlled world. And that is not the model Scripture gives us of true discipleship. To be a disciple in the model of Judith and Esther, of Deborah and Ruth, of Mary and Mary Magdalene means to find ourselves makers of a world where the weak confound the strong. The true disciple begins like prophet Ruth to shape a world where the rich and the poor share the garden according to their needs. The true disciple sets out like the judge Deborah to forge a world where the last are made first and the first are last—starting with themselves.

"Clearly, some people mean business," said Lisette. "That should help us."

"We have to decide how far to go with this and what we are doing exactly. Do we remove verses dealing with submission? Do we add back in deleted texts from other ancient Bible sources? Do we balance the teachings to feature roughly half women and half men? The question is really, how much should we aim to do?" Ron asked.

"Dan Brown brought to light through writing and media attention the 'conflation' of Mary Magdalene; how her story was confused with another story, but repeatedly told over time in such a public way that it was thought to be true for centuries to follow. Whether Mary was or was not the bride of Jesus, she was mentioned at least twelve times in the New Testament, which was more than any other woman. It is pretty clear she took a blow moving down from possibly Jesus's leading apostle to a penitent whore. Many people already acknowledge that in both the New Testament and in the Apocrypha she was one of the most important women in the movement of Jesus."

She added, "Mary was with Jesus and the apostles during his travels, right up until the very end. All four Gospels say she was the first to witness his resurrection, and she is continuously depicted as a founding leader of Jesus's early movement. Neither the Bible nor any other early historical sources validate the claim that she was a prostitute—most people think that this was a result of an error—or an intentional misinterpretation—given in a sixth-century sermon by Pope Gregory the Great.

"Hmm . . . one pope gave one sermon that either wasn't well researched or was somehow intended to lower the status of Mary Magdalene sometime in the sixth century and this caused people to lose perspective of one of Christianity's core founders for the next fifteen hundred years . . . it might be easier to hire a PR firm and start writing," concluded Lisette.

"I'm not in disagreement. There were strong examples of powerful women in the early Christian church, even in the Old Testament. Over time, they each lost their leader status and are now slowly regaining it. For us, I think the question remains: How much or how little do we do to restore women?" Ron asked.

"I say we include all the data, all the art, all the lost-and-found text, all the lost-in-translation verses, anything and everything we can find," she stated.

"That's the plan?" said Ron. "You think the evidence will speak for itself?"

"People, especially today, are not idiots," said Lisette, struggling to contain the broad smile now taking over her face.

11

AFTER MORE THAN A DECADE of research and testing, flying below the radars of governments, Spiker was waiting for precisely the right time and the right solution to execute his plan. He now sensed the day of reckoning was approaching. He could hardly wait.

Spiker no longer had the punkish, spiky hair he wore in his twenties. Male-pattern baldness put an end to that look. Gradually over the years he grew more into what became the skinhead look. Most people assumed it was his formerly spiky hair that earned him the nickname, but he got it in a more gruesome way in his younger years. From the time he began his journey into supremacism his inspiration was Vlad III, Prince of Walachia during the 1400s, more commonly known as Vlad the Impaler. Vlad was known for his resistance to the Ottoman Empire and its expansion, but perhaps better known for his particularly barbaric, torturous punishments he carried out on his enemies.

Spiker read all he could about Vlad. It seemed the ruler took great pleasure torturing, then killing, his enemies. It is not clear how many people Vlad may have impaled; by some counts it could be as high as 100,000, with the low estimates at 20,000. Spiker had confidence in German legends, which placed the number of victims at 80,000.

Vlad seemed to like impaling the best, but was also known for exacting other tortures: burning; sometimes skinning people; sometimes roasting or boiling people. He sometimes fed people their own friends or relatives. Sometimes he cut off limbs, or for variety caused drowning. More gruesome still, he was known to skin the feet of victims, salt the skinned feet, and let goats lick the salt off. These were just some of his torture methods. His real signature was impaling by tying a victim's legs to two horses then driving a sharp stake into the body as the horses pulled the legs apart. He took measures to make sure the victims didn't die quickly from shock, such as oiling the stake in an effort to avoid puncturing vital organs. He certainly appreciated a slow and painful death.

Vlad understood revenge. *A worthy hero,* Spiker thought at the time he began his personal transformation. Spiker continued to admire the determination of Vlad the Impaler. It would take him a long time to achieve his goals as well. Although his family was Aryan, he was the first member to step forward to promote and defend their people. Many white supremacists join movements in their twenties, to the surprise of those around them. Spiker was smart, and he was discreet.

Though he would have enjoyed exacting Vlad's type of slow torture on the masses, with the population over six billion, it would simply take too long; and anyway it would be nearly impossible to pull off that kind of genocide today.

Stupid satellites ruin so much fun. And he lacked the army it would take to kill people one by one, fun though it would be. He would have to settle on an effective, efficient, discreet solution. Through years of trying he was finally satisfied he had a solution that would work at some level but had the potential of working on a broad scale if deployed properly. Fortunately Joe's trust fund and financial strength were at his disposal.

Some twenty years earlier, Spiker had enjoyed listening to Harvard professor Erich Goldhagen's famous lectures on the Holocaust. Naturally, most people registered for the class to explore the professor's famous intentionalist-functionalist debate, the crux of which is: Why, when Hitler gave the order for the mass killing of Jews, did the people carry out the order? Most people were there to learn how to prevent another Holocaust.

Not Spiker.

Well, if one wants to secretly kill a lot of people and fast, there are ways to do that.

And, if needed, there might be high-level support in the United States, even in the White House. In his research, Spiker learned about a possible ally and debated approaching the top US science czar, John Holdren. While their objectives were different, an alliance might be explored. Holdren was well known for his opinions about overpopulation. Surely a swift reduction of, say, a third of the people who were threatening the planet might appeal to such a man who was now working for the White House.[15]

It seemed global population control was indeed a long-time concern of Mr. Holdren. In 1969, he coauthored with Paul

R. Ehrlich an article stating, " . . . if the population control measures are not initiated immediately, and effectively, all the technology man can bring to bear will not fend off the misery to come." By 1977 Ehrlich, along with Anne H. Ehrlich and John Holdren, coauthored the textbook *Ecoscience: Population, Resources, Environment,* putting forward arguments for forced population control, mass sterilization, forced abortion and adoption, and other novel ideas they claimed were not unconstitutional.

Later they would be opinions he wished he had kept to himself. Talk about the hot seat: a pending presidential appointment and more than a few skeletons in the closet. Yet, Spiker noted with some respect that Holdren never renounced his views, but rather issued a statement distancing himself slightly by saying, "no one really knows for sure" the right number of humans who "should" occupy the planet. But surely he had a good guess. Slippery. Spiker liked this guy.

Reaching for his copy of *Ecoscience,* he turned to page 787 and began reading that mass sterilization of humans by putting drugs in the water supply would have been fine by Holdren, provided they didn't harm any livestock:

> Adding a sterilant to drinking water or staple foods is a suggestion that seems to horrify people more than most proposals for involuntary fertility control. Indeed, this would pose some very difficult political, legal, and social questions, to say nothing of the technical problems. No such sterilant exists today, nor does one appear to be under development. To

> be acceptable, such a substance would have to meet some rather stiff requirements: it must be uniformly effective, despite widely varying doses received by individuals, and despite varying degrees of fertility and sensitivity among individuals; it must be free of dangerous or unpleasant side effects; and it must have no effect on members of the opposite sex, children, old people, pets, or livestock.

But what if Spiker had just such a sterilant and could assure Holdren that the White House would be completely removed from the plan? All he might need was help getting a new FDA requirement for a sanitization process to prevent E. coli, which his process did, along with sterilizing any woman who came into contact with it.

He noted that Holdren also suspected forcing the sterilization of women would be acceptable, so this might help him as well. He read Holdren's thoughts about how the government could control women's reproduction either by sterilizing them or by implanting a kind of "mandatory" long-term measure of birth control:

> Involuntary fertility control: A program of sterilizing women after their second or third child, despite the relatively greater difficulty of the operation than vasectomy, might be easier to implement than trying to sterilize men.
>
> The development of a long-term sterilizing capsule that could be implanted under the skin and removed when pregnancy is desired opens additional possibilities

> for coercive fertility control. The capsule could be implanted at puberty and might be removable, with official permission, for a limited number of births.

And this comment from 1977:

> Humanity cannot afford to muddle through the rest of the twentieth century; the risks are too great, and the stakes are too high. This may be the last opportunity to choose our own and our descendants' destiny. Failing to choose or making the wrong choices may lead to catastrophe. But it must never be forgotten that the right choices could lead to a much better world.[16]

Nearly impossible to believe that a man who had long held and published such radical views could now be leading science and technology in the United States. Spiker laughed to himself at what the rest of the world already knew: *American people with their precious power, the right to vote, rarely care enough about the issues to use it.*

Based on Joe's research, it appeared for the first time in history there was a fairly easy way to perform the unthinkable. In true scientific process any result, whether it proves or disproves a hypothesis, is valuable scientific data. Therefore, one person's scientific disaster might be very useful to someone else, as was the case with the discovery of the sterilant.

Joe found that a few years earlier a major consumer products company had a team working on creating a sanitizing mist to be used in public restrooms, hospitals, airplanes, and other places people could not or would not want to touch faucets. It would be a waterless way to wash one's hands without having to carry a bottle of instant sanitizing liquid everywhere.

Testing was going fine. Focus group data supported a successful launch. Branding would be a breeze, and demand would be high given the concern about avian and H1N1 viruses.

The formula started as a concentration of alcohols because alcohol sanitizes thoroughly. However, with alcohol, flammability is always a problem. Adding CO_2 gas with the alcohols would displace the oxygen and prevent combustion. Once the basic formula was stable, final ingredients were added for fragrance and moisturizing effects.

The testing and prelaunch phase for the product was roughly ten months. Then, in the tenth month, a group of research and development women were having a watercooler discussion about the strange fact that they must be entering menopause. What came out was that for exactly ten months, not one of these women had been menstruating. And never would again, it would later be determined.

Together the group of women marched into the office of the head of their company's consumer products division and explained the situation. An immediate phone call was made to their chief legal counsel, and within thirty-four minutes the project was shut down.

The only way Spiker got wind of the results was by monitoring a blog by one of the women on her daily struggles with infertility and how the settlement money she received from the company would never compensate her real loss.

Proprietary information—included the product's detailed formula—was easily hacked for less than $50,000 by a fifteen-year-old Russian kid who delivered it in less than forty-eight hours.

Joe discovered that corn was the most convenient delivery method for introducing the agent into the general population. Because it is used in almost everything big consumer products companies make and export, corn was an easy valet; indeed a worldwide Trojan horse. He examined the list of 145 everyday products that contain corn in some form.[17]

Spiker knew it was risky to go to Holdren. He might not even need the FDA—after all, he could treat the crops themselves with a simple "pesticide."[18, 19, 20, 21]

Note to self, he thought, *and start buying local organic because everything else is about to be poison.*

12

ANNEKE LOOKED UP from a tall stack of papers. "There are so many Bible passages that directly sanction and regulate slavery. I really had no idea how prevalent the practice was."

"Both Old and New Testaments?" asked Hala while watching a barge slowly making its way down the Ohio River in the gray, cold distance.

They had decided to meet in Cincinnati for two reasons. First, it was fairly equidistant from their homes in Washington, D.C. and New York City. Second, it was the relatively new home of the National Underground Railroad Freedom Center, an extraordinary resource for research on all forms of slavery, both historical and contemporary.

"It seems that way, yes, but many more in the Old Testament. But first, as a Jew, let me kick this off with a special quote from Rabbi M. J. Raphall in 1861, and remember that here in the US slavery was formally abolished in 1865. It starts by saying:

> [Slaves are] under the same protection as any other species of lawful property . . . That the Ten

> Commandments are the word of God, and as such, of the very highest authority, is acknowledged by Christians as well as by Jews . . . How dare you, in the face of the sanction and protection afforded to slave property in the Ten Commandments—how dare you denounce slaveholding as a sin? When you remember that Abraham, Isaac, Jacob, Job—the men with whom the Almighty conversed, with whose names he emphatically connects his own most holy name, and to whom He vouchsafed to give the character of "perfect, upright, fearing G-d and eschewing evil" (Job 1:8)—that all these men were slaveholders, does it not strike you that you are guilty of something very little short of blasphemy?

"Who can argue with this rabbi? It is pretty clear what the rules in the Bible were," said Anneke.

"So really Judaism and Christianity have to some extent already overruled the Bible by changing their slavery practices over time?" asked Hala.

"Oh yes. Equality of gender and race is still emerging, but it is setting the standard in most forms of both religions. Let's look at what the Bible itself actually says."

Anneke continued, saying, "Okay, this might get a little heavy but here are the most controversial verses, the ones I found in the King James Version. It is interesting to see how even Bible revisions over time have softened the language of these verses. Some children's Bibles today really sugarcoat the meaning of these. Exodus 20:17 states, 'You shall not covet your neighbor's house. You shall not covet your neighbor's wife, nor his male servant, nor his female servant, nor his ox, nor his donkey, nor anything that is your neighbor's.'

"And Deuteronomy 5:21 says, 'Neither shall you covet your neighbor's wife; neither shall you desire your neighbor's house, his field, or his male servant, or his female servant, his ox, or his donkey, or anything that is your neighbor's.'"

Anneke continued, "The mention of 'male servant' here means you could have a slave alright. And, as you'll see in a moment, you could beat your slave. You couldn't kill your slave without a punishment, but if you knocked a few teeth out or blinded the slave, that would be reason to let the slave go.

"It says in Exodus 21:20–21, 'If a man strikes his servant or his maid with a rod, and he dies under his hand, he shall surely be punished. Notwithstanding, if he gets up after a day or two, he shall not be punished, for he is his property.'"

"His money," Hala said with emphasis.

"Right, his money. And then in Exodus 21:26–27, 'If a man strikes his servant's eye, or his maid's eye, and destroys it, he shall let him go free for his eye's sake. If he strikes out his male servant's tooth, or his female servant's tooth, he shall let him go free for his tooth's sake.' You see my point: it was okay to beat slaves, just not to knock out eyes or teeth, it seems.

"There were some odd rules for owning and freeing slaves, which was called emancipation. Slaves in ancient Israel were automatically emancipated after six served years of slavery––that is, if they were Jewish. But, if a slave owner 'gave' his slave a wife, the owner could keep the wife and any of her children as his property. Can you imagine that? The rules seem so unfair by the way we have come to value humanity, but a big problem we face is that the Bible isn't really about fairness. These rules don't seem to make much sense to us, but I guess in more ancient times they had some framework to rely on for doing what they considered to be right.

"Exodus states that females could be sold into permanent slavery by their own fathers, but other verses contradict this; some required female slaves to be given their freedom after six years, so in this case we have to consider both.

"There were rules for buying back one's own brother, and by that possibly it also would mean a sister as well. Here's something strange, too: if a man was sold as a slave due to his poverty and his brother purchases him back again, then he would have to be considered a hired hand or guest by the brother. He would not be free to leave; in this case, he would have to serve until something called the 'Jubilee Year,' which occurred every fifty years. This would mean that depending on timing, one's brother could be his servant for the rest of his life. We don't know if this applied to sisters and women as well.

"See for yourself in Leviticus 25:39–41: 'If your brother has grown poor among you, and sells himself to you; you shall not make him to serve as a slave. As a hired servant, and as a temporary resident, he shall be with you; he shall serve with you until the Year of Jubilee: then he shall go out from you, he and his children with him, and shall return to his own family, and to the possession of his fathers.'

"There were many ways to buy a slave. One could purchase a slave from another, or from the state, or from foreign people who were living among them. These slaves would remain in slavery forever, unless the owner chose to free them. Which

I'm guessing was never. Except that it seems there was a little better treatment for Israelites, because an Israelite slave could have been freed by a fellow family member or by himself, if of course, he had the money. But the cost varied a lot also depending on timing, as the cost was based on the number of years to the next Jubilee Year, which could have been anywhere between one to fifty years. Male Israelite slaves were automatically freed during the Jubilee Year. Foreign slaves, it seems, were pretty much out of luck.

"Right here in Exodus 21:2–4, it says, 'If you buy a Hebrew servant, he shall serve six years and in the seventh he shall go out free without paying anything. If he comes in by himself, he shall go out by himself. If he is married, then his wife shall go out with him. If his master gives him a wife and she bears him sons or daughters, the wife and her children shall be her master's, and he shall go out by himself.' There is a similar law in Deuteronomy 15:12–18.

"And then, there is this troubling section in Exodus 21:7-11: 'If a man sells his daughter to be a female servant, she shall not go out as the male servants do. If she doesn't please her master, who has married her to himself, then he shall let her be redeemed. He shall have no right to sell her to a foreign people, since he has dealt deceitfully with her. If he marries her to his son, he shall deal with her as a daughter. If he takes another wife to himself, he shall not diminish her food, her clothing, and her marital rights. If he doesn't do these three things for her, she may go free without paying any money.'"

"I can't believe this stuff is in the Bible. Don't American black people have a really hard time with this? Why did they adopt this religion?" Hala sounded outraged.

"I really don't have any idea about that. Black slaves from Africa weren't forced to practice Christianity, were they? There must be sermons from black churches we can research. Hala, as a Jew I am embarrassed by this. There's more. Leviticus 25:44–46: 'Moreover of the children of the aliens who live among you, of them you may buy, and of their families who are with you, which they have conceived in your land; and they will be your property. You may make them an inheritance for your children after you, to hold for a possession; of them may you take your slaves forever: but over your brothers the children of Israel you shall not rule, one over another, with harshness.'

"And here's the one about the calculation in Leviticus 25:48–50: 'After he is sold he may be redeemed. One of his brothers may redeem him; or his uncle, or his uncle's son, may redeem him, or any who is a close relative to him of his family may redeem him; or if he has grown rich, he may redeem himself. He shall reckon with him who bought him from the year that he sold himself to him to the Year of Jubilee: and the price of his sale shall be according to the number of years; according to the time of a hired servant shall he be with him.'

"So, it is hard for us to imagine. A slave was simply someone's personal property that could be sold at the will of the owner. It's mind-boggling that this even applied to God's own people, the Hebrews. It seems, however, that special rules applied to Hebrew slaves: we see a lot of this preferential treatment of Hebrews over other peoples, which kind of goes against what we think of God today. Somehow we all go around with the idea that God loves everyone the same, that God treats everyone the same. Hala, it is the opposite. How can that be?

"Well, not surprisingly, female Hebrew slaves had it worse than the males. Get this, if a person bought a female Hebrew slave from the girl's father and she later did something that displeased the new owner, the buyer couldn't then sell her to a foreign owner. This, it seems, was a form of protection for the girl, or because she was a Hebrew. But, if the owner of that female slave required her to marry his son, which I know seems even more outrageous, then the owner had to treat her afterward as a daughter-in-law. Fine so far, right? Still seems like protection, right?

"But it broke down a little after that: if the owner's son married his slave and the son later married another woman, he was required to treat his slave wife as he previously had treated her. But, if the son violated this requirement, then he would have to free her; but she would leave without any money or means of supporting herself. So she would wind up free, having been enslaved, then forced into marriage, then abandoned and destitute—not to mention no longer a virgin, and so her chances of finding another husband in those times would have been slim.

"And so let's acknowledge the elephant in the room, slave rape. Hala, you will not like this, but the punishments for raping female slaves are here as well. I mean, come on! Why would women have silently put up with this unfair treatment for all these years? Ah, of course they were raped. They were treated as property. If a poor girl slave was raped during the time she was engaged to be married, it says the rapist must sacrifice an animal in the temple in order to obtain God's forgiveness. So, by my count, now we have a girl enslaved, which is bad enough; a girl raped, which is worse; and a dead, innocent animal. And the rapist suffered nothing. And if that wasn't enough, can you believe that the girl would have been whipped for having been raped while being engaged? True. And, while the girl slave would have been whipped if she had been engaged when her rape took place because it would have been wrong for her to have been raped while engaged to another man, there is apparently no punishment nor even an animal sacrifice needed if the girl was not engaged at the time. Get that! The Bible therefore implies that it was okay to rape women slaves as long as they weren't engaged at the time. Am I right that they don't teach this stuff in Sunday school?"

"Good question. I can see what it says here but I wouldn't know what they teach," said Hala.

"Leviticus 19:20–22 states: 'If a man lies carnally with a woman who is a slave girl, pledged to be married to another man, and not ransomed, or given her freedom; they shall be punished. They shall not be put to death, because she was not free. He shall bring his trespass offering to Yahweh, to the door of the Tent of Meeting, even a ram for a trespass offering. The priest shall make atonement for him with the ram of the trespass offering before Yahweh for his sin which he has committed: and the sin which he has committed shall be forgiven him.'

"In foreign wars, women were raped. But an Israelite had the right to take any foreign woman as a slave wife, even against her will; which I imagine, it usually was. First, he would put her through a period of ritual abuse. Then, if he later decided he didn't like her, he could decide to free her, but couldn't sell her to another slave owner. Go figure.

"Hala, this next one is just so awful. The Bible tells the men how to methodically strip the women of their dignity and then tells the men to rape the women. How can we reason with it? Listen to Deuteronomy 21:10–14: 'When you go forth to battle against your enemies, and Yahweh your God delivers them into your hands, and you carry them away captive, and see among the captives a beautiful woman, and you have a desire to her, and would take her to you as wife; then you shall bring her home to your house; and she shall shave her head, and pare her nails; and she shall put the clothing of her captivity from off her, and shall remain in your house, and bewail her father and her mother a full month: and after that you shall go in to her, and be her husband, and she shall be your wife. It shall be, if you have no delight in her, then you shall let her go where she will; but you shall not sell her at all for money, you shall not deal with her as a slave, because you have humbled her.'"

"So by raping the woman, the man forced her to become his wife?" Hala asked.

"Yes, unless the man later decided he didn't like the woman and then he was supposed to let her go free.

"But here's something entirely different in Deuteronomy 23:15–16, which says that if a slave runs away from his owner and comes to you, then you are not to return the slave to his owner. Rather, you are to let him live in any town in your area: 'You shall not deliver to his master a servant who is escaped from his master to you: he shall dwell with you, in the midst of you, in the place which he shall choose within one of your gates, where it pleases him best: you shall not oppress him.'"

"Okay, now that sounds better and, based on that, who wouldn't try to escape?" Hala remarked.

"Right, but look, here's a really disturbing section again in Numbers 31:7–18. In this next verse God ordered Moses to go to war against a group of Midianites for trying to convert some Israelites. The result was that the Israelites murdered all the male Midianites, but showed mercy on lives of the women and children. But Moses—the same Moses we are taught to hold up as a hero—got so angry at their mercy he committed what we would call genocide nowadays. He demanded the women and children murdered, sparing only thirty-two thousand virgins. Virgins! In the Bible—of my Jewish people and of all the Christian people—the group of surviving virgins was then split into two equal groups: one group of virgins was for the soldiers and the other group was given to the people of Israel. Based on a percentage system they were divided up so that the priests themselves got three hundred and sixty-five female virgins, presumably to rape or own as sex slaves."

"So then God—the same Christian and Jewish God who many believe wrote the Bible—ordered rape? This isn't possible. It is horrible. How is it that this has been here for thousands of years without any protest from all people, men and women? I mean, imagine a Christian-sponsored rape and abuse center for women handing out Bibles to comfort the women and they open to this page? What comfort is there?" Hala's disgust was unmistakable.

"But back to the topic of rape. Genesis 16:1–2 states: 'Now Sarai, Abram's wife, bore him no children. She had a handmaid, an Egyptian, whose name was Hagar. Sarai said to Abram, "See now, Yahweh has restrained me from bearing. Please go in to my handmaid. It may be that I will obtain children by her." Abram listened to the voice of Sarai.' Was Hagar happy with that? Who asked Hagar?" Anneke continued, on a roll.

"Genesis 30:3–4: 'She said, "Behold, my maid Bilhah. Go in to her, that she may bear on my knees, and I also may obtain children by her." She gave him Bilhah her handmaid as wife, and Jacob went in to her.'

"Rape, rape, and more rape. He 'went in to her,' my hat! That is a poetic way of saying he raped her and probably repeatedly until she got pregnant against her will. And that didn't end well for Hagar, who wound up getting thrown out, the poor thing. Here's another instance of raping a servant. It seems one wife could give her slave as another wife to her husband. See here in Genesis 30:9–10: 'When Leah saw that she had finished bearing, she took Zilpah, her handmaid, and gave her to Jacob as a wife. Zilpah, Leah's handmaid, bore Jacob a son.'"

"Why isn't there outrage? How can this be?" asked Hala. "What does the New Testament say about slavery? Did Jesus overrule it and stop it?"

"The Bible isn't easy reading. Few people do it. Most people have a verse, chapter, or book they read once in a while, but these kinds of verses are not highlighted and no doubt the churches and synagogues would like to keep them hidden right under everyone's noses. If you don't go searching for them, you'd never find them! But as sure as I am alive they are here and there are many. As for Jesus, I wish he had; but no, he didn't really go up against slavery and all this rape. In fact, not at all, it seems. Your Prophet Muhammad brought about more change and reform for the better treatment of women than Jesus did for the Christians, it would seem. The

New Testament is a very short part of the Christian Bible, of course, and it is not clear that by the time of Jesus's death that he had brought about all the change he had hoped for. This is my first time reading it; in Russia we were never allowed to read the Bible, and since I have been here in the US for fifteen years, I have only been reading Jewish Bibles. To me it seems that pretty much no one in any way opposed slavery. What is clearly such a crime in our day was such common practice in the days of Jesus that he really didn't address it much, surprisingly.

"Actually I read that one time Paul met a runaway slave, Onesimus, who was the slave of a Christian—presumably Philemon. Paul sent the slave back to his owner, which was forbidden in Deuteronomy 23:15–16, as I mentioned earlier. So maybe Paul didn't know that he was doing something wrong. Or maybe since he knew the guy was a Christian, he thought other rules applied. It is impossible to know."

Hala said, "We have our work cut out for us. There is just no way to argue that slavery isn't sanctioned by the Bible. It is a way of life in the Bible, and God seems to have been making many rules that would be completely unacceptable by today's standards. Do the Jewish people have anything in place, such as a proclamation, that voices opposition to this practice, or did they just let the era go by and accept it as something of the past? Or do they and the Christians actually think because all this is in the Bible that slavery is really still okay today?"

"I just don't know, Hala. I am new to religion, and am not so sure I am fond of it based on what I am reading. As a Jew, I am considered a Jew whether I practice religion or not. But what I would need to do in order to embrace it is voice some opposition to these things. Yours are all good questions, I think," said Anneke, who was as baffled as Hala about how they would find any solid footing on which to undo slavery. However, she was comforted by the thought that humanity had outpaced the Bible on this topic, although disturbed by the idea that the book had not been revised to reflect more humane newer practices and beliefs.

"Anneke, if slavery is so clearly sanctioned in the Bible, what we are asking people to do is to hold themselves to a higher moral and ethical standard than God set," Hala whispered, as though someone might hear her.

"It certainly seems that way."

"How can we realistically do that?" Hala wondered aloud.

Anneke sat back, musing. "You know, when I read the Bible it is with fresh eyes, as a person reading something for the first time. No one convinced me of its authority from an early age. I don't have years of commentary and preachers or rabbis telling me what it says or what it means. I just read what it says and from what I can see, it seems that God made plenty of mistakes, some of which He later apologized for, such as the Flood. The Bible to me reads like the reflections of a first-time parent making all the predictable mistakes and evolving through the struggle to find the right balance of rewards and consequences to achieve the desired behaviors a parent wants from a child. Various characters throughout the Bible argued with God, sometimes prevailing. Jesus himself, dying on the cross, said, 'My God, my God, why have you forsaken me?' Not the words of a man accepting his fate, but rather a loud argument at the fate he met that day.

"Actually, there are also examples of Jesus being 'wrong' and needing to be convinced of it, such as the story in which he initially refused to help a Canaanite woman when she asked him to heal her child. He ignored her at first and then explained that his mission was only intended for the 'lost sheep of the house of Israel.' Jesus told her that the Canaanites were no better than dogs. That would be considered entirely racist today to consider a group of people dogs. I mean, can you imagine a person in need of medical help going into a doctor and hearing that because of your race, you wouldn't be treated? I'm sure some of that goes on, which is kind of the whole point here, but one could argue that even Jesus was racist. Jesus a racist? It can't be, but it is. Yet when the Canaanite woman pointed out that even dogs have a right to exist, Jesus admitted he was wrong and changed his stance and finally agreed to heal the child. The Canaanite woman prevailed in the argument with Jesus on the grounds of morality, and he realized his initial stance was wrong. So if Jesus was God and also was perfect, why did he initially make a mistake and have to admit that he was wrong in the encounter with the Canaanite woman? That can be found in Matthew 15:22–28. So is the point that maybe people sometimes have to argue with God or Jesus because maybe those two aren't always right? [22, 23, 24, 25]

"God as 'in total control of everything,' is not really all that accurate," concluded Anneke.

"Well?" Hala asked.

"We need to formally argue with God on the issue of slavery," Anneke said.

"Merciful Allah, help us!" Hala exclaimed.

"It might not be a welcome idea in any religion, but . . ." Anneke trailed off.

"What are you trying to say?" Hala waited for an answer, holding her breath.

"Maybe, sometimes, we need to stare down God Almighty."

13

AFTER A NICE DINNER, Hala and Anneke retired for the evening, turning in early due to the weight of their undertaking.

But, at exactly 3:09 a.m., Anneke sat straight up in bed. She dialled Hala's room extension.

"Hala! I've got it! I know the plan! I—I—I saw the plan. Come down here, quick!"

"Wha, saw what, who showed you what?" a very disoriented Hala asked.

"God. A dream. Or was it? I saw a plan." Anneke was totally alert. "Come quick. I don't want to forget the instructions," Anneke said, and hung up.

Hala arrived in minutes, wearing a flannel robe and slippers. "Anneke, are you okay? What are you talking about? Did you have a dream?" she asked as she stared at a perfectly calm Anneke, who was at the desk scribbling.

"Hala, I am not a religious person, you know that. Maybe it was a dream; maybe it was God telling me something. I know how we can end slavery. I was shown the door through which we must go. It will not be difficult."

"Anneke, tell me what you saw," Hala said with an open mind.

"You know that verse I came back to twice, the one about the escaped slave? The one from Deuteronomy about not returning the escaped slave to bondage?"

"Yes . . ." Hala said.

"That is the door God has left open for us. Every church and every synagogue on this planet will agree to offer sanctuary when they hear that God has spoken.

"First thing in the morning, instead of just going over to tour the Freedom Center, I will call my friend Ted Bidault, a visionary leader who helped conceptualize and build the Freedom Center. We can ask him to teach us how the Underground Railroad was developed and how, hypothetically, to create an invisible global network of freedom conductors leveraging churches and synagogues."

"Are you sure?" asked Hala.

"It was the plan, Hala. Ted was in the plan," Anneke said, not minding how truly absurd she might have sounded.

Hala then fell to the floor and covered her eyes in prayer, for she had possibly witnessed or nearly witnessed the presence of God.

THE NEXT MORNING, Ted Bidault walked into his office, where Hala and Anneke were already waiting.

"Anneke, how are you?" asked Ted as he gave her a warm hug. Anneke had helped the Freedom Center restore a few treasured art pieces that had been damaged as a result of poor, damp storage conditions over the years. She had never charged for her work, knowing the precious value of the paintings depicting slavery and the tight budget of the fledgling organization.

"I'm well, Ted. This is my colleague, Hala El Feddak. Hala is the CEO and founder of the Muslim Women's Global Leadership Initiative and an expert on contemporary Islamic practices."

"Very pleased to meet you," he said with an impressed look, perfected over years of meeting with dignitaries.

"How are you, Ted?" Anneke asked.

"Well, I'm great,"—he leaned over to whisper—"just getting back from a little golf outing at the Greenbrier with a certain former US president."

"Must have been a good time. You always meet with the global who's who. You look great. Ted, could you tell us about the development of the Underground Railroad, please?"

"Well, sure. During the mid- to late-1800s, perhaps more than one hundred thousand enslaved people secretly tried to obtain freedom by securing the help of others. Since it was a secretive operation, no one knows the real count. The 'Underground Railroad' became a term used for the various routes enslaved black Americans took to gain their freedom as they travelled, often as far as Canada and Mexico. I have some interesting hand-drawn maps you can look at here on this wall. Over time, as the movement grew, the Underground Railroad became a large network of many different races: whites, slaves, free blacks; even some Native Americans acted as what we call 'conductors' by assisting the fugitive slaves along their way."

"So, it was an illegal freedom movement?" Hala asked.

"Quite right. In fact, there were grave consequences to

helping slaves escape, including fines, imprisonment, and worse in terms of social consequences."

"The movement relied on ordinary people who had the courage to act in the face of injustice, and do the right thing?" Anneke wondered.

"Right. Hundreds and thousands of times over many, many years until slavery itself was abolished."

Satisfied with his responses, Anneke briefly explained their mission and what she believed Ted's role would be.

He sat quietly and listened, then said, "I was never quite able to agree with the Bible on slavery—how could I? In the name of God, slavery still exists today. Well, some call it bonded labor, some call it human trafficking, others call it forced labor, and even sex trafficking. Whatever you call it, it is still around in many places in the world, including the United States. According to UN reports, as many as twenty-seven million people might currently be ensnared in various types of slavery. We call it 'contemporary slavery,' and it is one of the things we are helping to work on here by drawing awareness and creating forums for action. We know that possibly six to eight hundred thousand people may be trafficked internationally each year, with perhaps more than seventeen thousand people trafficked into the US. Most, maybe three out of four victims, are women and possibly half are children. The fight against slavery is far from over."

After a moment, he continued, "Even though contemporary slavery is banned in international treaties around the world, outlawing slavery does not prevent it. It is a huge global industry—the same size as drug trafficking and illegal arms sales. Enforcement of the laws is really tough because police in many areas of the world are too few and often are easily bribed. We believe that public awareness is critical so that slavery becomes more visible. If the public would become more engaged and outraged, we could bring about change faster."[26, 27, 28, 29]

"Ted, we might be able to ignite a wide—a really wide—global network of sanctuaries and safe houses," said Anneke. She set forth the plan as she had seen it so clearly hours earlier.

Ted listened carefully, taking notes from time to time. When Anneke concluded, without hesitation Ted agreed to advise them. Unofficially, until he built support, it was understood.

Hala said, "When we started, I was thinking only of how we would edit and omit references to slavery in the Bible, but now I see that the way to fight is not just with editing words but with a new form of action."

"Forced labor is defined as work or service exacted from any person under the menace of any penalty and for which the person did not enter into the agreement on a voluntary basis. Another example might be people trafficking, including recruitment, transportation, transfer, hiding or harboring people, or taking control or receiving people under threat, force, or coercion. Clearly in some cases abduction, fraud, and deception play roles. In some cases, abuses of power. That's how, more or less, the UN defines it." He paused, then added, "Slavery pretty much cuts across nationality, race, ethnicity, gender, age, class, education level, but seems to target women and children who are disadvantaged," he said matter-of-factly.

OVER LUNCH, Ted told the story of India's dirty work. "We hear about it all the time. People trying to sell or attract new slaves pose as recruiters for domestic workers and convince poor Indian villagers to board a train with the promise of work. They are told there is better pay in the bigger cities.

"Many people, possibly hundreds of thousands, have fallen for this. With India's growing elite, many believe they have real needs for various kinds of domestic help.

"But it's a trap, of course. Sometimes they are raped or beaten either by homeowners or traffickers. Threatened with death, few speak up. While some of them may be in nice suburbs working in nice homes, they are nonetheless enslaved there and have no way to break free."

Ted told them of a movement to combat this in India, explaining, "It involves the working women's association, Shramajivee Mahila Samity—SMS—which combats slavery by sending agents undercover in order to identify slave traffickers and help find missing people. Sometimes the agents pose as wealthy homeowners who might need a cook or a maid. They set up teams to learn about and investigate domestic labor agencies to check if they are really fronts for slave trafficking. SMS agents often interview former slave traffickers to learn the inside workings of the trade. Right now SMS is trying to establish government regulations. When SMS is successful in finding someone who's enslaved, one of the services it provides is helping people rebuild their lives once they return home. Anyone implicated might need to make financial restitution to the person. Often these people cannot just leave because their pay has been withheld and they have no means. Another service is helping women start businesses. Also, they teach awareness and how to prevent being targeted in the first place. Many hundreds of people have been helped by SMS."

"To SMS!" they toasted.

HALA AND ANNEKE spent the rest of the day touring the Freedom Center and learned a lot, including the fact that many people regard the Underground Railroad as the noblest initiative in US history.

They learned that the Underground Railroad operated for two hundred and eighty years, possibly from 1585 when the slaves from Africa landed at a Spanish settlement called Saint Augustine, Florida, all the way until the end of the Civil War in 1865. Often the Seminole Tribe and other Native Americans were the first to help along the way.

George Washington wrote a letter to William Morris on April 12, 1786, telling the story of how a Quaker helped a slave escape. And later in another letter described an escape "network." The Quakers were known to help many.

In 1833 Canada abolished slavery, which naturally attracted runaway slaves. Slaves made their way through various routes from the South all the way north until they reached Canada through a network of assistance. Sometimes a light in the window signalled a welcome to a runaway. But, with the disappearance of many slaves, the US eventually passed the second Fugitive Slave Act, which formally made it a law that US citizens had to apprehend runaway slaves or face punishments that included jail and fines, among other consequences.

The three of them stood for a long time in awe of an exhibit of a modern timeline of slavery, which began in 1585 and continues through the present day.[30] Hala and Anneke left with a great sense of hope and inspiration, with clear and precise divine direction, and with the support of the National Underground Railroad Freedom Center.

One day, God willing, their timeline would be equally inspirational.

14

COOLING DOWN from his five-mile lunch-break run, Joe collected a few letters from the highly confidential mail drop box. It was the only opening to the outside world from the complex itself. Gated, guarded, and recorded from every angle, the outer perimeter was sealed to the compound, but there was ample room on the campus to exercise and a fair amount of personal privacy once inside.

Joe took advantage of the opportunity to keep in optimal shape, running, biking, swimming, and playing hoops with the research and development teams. Odd, he always thought, that a mail drop box was chosen, rather than an anonymous box in town that a clerk could run to and fetch mail from every day. Sighing, he looked around at the expansive complex. With such extensive security, not many things could be tightened up, but this mail was a concern.

Spiker once told him the mail was safer in the hands of federally governed postal delivery people than anyone else, and he wasn't fond of the government. So, maybe he was right.

As he headed to his quarters for a shower before returning to work, Joe placed the mail on Courtney's desk.

"Ooh. Another one from mystery girl?" Courtney said as he handed her the mail.

"Huh?"

"Oh, nothing . . . just last month there was the same kind of letter."

"The letter is to Spiker, so how do you know about any mystery?"

"Naturally, I open all his mail and weed out the junk. Spiker hasn't read any personal mail in over a year so I keep it all in a box for him."

"So, what's the deal with this? Has he even seen it—is it from some psycho?"

"Orders were no personal mail and I am not going against orders. That man does not want to be distracted."

"So, what did it say?"

"It was oddly personal, yet distant. Like some old friend wanting to get back in touch but not sure if that door was still open. Kind of cryptic."

"Maybe it wasn't personal; maybe just a contact checking in with information—maybe he should see it and decide."

"Trust me, as a woman I know this tone. See for yourself."

Opening the new letter, she leaned forward enough for Joe to read over her shoulder.

> Dear Tommy,
>
> I tried writing once before but didn't hear back, so here goes again. It took me a long time to track down your sister so that I could get an address for you. Wow, you have vanished and are one hard guy to reconnect with.

She said you go by "Spiker"! How fantastic. I still think of you as Tommy.

Recently I was up in Boston and spent some time in some of our Back Bay stomping grounds—it brought back fun memories of the late '80s.

Just wanted you to know that I finally told my parents off and moved away from the community and I still feel awful about everything.

Don't know if you'll ever get back to New York, but if you are in town and would like to have coffee sometime, call me at 555-902-6626.

Michelle Mizrahi

"'Tommy'?"

"Did I tell you, or what?" Courtney placed the letter with its envelope in the box of personal mail and glanced up at Joe, who appeared a shade paler.

"Bury that and do not try to get his attention about it—whoever she is, she will likely fade away if she gets no response. Spiker will throw a fit if he thinks anyone is prying into his past, which I must admit, I had never really considered until now."

"Got it."

Joe left, having committed to memory a few assumptions based on the letter. Tommy Williams was possibly once the boyfriend of Michelle Mizrahi in the late '80s in Boston. She possibly dumped him due to family pressure and now is regretful. Joe had memorized her cell phone number. Mizrahi? *An Arab or Iranian name,* he thought. There was a healthy respect and alliance between white supremacists and Iranians, with shared anti-Semitic goals and all that.

Back in his room and freshly showered, he performed a computer search on his private laptop using the terms "Mizrahi Origin" and found something odd. "Mizrahi" appeared to be a name used for Syrian Jews and, even more interestingly, "Mizrahi" is a surname for Jewish people with Syrian origin, including the famous clothing designer. Other common Syrian Jewish names listed were Beyda, Ftiha, Esses, Dwek, and Douek.

Impossible, he thought. No possible way Spiker could have dated or loved a Jew. And he'd never heard Spiker express interest in any woman other than the woman who had dumped him in college. But he said she was racist, and this woman appears to be a Jew. A Jewish racist?

He went on to read about the Syrian Jews of New York, known for their refusal to intermarry—even with other Jews. He was able to learn that a century or so ago, sometime in the in the early twentieth century, the two Syrian-Jewish communities of New York and Buenos Aires each created rules to discourage intermarriage, and the rules applied to their own Syrian-Jewish community. That meant Syrian Jews could no longer marry other Jews. The ban is known within the Syrian community as the "proclamation."

Small gene pool, he thought. Maybe Spiker was trying to use this woman to learn about a Jewish supremacy movement—if there was such a thing. It sure looked like supremacy, with one group of Jews refusing to be contaminated with others. Maybe he was trying to understand their racial purity aspirations, which could make sense. He himself would have found it easier to accept Jews and other races if they stopped intermarrying and kept to themselves. Maybe that was what Spiker was doing back in his college years with this girl.

Preparing for his next meeting, Joe quelled a suspicion: maybe not.

15

THE SANCTUARY OF GRACE and Hope's meeting agenda was distributed. The framework for their meetings worked fairly well. They had selected the Palm Springs Ayurvedic and Tennis Center in Palm Springs, California, as their meeting place for several reasons. First, the weather was usually some form of beautiful in that part of California. Since many members were tiring of the dead of winter on the East Coast, the sun would offer welcome nourishment.

Second, the resort, having in recent years invested over $100 million in renovations, was both stunning and broke. The economic downturn and its devastating impact on tourism had driven rates way down; they were now unbeatable for a three-night stay along with group business-conference amenities.

Third, and perhaps the unstated but most compelling reason for the choice, was that the Palm Springs Ayurvedic and Tennis Center was also the home of the Patel Center, and Rahul Patel himself was often on-site. His was an offshoot center of a more famous Ayurvedic leader in the United States, in which Rahul touted his accessibility to his guests.

However, recently he had become less accessible as he spent more time treating celebrities.

Patel's gatekeepers proved impenetrable in trying to schedule a formal meeting with him. However, they knew he was in town and running one of his Whole Health Healing seminars that week at the Palm Springs Ayurvedic and Tennis Center, so while the chance of meeting him was slim, the task force members would still explore it.

Larry, the group's finance wizard, and Lisette served as the welcoming committee and introduced the meeting's objectives:

- To discuss the requirements of adherents to this faith
- To delineate the rites of passage of the faith
- To explore financial means to grow the faith

There were no suggested revisions so they called on Anneke for the opening prayer.

"Master of the Universe, we thank you for all the gifts of life. We call on you to protect us and all those near to us, and all life itself. O most high and powerful God, give us clarity in our mission, courage to meet any challenge, and patience to overcome obstacles so that we may navigate the path you have brought before us. Amen."

Before the meeting continued, the group members saw two strapping African American men standing in the doorway with their heads still bowed in observance of the prayer they'd overheard. As they looked up, there was a commotion coming from Monisha as she tried to get her size-eighteen figure untwisted out of a seated yoga position she had been attempting.

"My, my, are you two lonely already? Can't you guys stick to the plan? You were supposed to be havin' a look around while I sit here in a pretzel and labor away at savin' the world."

The group was taken aback. Not so much that Monisha brought guests to the resort, but at the sheer size of these men. The first man stood about six five and was easily 330 pounds of solid muscle. The second man stood about six three and had possibly the widest shoulder span and trimmest waist of any man on earth. Monisha said to the group, "This is Miles, my husband, the big one in the expensive new golf getup. Now he is supposed to be walkin' the fairways and following the path of the golfin' legends. And Lemar is our nephew, sportin' the hot new tennis look."

"Hello, everyone. And, sorry, babe. We must have got the time wrong and thought you were on your morning break. We'll check back later," said Miles, knowing that the early intrusion would cost him most of his peaceful evening.

"Monisha, I thought you told us your husband was a carpenter," said Ron.

Monisha sighed. "Yes, yes, I did, but that would be his moonlightin' profession, in the rebuildin' efforts, you see. Miles is more commonly known as number fifty-two, middle linebacker, for the New Orleans Saints. He jus' comin' off his fourth winnin' season.

"And Lemar, well, he's a fine boy. No doubt about that. As smart and handsome as they come. But, you see, Lemar left for Iraq just after Katrina, in which he lost his mama, Miles's sister. And with the special forces and all that frontline exposure over there, his re-entry has been a little rougher than expected. He jus' needs love like we all do. Too bad that post-traumatic stress clinic didn't give him what he needed. Even took him to therapy. Finally I jus' bought him an iPod, loaded it up with Deva Premal and all that relaxin'. Sweet boy, really. All I can say is that it is one very good thing he took up tennis. You know, for a kid who never grew up playin' a rich sport like that, he jus' loves to listen to that iPod and knock the snot out of tennis balls. That boy beats the ball machine now at full velocity and spin. It's the only thing that makes him feel any better."

After a brief moment of silence, Ron was asked to give the opening remarks, which he completed in less than five minutes. Lisette offered the recap and review: "Since our last meeting, we have each made respectable progress toward our research goals. We have now secured a web domain in the name of www.sanctuaryofgraceandhope.org as a private repository for our research and planning as well as functioning as a private, encrypted e-mail system for group members."

Ron and Lisette were meticulous in their presentations of information, which lasted just over an hour. "We will now go around the circle and provide brief topical updates, starting with you, Larry."

But before he could speak there was a soft knock at the door. Ron opened the door only slightly, expecting to see the catering staff members who had come to set up their working lunch.

To everyone's astonishment, stepping out of the field of infinite possibilities and right into their conference room was Rahul Patel. "Namaste," he offered as he scanned the room, making eye contact with each person, his signature group-facilitation technique of saying, "The me in me sees the you in you."

"My session is on break down the hall and I am told you requested my presence here."

T. Pumpkin Rowe greeted Rahul on behalf of the group and congratulated him on his efforts to spearhead the Alliance for a New Humanity, as well as on the success of his recent book. The group expanded their circle and he took a seat.

And then it happened. Gunfire.

Somewhere near. Run. Duck! Quiet. Everyone huddled together in silence under the long banquet table. What was it they heard—two or three shots? Screams? Running? What was happening?

"Call nine-one-one," said Lisette, "and leave the connection live."

Ron reached for his phone.

Footsteps approaching. Door opening. Men. Two.

"Is he in here, the Antichrist?" the first voice said.

"We're gonna find him and send him straight to meet his maker," responded the second voice.

As their feet made their way back through the door, Rahul said, "Go, all of you, and leave me here. They are after me. Radical Christians."

Monisha took his hand and said, "Come now with me," and the group followed them into the darkened main auditorium. "Split up and stay down," she said and she headed to the balcony level to see if she could get cell phone reception there.

Larry and Ron checked their iPhones to see if anything was on Twitter yet about what was happening. Nope. Larry tweeted: "With Rahul. Safe. Need info. Now."

Lisette and Ron headed to the front, near the stage in the shadows.

Rahul kept himself far away from the others in case he drew fire or needed to surrender.

Hala rushed to the middle and left. Anneke moved far back and right.

Ron tried a few places but wound up not far from Rahul. That scared him, and he curled up in a ball on the floor.

Larry got a tweet, but not the one he was hoping for: "Oprah Winfrey is now following you on Twitter." *Oprah. She knows something is up. Good. Will someone please tell us what in God's name is happening here?*

Just then, the men blasted through the doors and shouted, "In here!"

One of the men commanded, "Last room, get some lights on!"

As they moved across the stage scanning the room, one shouted, "Over there!" and pointed toward Lisette. "You, where is he?" Lisette froze in place.

"I don't know," she said. "Who?"

"Rahul Patel," said the gunman.

"I am with another group," she replied in a convincing tone.

"Last person who lied to me just ate a bullet, lady. One more time, where is he?" He aimed his gun at her.

Just then, Monisha took a giant leap of faith, and launched herself off the balcony toward the gunman.

He pivoted. She splatted.

Rahul emerged from the shadows and said to the first gunman, "Stop. Here I am, let her go. I know you are after me because of the book I wrote on Jesus."

The first gunman sprinted toward Rahul but then hit a solid brick wall.

Miles. Miles lifted the man and handed him over to San Diego's SWAT team, already in position outside the auditorium.

By now the second gunman was in position for his shot. He would not miss. The world would be rid of the Antichrist today and he would make sure of it.

In the back of the room, Lemar was improvising, calculating angles and quickly unpacking a pink tennis ball he bought over at the Aptera Classic in honor of breast cancer awareness. *It might not work,* he thought, *but it's the only chance I've got.* He had been doing cone practice for months to perfect his ball placement. Reaching for his Babolat tennis racquet, recently strung to fifty-seven pounds for maximum control, he tossed the ball high. *Whack!* Andy Roddick would have been impressed. Traveling at 125 miles per hour, the ball hit the second gunman in the left temple. Game over.

THERE WERE HOURS of debriefing and treatment for all those in the conference center that day. Larry couldn't make any sense of it. Ron was pale and faint from the ordeal. Monisha was all revved up with adrenaline and talking nonstop. Lisette was quietly recovering, and Rahul was spending time expressing his gratitude to everyone.

By late afternoon Lemar was finally allowed to leave the building and he headed toward the stairway that led down to the tennis courts. He was fine; even his aunt was miraculously fine. He kept reviewing the situation. No one in the group sustained injuries. There were two gunshot wounds in the other group but the victims would recover. In some ways, for a recent soldier, it felt like a normal day to him; he wasn't all that rattled.

Something clicked. Maybe life did make sense. He had saved the day.

16

"MS. CONIHAN, you've seemed distracted all day." Spiker was not happy.

"Its nothing. My dad is trying to help out a group with some possible Bible revisions and some freaks broke in and tried to kill one of their advisors yesterday at a conference. He's okay."

"Freaks?"

"You know, extremists."

"I see." As Spiker left his office for the day he took a long walk across to the research and development building. He wondered what his family and friends would think of him now.

Later that night Courtney's words haunted him. Spiker stared at his dark ceiling, knowing what came next: tears. About twice a year he had a similar dream, not the kind of unrelenting, recurring dream that haunts some unfortunate people, or the kind of sleep terror that causes one to wake drenched in sweat with heart palpitations. And not even the kind of eerie, nonsensical psychobabble of the mind as it tries to make sense of the day's events.

Worse. It was the kind of dream one has in a half-alert state in which the dreamer can sense the act of dreaming, creating the drama as it plays out on the great movie screen of the mind, while the dreamer observes it. He wasn't even sure if it was technically a dream, or something else. It was a story that took all night to tell, sometimes not finishing by morning. He noticed the clock advance by a few hours each time he tried to shake the dream and return to normal sleep. That never happened. The dream would play again, taking its time to recapture each raw emotion, every climax and plummet.

The dream had a pattern. He was sportive, she was impish. He was wild, she was witty. Intoxicated by her pheromones, he could not break himself free and never wanted to, as though caught in the lotus's lair of Greek mythology. In his arms, she was…his.

There was a synergy they had, in which they were a force that was greater than the sum of both their equal parts. Rare human electricity set their bodies on fire. He never imagined being telepathic with a person, but he suspected theirs was the kind of strong connection that would alert him across the planet if she were ever in danger. But he would never let any danger come to her. He would instantly give his life to protect her.

In Boston, in college, it had started. He was running along the Charles River after class. She was roller-blading with a friend. Rather, she was attempting to roller-blade, but in the learning process had turned herself into a heedless, giggling, spandex-sporting missile aiming for anything or anyone who could help slow down the wheels under her feet.

One minute he was headed up a very slight incline, enjoying the sight of the rowers and their sleek shells practicing hard as they always did out on the Charles. *Possibly the most self-punishing group of athletes alive,* he thought. The next minute, *BAM!* Something had knocked him flat.

When Tommy caught his breath he walked over to help untangle the neon-clad woman, starting with the wires of her Walkman, then her headband, which was twisted with her sunglasses, finally helping her up. He turned around to see a second roller-blading woman heading down the incline he had been planning to jog up, but this one seemed to be able to control her approach. Nonetheless, he stepped out of her path.

"Ladies," he said.

Sylvia was the first to speak. "She is soooooooo sorry. Michelle was trying to get a little practice. This is only her second time. It was my all my idea; I hope you can forgive her. Are you okay?"

Tommy looked over at Michelle, trying to determine if he should be angry or let it go. "What on earth were you thinking? You could have killed us both."

"You know, I am very selective about whom I throw myself at along this path. Look at all the gorgeous guys running by, and I chose you. You should feel special," she said, rapid-fire.

Tommy shook his head. Looking at Michelle he retorted, "You know that will cost you dinner, right? That's Cambridge etiquette. If you had knocked me down on the Boston side of the Charles, I would have to buy you dinner, but since you knocked me down on the Cambridge side, well, that's just the way it is."

"It was almost a perfect strategy, then. Do you cross over and jog back on the other side? 'Cause, ya know, I could go wait over there and try again."

Tommy was impressed with her speedy wit and playfulness. "Too late, I'm afraid. Now write your phone number here. I'll be ready Friday at seven."

17

October, Cambridge, Massachusetts

"MICHELLE, MICHELLE. There is only one sun, but it is bright enough to light the planet. There is only one Paris, but who needs another? Only one Mona Lisa, only one Grand Canyon, and only one Tigger. There is only one God above. There is only one time we will walk this earth. Walk with me, Michelle. You are my one."

"Not bad," said Tommy's mother, Corrine.

"Not bad? I worked all night on that. And the night before."

"Seriously. You should go with that. It's very sweet."

"I wouldn't be calling you if it was good enough. You're the writer in the family."

"You can write, Tommy."

"Mom, I'm a chemist and a scratch golfer. I'm only capable of cooking soup. I can't find matching socks. I've turned all my white clothes pink trying to do laundry. I can't even find my car keys half the time. I forget people's birthdays and get lost on my way home. I know for a fact I cannot express myself."

"Tommy, she'll love it. She'll say yes, don't worry. She adores you. And we adore her."

"I don't know. She doesn't like to talk about it. Mom, she has to say yes. I can't imagine life without her. But this poem or whatever it is needs to be better. Come on, work your magic on it?"

"What time do you need it?"

"By eleven, we have a meeting with that rabbi I told you about."

"Huh. I'll have to skip my tennis match. Well, let me think about this. Can I use some Jewish expressions and learn to play mah-jongg with a group of ladies every week?"

"Mom, if you get this right, I'll pay for some Yiddish lessons and I'll throw in a brisket."

"And you'll spend the Christian holidays with our family, right?"

"Fine."

"Deal."

18

"KITTEN, WAKE UP, we have somewhere to go."

Michelle's long, tight curls spread clear across the pillow and over the side of the bed. As she sat up and looked around, it seemed to be about midmorning. Thoughts of their night together drifted back into focus.

"I'm not so sure I'm done with you yet."

"Come on, I've been waiting to surprise you with something."

"Okay, give me twenty minutes and I'm good to go."

As she showered, she wondered if today would be like the day Tommy planned an all-day whale-watching trip. Or the time he had the car all packed and they went skiing just for the day. Sometimes they took the ferry out to Nantucket for an afternoon. In the fall they drove through the foliage in the White Mountains and spent their nights in Conway. It was a blissful way to spend their time at college.

In the two years they'd been together, she always maintained an official residence with Sylvia for the sake of her parents, but in reality hadn't spent a single night there. For a while, at least, she was willing to put up with the deception, although it was gnawing at her.

She and Tommy were never apart except when she went home to Brooklyn, or in the summers when she spent time with her family in the Jersey Shore town of Deal, an exclusive Syrian Jewish community few people knew about.

Tommy was from Darien, Connecticut, a coastal suburb of Manhattan. He went home regularly, and Michelle was always invited. His parents adored her and despite their centuries of Episcopalianism, didn't seem to mind the fact their son was dating someone Jewish. Darien had been somewhat famous for its history of excluding Jews, but in recent times had progressed. Now it accepted Jews, a few at least, but had serious concerns about other ethnicities moving in. But Michelle always felt welcome.

"Where are we heading?" She looked ready for anything. Except for what actually came.

As they approached Natick, Tommy pulled into Temple Israel.

"Michelle, I've been meeting with Rabbi Milner, coming here once a week while you go to yoga and lunch with Sylvia. I told him I want to marry you and I want to convert to Judaism. Three times he turned me away. I found out that that is what rabbis are supposed to do, but I took it a little hard the first two times. Anyway, today is the day—and I want you to be there."

"What are you talking about?"

"I could never be without you and I see the way you are about your family and religion, so I started studying. Fortunately for me, my parents took care of the circumcision when I was a baby so I don't have to do that, but I would have. Come meet him, he's an awesome guy."

"Wait, you really don't understand."

"What? I know you won't convert for me, so I will convert for you."

"No, you really don't get it—there is no way we can marry."

Tommy looked completely baffled and could barely move. Somehow he followed.

As they walked into the office of Rabbi Milner, he greeted them warmly. "Hi, kids."

"Rabbi, hello. I am so sorry—this is a terrible mistake. I am from the Syrian-Jewish community—are you familiar with it?" Michelle asked hopefully.

"Not specifically, but we have a lot of Sephardic-Jewish communities that we regularly partner with in marriages and other events."

"Rabbi, this may be news to you. Can we please call my rabbi so that you can hear for yourself what I am up against? I have never loved anyone so much and would marry Tommy in a second, but our community is not allowed to intermarry with anyone, not even other Jews. I don't think this conversion should happen because then Tommy will have to live his life as a Jew, without being able to marry me in the end. I very much appreciate your effort, but will you do me a favor and talk to my rabbi? I know it sounds ridiculous but that is the truth."

Rabbi Milner asked for privacy for the call.

As they waited, Michelle held Tommy's hand. "Believe me, I would marry you. Our time together is more precious than gold, but you know that I have always tried to tell you it would end because of my religion, and I guess we are at that point."

"End? What are you talking about? We're still young. We'll have children and your parents will eventually want to see their grandchildren. Once they know me they will accept me. Once they see how much I love you, how I would give anything for you . . ."

"Of course they would love you. They want me to have someone just like you. All parents want their children to find love. But if we married, they would be shunned, blackballed—and I would be excommunicated. They just won't do that for love."

"Then you'll have to leave them and be with me."

Rabbi Milner walked through the door. "Please come with me to the library." As he picked up the fax that had just arrived, he began, "I learned something new today. Michelle is right. There is a rare proclamation that applies to her community, and she cannot marry you. I am sorry to bring you this news. I am taken aback by the news myself. The ban is based on the right of a community to promulgate 'takanot' and prohibitions. This is laid out in an ancient text called the *Shulhan Arukh* and goes back to Talmudic times, when the leader Rav found a problematic situation regarding oaths in the Babylonian community. The words translated to 'He found an open valley and built a fence.'"

He continued, "The Syrian community feels that the current situation in America regarding conversions, *'gerut,'* done for the purpose of marriage, is a total sham and a travesty of the Jewish tradition. But actually this rule exposes the strength and force with which the community feels the need to protect its heritage and traditions. The ban is not intended to deny the legitimacy of a particular conversion. There is a strong need to 'be a member' in this community if one wants to get anything practical done, such as business, getting children educated, and anything social. The ban really is a complete social ban and restricts access to everything and it gives permission for members to shut nonmembers out. The only two loopholes are for people who converted prior to 1935 and those children adopted and immediately converted at birth."[31,32,33]

Rabbi Milner concluded, "Tommy, there's just no loophole here, no way in for you. Why don't you reconsider your conversion? We would be lucky to have you, but I think you two have some talking to do."

That talking never took place.

The car ride home was silent. Tommy didn't drive toward his house, but straight to Sylvia's house to drop Michelle off. He could send her things from his house later.

The tension mounted in the car Tommy drove—his father's old maroon Volvo 240. It was a sunny day, but everything about it made it seem gray.

Tommy kept his eyes on the road. Michelle looked out the window.

There was plenty that could have been said, plenty more that should have been said. But in the end absolutely nothing was, as they became two people who shared some moments in what was quickly becoming history.

As Tommy approached Sylvia's house, Michelle opened the car door and got out, but as she closed the door Tommy waited a few extra seconds to see if she came to her senses and apologized.

Nope. It was really over. He had never had a real breakup; just casual girlfriends with easy partings of ways with no feelings hurt either way in the past.

He pulled away, not looking back to see what—if any—expression she wore on her face.

Tommy was unprepared for every minute he was now suffering through on his own.

19

"WELL?" DEMANDED CORRINE, sounding a bit unnerved. She had tried the call eight times.

"Mom, I'm not coming home this weekend for the father-son golf tournament at the club."

"What are you talking about, Tommy? How did the whole thing with Michelle go?"

"I'm fine. It's fine. I gotta go, Mom."

"Oh no, don't tell me! She didn't?"

""I gotta go."

"We love you, Tommy," Corrine tried to say as she heard the line go dead.

After dropping Michelle off at her own home with Sylvia, Tommy didn't feel the same. His outlook was different. He was on edge. His expressions were openly bitter. His appearance began to deteriorate. He withdrew.

Tommy's next twenty-plus years would be a progression of rage. A sweet, wholesome American boy would slowly become unhinged.

20

AS MICHELLE WAS FUMBLING around for her keys to Sylvia's place, she found an envelope in her handbag. It was a small, smooth, beautiful chocolate-brown envelope with sculpted silver and blue edges. There was a hummingbird embossed on the back flap. She knew Tommy had placed it there, and she knew if she opened it, it would make her cry. She would absolutely crumble. She couldn't read it now, maybe not ever. She held the sealed note and debated throwing it away, knowing she had made the only decision she could.

She couldn't go back now. He might not even want her.

Michelle put the envelope away in a drawer, just in case a day ever came when she was strong enough to handle its message.

What had she done? What had she lost?

She would not allow herself to wonder about the message inside.

It was over. Suddenly and without warning, just over. There was a hole in her heart shaped like Tommy.

It was early afternoon and Sylvia was not home. Michelle thought about going to the gym, but could not bear the thought of being seen in public. She needed something to numb the pain. Two full bottles of Silver Lake chardonnay later, Michelle passed out on the small living room floor and didn't wake up until the following morning.

21

AT THE RESORT, each member received a call from Rahul Patel with an invitation to join him for dinner at his home in Del Mar the following day. A car service was being arranged to pick the group up at 2:00 p.m. and drive across the desert and along the scenic coastline, which would allow them to see some of the local sights. By any measure, that route featured some of the most breathtakingly beautiful vistas in the country, complete with all the wonders of the marine environment including dolphins, pelicans, and seals, and also the very chic village of Del Mar, with its artistic shops and creative restaurants.

Finally, the group would arrive at Rahul Patel's home, where a spectacular Ayurvedic feast would be prepared.

The next morning, the group met for the sunrise yoga session at the the Palm Springs Ayurvedic and Tennis Center, right outside the conference center, and made up for lost time with an early start. Many people reported having nightmares or lost sleep. As the day got going they spent a lot of time in discussion about the horrific events of the previous day, and after much-needed reassurance, began the process of reworking their meeting agenda, paring down the "nice-to-have" from the "need-to-have" items.

The first topic they discussed was "peacefulness" as opposed to "nonviolence," in case even the mention of violence further helped bring the reality of violence into existence. Not certain about the quantum-mechanical specifics of "thoughts becoming things," everyone agreed with the comment in *The Secret* that there must be some wisdom in being extremely careful with their choice of words; after all, Mother Teresa purposely attended peace rallies and would never attend an antiwar protest.

The second topic was the reverence for personal power. This seemed to be the central and unique component of a hidden biblical message. Recognition of the cocreating ability each person holds to influence either positive or negative change in the world, the group knew, was a key lever to one huge quantum leap forward in humanity; there would be exponential impact when groups combined to cocreate. This would be a new concept to many who had never learned of their power and only learned of God as a distant entity, not a force within, as well as an old one since the power of prayer—and the power of praying in groups—was a common theme to most Christians as they followed Jesus's direction "When two or three are gathered in my name."

Their third topic, "giving," would be a very hard sell because it required a new "abundance" mind-set. In the economic downturn most people feared scarcity. Unemployment in the United States hovered at about nine percent officially, but the true number was closer to sixteen percent. While the GNP was growing slowly, it wasn't by any means a measure of economic recovery. All the great economic minds predicted the United States was still headed into, not out of, something like another Great Depression. Whatever caused it—the failure of capitalism, the rise of corporatism, the greed and subsequent speculation with the creative securitization of mortgages, now migrating into the securitization of life insurance—no one was quite sure what was going on with the economy. To this group it was all mind-numbingly complex.

Courage was one thing they all felt certain they could bring about. Just the day before, their own Monisha, at 220 pounds, had hurled herself through the air without regard for her own personal safety, in the name of all things good. And she emerged unscathed. They would lead this way, leveraging the list of courageous people they were studying as human examples of Gandhi's motto "Be the change you want to see in the world."

After lunch, and having made decent progress on their agenda, the group agreed to take a break from thinking until the dinner discussion with Rahul. His car then arrived for them. Having enjoyed all the sights and raw natural beauty in the trip from Palm Springs, the group arrived at the Patel residence just before five o'clock.

As they gathered on the veranda, Rahul Patel addressed the group. "This may surprise you, but nothing ever goes wrong. The universe in its unfolding majesty holds many secrets. What we experienced yesterday was terrifying. I knew that I would not die yesterday because I know the exact date of my death and it is reassuringly far in the future. But I did not know if my presence would bring harm to you. Fortunately, that did not happen, and for your many acts of bravery and courage, please accept my thanks."

Lisette replied, "Rahul, thank you for inviting us. We are big fans. Most of us are familiar with your work and have read a number of your books. I have been to several of your seminars, and was even on your course for instructors in Ayurveda—the nutrition focus."

"Well, what happened, what stopped you?" asked Rahul.

"Oh, I may get going again with it, but at the last session I learned of the importance of 'life force' in food, and that eating food that has happy molecules can even make a person feel happier, and the reverse. To eat unhappy food is to take into our bodies unhappiness. So I haven't stopped; I was just slowed down because I was trying to avoid being a hypocrite, and start with myself before preaching all this to others. And let me tell you, it takes a whole lot of work to find a formerly happy chicken to cook for dinner."

Rahul Patel smiled.

"What about you—how are you doing?" Rahul asked Ron.

"Well, my brain is a little numb, but my fashion sense is still intact: Are those turtle-green Versace glasses?"

"They are!" Rahul chuckled.

"How often do you get death threats?" asked Larry.

"I don't know—I think quite a lot. Not so many with my books on Buddha. The Buddhists were too busy being happy to bother with me. But, ever since I wrote about Jesus, it has been a steady stream of threats. I ask my staff not to notify me so that I don't become paralyzed by the fear, but there are some people who don't even read the books and become enraged, feeling it is their duty to kill me. This was a risk worth taking when I wrote them, the only way to bring about change," he said. But he added, "Today, in a childish way, I am enjoying having Lemar and Miles here. I still enjoy safety like everyone; I just learned to take more risks. We each know that every day there are risks of going out of our homes, driving our cars, etc., but we still do them. I consciously try to avoid violence and bring peace to every situation. Once I talked a group of muggers out of hurting me or killing me."

"But how did you know you weren't going to die yesterday?" asked Hala.

"A while ago I travelled to India at the request of a close friend. This friend insisted that my prediction had been found on an ancient astrological writing on birch bark. In Sanskrit, birch is 'bhurja.' These writings were done for thousands of years up until about five hundred years ago, so all the writings are ancient. Today these astrological predictions are scattered around India but can still be read and interpreted by some special readers—they cannot write them today, just read them.

"Growing up in modern India, I never had an interest in astrology, which is called 'Jyotish'—I considered it nonsense. But later, having proven myself in Western terms, I was called back and dared to explore some of India's ancient mysteries and truths. So I agreed to have this reading done. There were some things I didn't understand; some numbers, like thirty-one, that I still don't know the significance of; but the reader knew every facet of my life and asked if I really wanted to know when I would die. After some careful thought, I said I did, and it is not soon. Would you like to see the reading? I have it here at the house."

"Yes," the group members said, and Rahul agreed to bring it out after dinner.

AFTER A BANQUET in classic Ayurvedic fashion in which meals are prepared in all the colors of the rainbow, as well as incorporating the six tastes of sweet, sour, salty, bitter, pungent, and astringent, the group retired to the living room to see the ancient writing on birch bark from India.

Pumpkin was enjoying the experience of being with a *real* Indian family for once in her life. Yesterday's brush with death also left her feeling remarkably light and burden-free. She said, "Rahul, you know Christianity as well as anyone and have written two books on Jesus. We know your focus is Christ-consciousness, which we all agree is the true centerpiece of his teaching. Do you think it is possible for us to significantly revise the Bible, both the Old and the New Testaments, to remove references to violence, genocide, subjugation of people as in slavery, and better feature equality in race and gender—the way Jesus himself lived?"

"Anything is possible, of course," Rahul Patel said. "But because many people believe the Bible is real history, they may not agree with your rewriting it. The others who value the Bible as literature may be more open to a new interpretation. Certainly, it will be welcome to half of the existing Christian population, the women. Other minorities are certain to like it as well, so within Christianity your work may start a reform movement. I say keep going and see where it takes you. If the universe wants a new Bible, by God it will arrive."

As the evening came to a close, Lisette said, "Rahul, you treaded very lightly on your suspicion that Jesus spent time in

India. I saw an interesting BBC show that also alluded to his time there; it also mentioned KrishnaTube.

"Then, just before I got into my graduate studies, I started doing my own research on the connections. I read Holger Kersten's compelling book, which tried to present irrefutable evidence that Jesus had lived in India; that he somehow survived his crucifixion and finally died there of old age. His conclusions were that in his youth, Jesus followed the ancient Silk Route to India. Over time he learned Buddhism and became a spiritual master. The writer's other conclusions were that after Jesus survived the crucifixion, he returned to India to die in old age; and, finally, that Jesus was buried in Srinagar, the capital of both Jammu and Kashmir, where he is still today revered as a saint. The tomb of Jesus still exists there.

"I've been studying this for a long time. Not many people know that the Cochin Jews were traders from Judea who arrived in the city of Cochin, India, in 562 BC, and that the Bene-Israel Jews arrived twenty-one hundred years ago—just before Jesus was born—after a shipwreck stranded seven Jewish families from Judea at Navagaon near Alibag, south of Mumbai. So really there were established Jewish connections in India at the time of Jesus.

"Then I got going on a hunch. The three Magi, or 'wise men,' as some Christians know them, were said to have come from the East. Magi were ancient astrologers and Northern India was the epicenter of Jyotish astrology at that time. So I got out an ancient map of the Far East and found this: Bethlehem's geographical coordinates are 31°43′0″ North, 35°12′0″ East, and Jammu, India's geographical coordinates are 31°14′29″ North, 77°2′12″ East. In Jammu there is a tomb of Jesus, which still exists today, due east of Bethlehem. Rahul, Bethlehem and Jammu are both located on the 31st latitude—you said that thirty-one is your significant number, correct?"

"Yes, it is," he said, knowing that the student had become the teacher.[34, 35]

22

IN ORDER TO FINISH all their slated work, the group agreed to stay an extra day at the resort. The opening prayer was given by Lisette.

"First I would like to share a quote from Robert Collyer: 'God hides some ideal in every human soul. At some time in our life, we feel a trembling, fearful longing to do some good thing. Life finds its noblest spring of excellence in this hidden impulse to do our best.'

"Heavenly master of all," she continued, "great creator divine, help this group of your devoted people as we strive to bring peace to your great creation of humanity. Let us reach high and recognize this opportunity is rare. Remove our obstacles, center us on the mission, and give us the courage to proceed. In your holy name I pray, amen."

Next, the celebration of courage was given by Anneke.

"In these past few weeks I have learned a lot about slavery, both historical and contemporary. I have learned a lot about the plethora of ways the Bible has sanctioned slavery, and I have learned about how horrible a practice it truly is on every human level. I have been spoken to by God our creator and called to action. I will do all that I am required to by this high calling.

"In Cincinnati, at the National Underground Railroad Freedom Center, I learned about a slave named Araminta Ross, who many people learn about as Harriet Tubman. She lived from 1820 until 1913. This was a woman who did many things and showed great courage and bravery. She acted as an abolitionist, a humanitarian, and even a Union spy during the Civil War. Once she escaped slavery, she didn't go to Canada where she would be free and safe from being caught. She stayed behind and completed some thirteen rescue missions of others who were enslaved, ultimately helping over seven hundred people escape.

"She had a sad story, beginning in Maryland where she was born into slavery. I learned she had been repeatedly beaten and whipped. She had a failed attempt to escape, which also likely brought upon her more beatings. Eventually she did succeed in escaping and soon returned to help her own family. Over the years she is said to have not lost anyone she was helping and she was known to be very tough with her rules about escaping, and threatened to kill the escapees if they turned back or made too much noise.

"While running errands one day, she tried to stand up for a slave who had left his farm without permission. She refused to help capture him and enraged the owner. He threw an object at her, hitting her hard in the head and knocking her unconscious. She didn't receive any treatment but slowly recovered. Along the way her faith was deepening in God. She never believed what the Bible said about slavery; she rejected that and formed her own opinions. She began having visions she believed to be from God, which she heeded.

"That is the story of Araminta Ross, otherwise known as Harriet Tubman. By now you all know that I believe God may have recently spoken to me, in a dream. In this way, I can identify with her sense of clarity and direction. I have never prayed in my life, actually not once before I joined this group. Before God called me to action, I wasn't sure there was a higher power. Please, would you all help me pray right now, that I can lead in courage to help those who are in need to escape bondage?"

Larry led the group in prayer. And from that point on, the group felt that someone in a higher place was watching them, waiting to help.

Harriet Tubman was added to the list of names of the courageous.

"Do you think the churches and synagogues will agree to help us? I mean, this does take us outside of our project goals. Aren't we supposed to stick to identifying the problematic Bible verses?" asked Lisette.

"I'm happy to do this extra part on my own; maybe it's a new calling, but if anyone wants to collaborate it would be great," offered Anneke.

"I'm in," said Pumpkin. "After Anneke's late-night calling, I drafted this letter to the under-secretary-general of the United Nations and copied a long list of churches in places where the slave trade is thriving."

The United Nations
Under-Secretary-General
2 United Nations Plaza
New York, NY 10017
And to:
The World Council of Churches
150 Route de Ferney
P.O. Box 2100
1211 Geneva 2, Switzerland

Dear Bishop, Cardinal, Reverend, Priest, Pastor, Rabbi, Minister, Deacon, Brother, and Sister:
God Almighty has on this day called you into action in a new plan to rescue from slavery and bondage all those held captive within your geographical reach. God's plan, as revealed to Anneke Lebner, directs you to follow the Law as set forth in Deuteronomy 23:15–16: "Thou shalt not deliver unto his master the servant which is escaped from his master unto thee. He shall dwell with thee, even among you, in that place which he shall choose in one of thy gates, where it liketh him best: thou shalt not oppress him."

Take this time to make preparations. Some of you may receive a steady flow of these God's servants who have been lured astray. They are coming to you for refuge and you will support them. If they choose to remain with you in your community and have no homes to return to, you are instructed to settle them in your community. If they need to be returned to their homes from which they have been taken, you will see to their safe return.

Therefore, set aside time before they come to you to reach agreements with your local government and remind them the cost of keeping their people safe is equal to the cost of their sovereignty under the Responsibility to Protect terms outlined by the United Nations.

As these enslaved people reach you, you will register them with your parent organization and your government. God will bring numerous volunteers and you are directed to meet with each person who offers support in your community to determine and organize individual roles and responsibilities.

Make haste, for some are already on their way to you, entrusted now to your care by God in accordance with a divine plan. Godspeed.

Sincerely,
The Founding Members of the Sanctuary for Grace and Hope:

Lisette Colliere, *Faculty, University of Pennsylvania Department of Religious Studies*

Ron Goodman, *Senior Researcher, Institute for Philosophy and Religion, Yale University*

T. Pumpkin Rowe, *Author*

Monisha Ray, *Board Member, The Civil Rights Museum, Memphis, Tennessee*

Anneke Lebner, *Chief Art Conservationist, The National*

Gallery of Art, Washington, D.C.

Larry Conihan, *Esq., Jazz Musician, and Sloan Business School Professor, Esoteric Finance, Massachusetts Institute of Technology*

Hala El Feddak, *CEO, Muslim Women's Global Leadership Initiative*

"That would get my attention," said Ron.

"Mine, too," said Lisette.

"Any God-fearin' preacher on this earth would be shakin' by the time they finish readin' that," said Monisha.

All agreed the letter was good to go and everyone waited for Anneke to chime in. She had been staring out a window at the perfectly manicured fairway while it was being read, considering the full impact of the undertaking.

Finally, Anneke spoke in a calm voice and with full authority.

"Let it fly."

23

ALL SETTLED into their new complex, Spiker spent the morning reviewing the options Joe presented. Agrochemical giants like Bayer, DuPont, and Monsanto controlled most pesticides, which could be divided into three main categories: herbicides, insecticides, and fungicides.

He learned that every year over $10 billion in pesticides were sold in the United States for crops, including corn (25 percent), soybeans (20 percent), and cotton (10 percent). About a quarter of pesticides are used for lawn, garden, and other household applications.

Interesting. Now, was there a way to grab market share in a hurry?

The challenge would have been easier a hundred years earlier. The Insecticide Act of 1910 put in to help protect farmers from misbranded products, not so much for public safety. Later, in 1947, Congress created the Federal Insecticide, Fungicide and Rodenticide Act, which was supposed to better control their transportation; certain pesticides being transported over state lines had to be registered with the US Department of Agriculture. By 1954 there was a systematic approach to addressing public health concerns, which until that time had been brought before Congress. Congress created the FD&C Act, which was meant to deal with issues related to food, drugs, and cosmetics. Somewhere in the FD&C Act there was a directive for the FDA to establish appropriate or acceptable residue tolerance levels.

The way that tolerance levels were established incorporated a risk/benefit analysis in which public health risks need to be weighed against the benefits to the country's food supply.

Congress later passed the Federal Environmental Pesticide Control Act in 1972, which required all pesticides made in the United States to be properly registered with the EPA. The Toxic Substances Control Act of 1976 then required chemical testing and placed new requirements on the product manufacturers to determine threat levels to either people or the environment.

Most of the industry was controlled fairly tightly, but if a public health crisis emerged, changes could be swift.

Instantly, E. coli came to mind! E. coli outbreaks were not only on the rise, but they were keeping the good people at the Centers for Disease Control awake at night because strains of E. coli were growing stronger and becoming drug resistant; this was already happening on a global scale. Arctic birds at the polar ice cap already showed signs of drug-resistant E. coli. This had the makings of a true public health nightmare, and Spiker was certain this would help him heighten urgency.

In an effort to keep the public safe, it seemed that overuse of antibiotics in the food supply had created a giant problem with infectious diseases. Simply put, with antibiotic overuse, bacteria mutate just enough to prevent those antibiotics from destroying them.

Nice. Spiker liked unintended consequences.

Well, the public may not be as frightened of E. coli as they should be, but people in Washington at the EPA and FDA were certainly receptive to solutions and preventions.

Maybe, he thought, *if a small, "specialized" firm introduced a fast-acting agent to be applied during the crop stage of food production that dramatically lowered E. coli pathogens during the processing stage, that agent would become a public heath imperative.* His agent would then be mandatory. With Joe's commitment of a higher level of funding, he could acquire a small pesticide company and reoutfit it with this new agent and leverage the distribution channels of the larger corporation.

A plan had emerged. Within twenty-four hours the shareholders of some small-time pesticide company would be cheering as the value of their stock went through the ceiling.

As Spiker pondered a list of potential companies to acquire, he reached for one of his favorite bedtime-reading books from the shelf: *How to Lie with Statistics,* by Darrell Huff.

24

"WHAT DO WE DO about all the contradictory stuff in the Bible? Is it worth pointing all this out to people, or are there bigger battles we should try to win?" Ron motioned to Lisette to join him at a large table where pages of verses were spread out.

Lisette was open to any amount of revision in the Bible. She had been taught from an early age never to question scripture. As a child, she did as she was told. By the age of fifteen, she feared she would not stop growing. As she grew taller and taller, eventually reaching six foot one, she had become the anomaly in her high school, sometimes teased and shunned. She saw no connection to the mercy and acceptance she had been taught. The small girls' school had no basketball team or other way that she could possibly turn her height into an asset, and she was left to deal with her awkwardness alone. The possibility of a boyfriend seemed nonexistent. Frustrated and lonely, she started reading the Bible for relief and answers. Lisette found some relief there, as many do, but she didn't like some of what she was reading. One day, she would find a way to set straight these teachings.

That day had come.

"The early church leaders feared that people would have a lot of trouble with all the contradictions but, in reality, not many people read the whole Bible—just bits and pieces now and then. Most people are taught not to question the Bible, so when people read something that seems oppressive or violent, for example, they just file it away in their own mental box of things they will probably never understand. Many people don't know how many contradictions exist, and some may not really care, I suppose. Ugh. There sure are a whole lot of verses to go through," she said.

Ron looked at his notes. "Even the four Gospels conflict each other regarding the order in which things happen, as well as the specific things they report. John says that Jesus's cleansing of the Temple was the beginning of his public ministry, and in the other three Gospels, they say the cleansing was at the end. In addition, there is a huge discrepancy in the accounts of Jesus's resurrection appearances to his disciples.

"Matthew says Jesus told the women at the empty tomb to go find Jesus's disciples, that Jesus would meet them or be waiting for them in Galilee. In Matthew, after the women do this, the Gospel is ended. In Luke, however, he appears first on Easter in Jerusalem and nearby on the Emmaus road, and tells them to stay in the city 'until ye be clothed with power from on high,' but in Acts it is fifty days later."

Ron continued as Lisette listened carefully, considering the merit of including these verses as part of the group's larger effort.

"Here are some I noted, such as whether God is tender or not. Psalms 145:9: 'Yahweh is good to all. His tender mercies are over all his works.'

"Jeremiah 13:14: 'I will dash them one against another, even the fathers and the sons together, says Yahweh: I will not pity, nor spare, nor have compassion, that I should not destroy them.'"

He glanced up. "It seems confusing as to whether God is in favor of war or peace. Exodus 15:3: 'The Lord is a man of war: the Lord is his name.' Romans 15:33: 'Now the God of peace be with you all. Amen.'

"And here are three Easter contradictions to consider. Matthew 28:1: 'Now after the Sabbath, as it began to dawn on the first day of the week, Mary Magdalene and the other Mary came to see the tomb.'

"Mark 16:1: 'When the Sabbath was past, Mary Magdalene, and Mary the mother of James, and Salome, bought spices, that they might come and anoint him.'

"John 20:1: 'The first day of the week cometh Mary Magdalene early, when it was yet dark, unto the sepulcher, and seeth the stone taken away from the sepulcher.'

"Here's another tough one. John 10:30: 'I and my Father are one.'

"John 14:28: 'You heard how I told you, "I go away, and I come to you." If you loved me, you would have rejoiced, because I said "I am going to my Father;" for the Father is greater than I.'

"Here are three quotes about wisdom. Proverbs 4:7: 'Wisdom is supreme. Get wisdom.'

"Ecclesiastes 1:18: 'All things are full of weariness beyond uttering. The eye is not satisfied with seeing, nor the ear filled with hearing.'

"First Corinthians 1:19: 'For it is written, "I will destroy the wisdom of the wise, I will bring the discernment of the discerning to nothing."'

"Let's figure out who should die. Isaiah 14:21: 'Prepare for slaughter of his children because of the iniquity of their fathers, that they not rise up and possess the earth, and fill the surface of the world with cities.'

"Deuteronomy 24:16: 'The fathers shall not be put to death for the children, neither shall the children be put to death for the fathers: every man shall be put to death for his own sin.'

"And what exactly happens to the righteous? Psalms 92:12: 'The righteous shall flourish like the palm tree.'

"Isaiah 57:1: 'The righteous perishes, and no man lays it to heart; and merciful men are taken away, none considering that the righteous is taken away from the evil.'

"We can't tell what became of Judas Iscariot, although the newly found Gospel of Judas is a very good read. Acts 1:18: 'Now this man obtained a field with the reward for his wickedness, and falling headlong, his body burst open, and all his intestines gushed out.'

"Matthew 27:5–7: 'He threw down the pieces of silver in the sanctuary, and departed. He went away and hanged himself. The chief priests took the pieces of silver, and said, "It's not lawful to put them into the treasury, since it is the price of blood." They took counsel, and bought the potter's field with them, to bury strangers in.'

"Oh, this gives me a headache. It goes on and on. There are over fifty others as well. It becomes nearly impossible to read the Bible literally; it's just so confusing. How are people supposed to make sense of it all?" demanded Ron.[36, 37, 38, 39]

25

T. PUMPKIN ROWE focused on the controversial issue of land acquisition and the conquering rationale in the Bible. Larry offered his help, but for the most part this was her moment. Fifty-five years in the making, she knew this category cold.

Thalia Cabot was her grandmother's older sister who, for unknown reasons, willed to Pumpkin the family compound at Penobscot Bay (which, even with the downturn in the real estate market, had been valued at $43 million). She was twenty-two at the time. She also had one of only two French schooners built in the 1840s. Pumpkin spent the better part of her life trying to peel back the onion and understand what made her the rightful owner of these gifts of land and sea.

Pumpkin had only one sister, Paige, who had long been distanced from the family. She had married a peacenik in the sixties and spent many years abroad in the peace corps, and by the time she surfaced again in the States she didn't make it back to Maine until her aunt's estate had passed hands. Paige's only son, a polite and grounded whiz kid, was Pumpkin's only nephew; and as his aunt, she spared no expense on him. She gladly paid for the best education possible, and he always brought home top grades. The two shared something special, and although they were from different worlds, they were still family, and their strong connection remained. Pumpkin had no doubts that her nephew's dreams would be realized; she truly believed the world was a better place with him in it.

He had just become the President of the United States of America.

She became the temporary figurehead of the task force since it was her idea to begin with. Many days, she spent her time searching land records to better understand the original inhabitants. Recorded as far as Pumpkin could trace back were Algonquin-speaking peoples. Shortly after the first European settlement in the early 1600s by the French came the first English settlement in Maine called the Popham Colony. Refusing to be derailed by the thought of the French and English and their long, bloody history, she marvelled at how Maine had become the poster state of Episcopalians, when in fact that denomination represented only eight percent of the population.

Her mind refocusing on the present, she wondered what caused all the anxiety about reinterpreting the Bible one more time. With thousands of forms of Christianity in the modern world, who would even notice? Some of her fellow task force members had openly voiced fears about their work attracting the attention of right-wing fundamentalist abortion-clinic-bombing radicals, maybe some Vatican spies, or well-intentioned religious freaks. Would schools even accept their children? As does most everyone, the group feared the unknown. Heresy, as their work could be named, for calling into question what is written in the Bible, was punishable by death for hundreds of years. Over the centuries thousands of people were ordered to die by the Church itself for heresy.

Pumpkin had nothing to hide or prove; she was an heiress. But percolating just below the surface of her hard exterior was her adversary, guilt. She never knew how to shake it, no matter how she tried. New England's finest psychiatrists and Sedona's finest self-help workshops couldn't do it. On the hundred or so levels of consciousness that exist between the extremes of being alert and dead, guilt pervaded even her dreams as she tried to wrestle with her good fate.

Those things that limit us, thoughts or suspicions in our minds, fears put there by others or conjured up by the self; that was her battlefield—the Wild West of her own mind. If only she could do it—tame the bucking bronco of guilt. But the goal was elusive, as the freeing of the spirit to reach its full potential and possibly achieve maximum impact in a human life requires the clarity of what is, the confidence to move on, the courage to stare down one's past and an extraordinary level of comfort in one's own skin to create the present. She wasn't there yet.

Her parents and grandparents told the story of the Deerfield Massacre numerous times, and the fate of twenty-nine of her family members: eleven of them killed and scalped there, and the rest marched toward Canada, four more dying along the way. It was French and Native Americans who had attacked her ancestors' settlement in Massachusetts. Although it took place in February 1704, her family spoke of the attack as recent history. Forty-one colonists were immediately killed and perhaps a hundred and twelve were taken captive, including children. They were forced to march for months toward Quebec, some three hundred miles away in the dead of winter, and the story was that over twenty of them died during the journey. Some of her ancestors eventually managed to make their way back to New England. This family encounter with "the natives" resulted in a permanent disdain for indigenous people. Pumpkin was determined to close that old gap of relationships somehow.[40, 41]

This was about the same time the Salem witch hangings were happening. In the name of God, nineteen people were killed for being witches and nearly one hundred and fifty others were accused of being witches. The people of Maine nearby were on edge, her ancestors among them.

By 1702 Harvard and Yale had already been established to serve as training schools for new clergy. *Well,* she thought to herself, *how many know that?* At the time, the church was more powerful than the state in America. Imagine that.

One of the ways the ministers measured progress was by the numbers of Indians converted to Christianity, who would then be called "praying Indians." *For all our modern-day "respect" for religious freedom, they sure didn't have much back then,* Pumpkin mused. The early settlers believed that God had sanctioned them to take the new land by directing their king and leader to lead such action. Questioning the king's orders would be like questioning God—unheard of.

There was a knock at the door. *Hmmm,* she thought, *I wonder if that could be the newly wealthy Mashantucket Pequots of Connecticut coming by with a cake or a peace pipe.*

Larry Conihan, the celebrated musician and an elite task force member from Boston. Strolling in like an afternoon breeze through a bay window, he greeted her with, "Hey there, brain trust, whatcha working on?"

"Not much. It's slow going trying to untangle the right and wrong of four hundred years of land ownership in my own backyard as a way of working up to the biblical challenge of taking on the preceding six thousand years."

"Oh, all that Indian stuff," he responded.

"Larry, I value your help and appreciate your company. Let's enjoy a nice evening, a lobster bake, and even a sunset sail. You can help me untangle this web, and you can help get this question answered. But in my presence, don't refer to Native Americans as 'Indians.' Having plundered and killed most of these people, we must refer to them as they were." She took a deep breath and began reciting a very long list of 170 tribes: "Ababco, Abenaki, Aberginian, Abittibi, Abnaki . . ."[42]

"Ouch," he said. "That brain of yours is frightening."

"You have no idea," she said as they headed down to the beach.

AFTER DINNER Larry said, "We have many rough days ahead as we delve into these task force subjects. I want to help as much as I can. But just so we're clear, I'm on your side. We do all share a land that may have been taken by means we don't employ today, and hopefully will never again. Personally, I empathize with your effort. While the Native Americans were being diminished here, most of my ancestors were being killed and sent on death marches by the Bolsheviks and Cossacks. A bunch of my other ancestors died in the Potato Famine."

"Good to know your history," Pumpkin said. "Larry, I realize you may not see the relevance of my work just yet. I leave you with two words to ponder until next week when we reconnect on this: Iraq and Afghanistan."

26

MICHELLE DECIDED to read Tommy's letter. It had now been over twenty years, and she hadn't heard back from him once. Probably never would. For the sake of closure she finally wanted to read it and then she hoped she could allow herself to move on.

The envelope with the hummingbird was as beautiful as she remembered. Opening the flap, she slid out two small pieces of vellum that read:

> Michelle, you are my one love and I was meant for you. We share the same amazing spirit and can never be apart. No type of religion, no amount distance, no complicated relationships, and no oppressive society can separate us. Not in this lifetime. In this lifetime, you are mine and I am yours. From this moment on, we walk this earth together with our heads held high. When I see you, I see only joy, I see pure love. I see my whole life yet to live, I see our happy, hopeful, healthy children. I will remain the luckiest man alive, safe in your arms, until the end of time.
>
> Love, Tommy

Michelle carefully removed the second page and held her breath as she read:

In the name of the one sun that lights the world,
In the name of the one moon that finds its way back each night,
In the name of the one universe in all her majesty,
In the name of the one love we share,
I know you are my one. Will you marry me?

Any air that was left in her lungs exited her body. Michelle's knees went weak and the last thing she would remember that day was the feeling of falling backwards, hitting her head on a wall, and sliding down into a very quick state of unconsciousness.

27

FOR THE MOST PART, Larry worked alone to find a strong financial model that would work for the group and its mission. If anyone was capable of devising a plan, he certainly was, having earned his doctorate in mathematics at MIT, following a master's in finance at MIT's Sloan School of Management, where he now taught an occasional course. He loved music, loved his legal cases, but his main love was math—at least ever since his wife left him for a younger man. Now, with his daughter recently graduating college, he was left with one low-maintenance seagull in his life. A one-legged seagull, which resulted from the gull's near theft of his steak dinner one night a few years back.

His aim was to keep it simple, so that not only the group, but also the average churchgoing person could understand and adopt the new financial model. "Simple" was often the hardest thing to achieve, but he felt pretty good about what he was about to propose.

Today he was conducting his eighth focus group with fifteen people, this time seven women and eight men. Three Catholics, two Presbyterians, one Armenian Orthodox, three

Jews, three Baptists, two Methodists, one Congregational and one Episcopalian. He felt the need to test some assumptions, get some early reactions, and make any adjustments necessary.

He began by introducing himself and stating the mission of the Sanctuary for Grace and Hope. As Larry explained the group's mission, he underscored that the group planned to issue a new version of the Bible, which could be exactly the same as whatever current Bibles they might be used to, but with references to violence, slavery, and genocide deleted and anything that implied gender preference neutralized. This new version would be "phased in" as an alternative for those who do not want to lean on a source of religious guidance that promoted actions that demean or dehumanize people. He explained that in order for the group to succeed, it would need to bring about change from within churches and synagogues peacefully and patiently over time. As he had done the previous seven times, he explained that the rapidness of the change would depend on several things.

First, it would depend on how many people would want a Bible reflecting their beliefs about what is good and worthy of their study and practice—especially what they want their children to learn when they read it—the reason for this focus group.

Second, it would depend on how comfortable people felt in challenging their own faith organizations to reform their messages.

Third, it would require people to be willing to vote for the change with their money.

"How does that sound so far?" he asked the group.

Each time he ran a session, he was getting better at his group-facilitation skills, and checking in with people frequently was the fastest way to move through the predictable range of questions.

"So, you actually want to revise the Bible?" asked a Catholic man with "Bob" on his name tag.

"Yes. Correct, Bob. Our hunch is that people are hungry for change in a positive direction toward a more peaceful coexistence on the planet."

"Well, I can already tell you I would sign up to do this at my church," one of the Catholic women said. "We are long overdue."

Marie, a Methodist woman in her thirties, said, "I really [illegible]e what's wrong with the Bible the way it is."

[illegible]swered, "A lot of people don't, Marie, and you [illegible]t. Tell me, do you have children?"

[illegible]vo," she said.

[illegible]re they?"

[illegible] a nine-year-old son and an eleven-year-old [illegible] Marie said.

[illegible] ages," Larry said. "Do you teach them that slavery is a good or acceptable practice?"

"No!" Marie said instantly.

"Do you teach them that genocide is sometimes okay, or that women should be subservient, and not allowed to hold senior positions, or that racism is okay?"

"No, of course not," she said.

"Do you let them read violent literature, or watch R-rated movies?"

"No, I only let them watch PG movies," she said.

"Well, that's probably good. Most people are like you and want to expose their children to positive examples of goodness in humanity as a way of setting them up for success in life and in their own relationships. Most people don't try to raise hateful, war-bound children. The Bible as it is written now has numerous references to these things—and most people don't even know that.

"There is a code of teaching within most faiths, which leans on something called 'orthopraxy,' which implies a correct action or correct activity. Orthopraxy places emphasis on ethical conduct. In other words, the church has already overruled the Bible in matters of genocide, slavery, violence, racism, and sexism, but most people don't know that. There is a document that pastors, priests, even rabbis must sign before they are allowed to teach, so most do not actually teach the darker practices described in the Bible, or they risk getting in trouble by their religious authorities, but they are there. Have a look at this list of verses," he said, as he handed out a pamphlet. "Split up into five groups of three and take the next fifteen minutes to discuss these verses and be prepared to tell me which ones are worthy of your study, and which you feel comfortable having your children read when they read the Bible by themselves. You can read from your own Bibles if you brought them along or there is a large selection in the back of the room you can select from."

After the small groups had been working for a few minutes, Larry greeted Ron, who had stopped by.

"Thanks for your visit," Larry said.

"I was in the neighborhood, thought I'd see if you needed some help." Ron looked hopeful.

"I appreciate that. Right now, the group members are doing an exercise in awareness. It is exactly what I have seen the past seven times I have done these two-hour sessions. They are realizing for the first time that what they stand for, what they teach their own children; some of the things that make them feel like 'good people' or 'God's people' is in direct conflict with the Bible. They have to get there on their own, but watch what happens next," he said.

"Okay everybody, pick one person from your table to speak on behalf of the group to tell us which of these verses is worthy of keeping. Group one?" Larry prompted.

"None, it seems," said Charlotte, a Baptist woman.

"Group two?" said Ron.

"We decided they really don't do anybody any good," said Raffi, an Armenian man.

"Group three?"

"We agree they all should go," said Marie.

"Group four?"

"They're out!" said Marni, a Jewish woman.

"Group five?"

"We agree with everyone. Uh, none of us knew about these verses," said Bob.

"Well, you are in good company. People everywhere, from all lifestyles, from all religious denominations, and from many different religions themselves, agree with you."

"How are you going to be able to convince the religions to adopt a new Bible?" asked Paul, a Presbyterian.

"We are going to set up a system of rewards and consequences. Those who adopt or at least offer the new Bible as an alternative to what they are currently using will get the rewards of a lot of new members. Those institutions that resist will be faced with a whole lot of people who for a one-year time period will withhold their donations and pledges. In the interest of long-term positive change, we feel confident people will be willing to be bold and push back with the almighty dollar for a year against their institutions."

Herb, a Jewish man, said, "In our community, change is so slow it is almost imperceptible, happening in tiny steps over thousands of years, but slowly it does come. We have women rabbis now. So, I guess I would be willing to try."

Other people said similar things and no one voiced resistance to the goal. Then finally, one of the Baptist men said, "I don't think it really is possible. Things are the way they are, and they will stay that way. I don't think change will be possible even though I agree with everyone."

"Yet slavery was abolished, women vote, and we have a biracial president," Ron threw out for consideration.

If one universal thing was true, Larry mused, *it was this: Asking people to consider change always brought objections*. People are naturally change-averse. Objections and concerns need to be fully resolved and overcome, and in order to do so you cannot pretend they are not there—cannot go around them or bulldoze through them. Something he learned during his business-school days came to mind: you must meet people where they are and understand their concerns.

He decided not to press on until the group members expressed all their worries. "Tell me why you think this can't be done," Ron said.

"Well, the elders will resist it, try to quiet us down," Jean, a Congregational woman, said.

"People could be blacklisted socially," Marie said. "My kids go to a church school, too."

Marni said, "Every time Jews have tried to bring about change, God has a way of crashing down on us."

"Oh," Larry said. "Well, these are some valid concerns. Change is often hard for people to get their minds around, and many people do fear change. Others never try because they feel it can't be done. Why don't you spend the next five minutes putting together a wish list of the kinds of changes you would really like to see, if it were possible, just to give them all consideration?"

The group members came up with fourteen common themes. They happened to be themes he was well familiar with.

"Okay, these are all good. In fact, many of these are the same ones our group arrived at. Let's leave them alone for a moment.

"This is not a lecture session but you may find these facts interesting from the website pewforum.org. In brief, it seems that Americans change religions fairly frequently. As we can see on this chart, many—even as many as fifty percent—of Americans change religions at least once. Statistics say that those who change religions often do so before age twenty-five, and those who change once are likely to change more than once.

"I have reviewed information that indicates as many as sixty-six percent of Catholics who later decided to move away from the Catholic church, and maybe fifty percent of Protestants who decided to try a different Christian denomination agree that the reason they no longer practice the faith they learned as children is due to the fact that they do not believe in the teachings. This shows a lot of personal questioning of teachings as the core issue for people who change or keep looking for new faith systems.

"Perhaps a lot of people move away from their own religions because they see examples of hypocrisy or they realize on their own that the institutions are money-focused, or that perhaps the rules are impossible for them to live by and therefore set them up for failure in life.

"Catholicism used to be considered impossible to change, but because it has sustained the biggest loss of members, it, too, is changing, at a rate perhaps too slowly to avoid the fallout. Nevertheless the church over the centuries has adapted to demands for change. In times of real need the Catholic Church changes quickly. Recently, the sex abuse scandals are driving Catholics out of the church in record numbers, motivating quick changes in policy to bolster confidence."[43]

"What about the Jews?" a woman asked.

"Well, Jews are also in crisis. According to the Israeli Ministry for Foreign Affairs, the rate of intermarriage among Diaspora Jews continues to worry those who want to preserve the race and religion. It appears that the rate of intermarriage among American Jews is over fifty percent. This is a much higher rate of intermarriage than in previous generations; for example, thirty years ago the numbers were closer to ten percent, so this is cause for concern to certain Jewish communities who fear losing their heritage.

"In terms of real loss of numbers, there were less than eleven million Jews living outside Israel and currently there may be as few as eight million by some estimates, which could be considered a substantial loss. Due to factors of high assimilation and low birth rate, Judaism is also at risk.[44]

"We therefore see that the organizations we assume to be strong and unchangeable are really in need of change in order to survive."

The group members took in this information, and it hit them each in a different way, but they all got the same message: if they encouraged change, they would actually be helping their religions in their own way.

"Religions will change or they will die out. And actually, everyone wins with this kind of positive change. Everyone gets to keep his or her church of choice. People have religions they can really believe in and be excited about, not feel conflicted about. The religions can do a better job of taking care of their people and their charities with more money down the line, etc. You may not believe me, but this change is not hard to bring about. It does require courage and action—and it really is all about money. In these already-threatened religions, money is power. A significant drop in collections would prompt swift action. What we hope for is change over a twenty-five-year period. We think that most people over time will begin to feel good about the new Bible, to the point where the old Bible will become an artifact.

"By my math the tipping point is just over a quarter of the people—so if twenty-seven percent of any of the congregation withheld contributions for a year in order to prompt swift change, change would be immediate because not one of these institutions would prefer bankruptcy as an alternative to change.

"In the meantime, if people still want to give to a good cause, they could be encouraged to loan money through Kiva, which will do enormous good in developing countries, and will give people a sense of 'doing good' in the global community while they are withholding donations to their own churches, and thereby not supporting their local church community. Funds will be fully repaid—usually in under a year—so individuals and families can decide to loan it out through Kiva again, or donate it to their church or synagogue. Thereby the local community church can collect all its contributions within a year, if it changes quickly."

"What is Kiva?" a Presbyterian woman asked.

"Kiva is a great way to do something good with a little bit of money each month, but it is money that gets repaid, so that you would be able to give the money to your church or charity again in the future. It is a way to lend money to people mostly in developing countries who really need economic support to start businesses. By lending money, often very poor people can meet their needs. For anyone with Internet access, it's a simple process, and loans can be made in small amounts such as twenty-five dollars at a time, so if a person usually puts twenty-five dollars in the collection plate, now they can donate it through PayPal to Kiva. It is a vehicle for doing good in the world without permanently giving your own money away. So far almost a million individuals have lent a quarter of a billion dollars to individuals, families, and small teams to alleviate poverty. Nearly every cent has been repaid on time."

The group was fascinated. By the end of the two-hour session, Larry and Ron had fifteen eager people willing to try to bring about change in their own faith communities.

As the group dispersed, Larry said to Ron, "Another win; a one-hundred percent acceptance rate in less than two hours. I have replicated this now eight times."

Never imagining he would say these words to a math guy, Ron told him, "You rock."

28

FOR A FEW MINUTES, Larry was blown away. The change that seemed distant and theoretical now seemed real and possible, actually even within reach. As the group dispersed with their action steps, Larry noticed three young people who had walked into the room—and not just any three, it turned out.

This particular three-member team was from the University of Washington and had just beaten the math powerhouses at MIT, Yale, and the University of California, Berkeley, in a prestigious mathematics competition. It was not the first time; in fact, during the previous three years they had won four top awards. The Consortium for Mathematics and Its Applications hosted an annual mathematical contest in modelling. Out of the participating teams, just seven—including this one from UW—were winners. They were quickly greeted by Matt Stevens of Harvard, who had also just walked in.

Larry was used to big math, and for the past twenty years had considered nothing to be more fun than solving some of the largest, most complex math and finance puzzles in the world. He was happy to take his place among some other fairly decent math whizzes.

Feeling a bit too alone in the magnitude of the financial implications of the task forces goals, Larry had asked Ron to call his sister, who had just moved to Cambridge after accepting a fairly new Harvard Business School professorship in the field of data warehousing, to see if she could coordinate a meeting with Stevens, the prestigious finance expert and Baker Foundation Professor at the Harvard Business School. Stevens had received his BS degree from Yale, and his MBA from Harvard. His help as a sounding board would be welcome.

Ron, who was still discussing the session with Larry, was asked to join them for their lunch meeting. He couldn't imagine he was going to understand much from the heavy-hitting math nerds . . . eh, *stars*. It just seemed impolite to decline, so he figured at a minimum it would be a nice lunch. A meal is a meal, even if the conversation is way over one's head.

As lunch got under way, Matt said, "It was humbling to learn that 2,062 languages have translations of at least one book of the Bible, particularly because I never knew there were 2,062 languages."

"True," said Ron. "It appears as of 1804 there were just over 400 million copies of the Bible in circulation. By the 1930s there were 1.3 billion copies, and by 1975 there were 2.5 billion copies sold."

Larry added, "A friend in the publishing world explained that there are so many ways of publishing, including digital media, podcasts, e-books, etc., that timing the release of a book is an issue as well. No one yet understands how e-books compete with print books and no one wants to give up profits. For example, a hardcover Bible might ordinarily sell for about $30, while a typical price for any kind of e-book might be about $10. Amazon.com sells their e-books for the Kindle at $9.99, so perhaps that is now the de facto price for bestsellers, causing concern to publishers that profit margins will erode over time. Books have low margins to begin with. As for timing of the e-book release, the jury is still out. Maybe e-book buyers would get upset if they had to wait longer, having invested in their nifty iPads or Kindles. One analyst, Steve Weinstein, argues that global e-book sales at Amazon could reach $2.5 billion by the year 2012."[45]

"In our case, we hope demand will be so high that the e-books will have to be offered first, maybe even before we can print new Bibles," Ron contributed.

"Tell me, dream team, what have you got?" Matt asked.

"Well, for more than forty generations the Bible has remained the bestselling book of all time with buyers primarily counted among the nearly two and a half billion Christians and Jews in the world," recapped Andy Sorensen.

"Continue," said Ron.

Suzanne Roberts interjected: "Over a period of twenty-five years, starting in 2012, if we phase out the old Bible and phase in the new Bible in a staggered release, beginning with electronic versions at zero marginal cost, and then we experiment with giving away one thing to sell something else, such as a free immediate download or link with a preorder for hard copy . . ." she trailed off.

"Yes?" asked Matt.

Roger Ramos picked up. "Good thing you are all sitting down. Basically, maximum print capacity for all the large publishers combined, assuming they would all agree to do this, is about one hundred million copies per year, which would run for twenty-five years to replace and offer alternatives to the current Bibles in existence."

"Go on," said Larry, wondering if they would reach the same conclusions he had.

"So, if we are very conservative in our estimates, and make a profit of one dollar on each Bible, and invest that profit at eight percent compounding interest, we conservatively predict you will have eight billion, six hundred fifty-nine million, two hundred thirty-seven thousand, two hundred thirty-four dollars and three cents in net assets in twenty-five years' time," said Suzanne with a straight face.

Ron dropped his fork. "Billion with a *b*?" he said, astonished.

"By comparison, the assets of the Roman Catholic Church are estimated at under one billion dollars. Professor Thomas J. Reese, an American Vatican expert from Woodstock Theological Center at Georgetown University, says in his book, *Inside the Vatican,* that he found the Holy See ran a deficit from 1970 until 1993. The budget of the Vatican City itself is one hundred thirty million dollars annually," Matt added.

Larry cut in. "There is one problem. It seems Christianity has no central governing authority or single buying source for Bibles. Each church, in other words, each denomination, would have to somehow endorse and adopt the new Bible. Therefore parishioners at the grassroots level would need to show demand in order to bring about change in their own churches."

"How many denominations are there—more than a thousand?" asked Ron as he remembered the various groups represented in the latest focus group.

Larry replied, "Way more. More than twenty thousand denominations of Christianity. See for yourself." He handed Larry a list and motioned for him to pass it around.[46]

"So, I'm sorry to interrupt, I just can't get my mind around this. *Eight* billion dollars is what we can expect from the new Bible?" Ron asked.

"Not really," said Suzanne as she sucked in a deep breath. "It's just that in your case the costs of distribution and production are very low, the content is very stable, the electronic 'teaser' and the huge 'gift' aspect of the Bible imply that even if we sell the Bible at half price the entire time, we think the better estimate is closer to a profit of two dollars per sale, meaning that a more realistic estimate is twenty-two billion, eight hundred fifty million, four hundred thirty-nine thousand, two hundred seventy-five dollars and thirty-three cents in true projected net profits to your organization."

There was a stunned silence as the figure rang in their heads.

"Show me your math," said Larry as he and Matt began clearing the dining table so they could examine more than four hundred pages of equations.

As Ron eased away from the table slowly, he knew the task force had no immediate need for profit, stakeholders, or annual dividends. He briefly short-circuited his brain when he tried to imagine that money gaining interest somewhere.

He thought about the group; would greed enter and take hold of some of the members? These were mostly academics flattered to be participating in the task force, but would one or two make a power play when money entered the mix? Perhaps they should address with the president directly in their next progress-update call.

He remembered seeing a quote from Albert Einstein in a subway station in Back Bay: "The most powerful force in the universe is compound interest."

29

IT WASN'T HARD at all to gain market share with a pesticide that also had a guaranteed E. coli prevention feature, provided the company didn't actually need to make a profit and was willing to even lose money. Low cost, high results . . . no corporate buyer with P and L responsibility could resist a deal like that.

Bigwigs in Washington would spin the new product as the result of years of research and development with public health foremost as their concern.

Spinach growers would celebrate.

Industrialized meat manufacturers would launch new marketing campaigns, still reeling from the mad cow outbreak and trying their best to court a somewhat leery public who were watching films like *Food, Inc.* and starting to buy grass-fed beef.

It would take three weeks for the product to be fast-tracked through EPA and FDA approvals; meanwhile, manufacturing would begin, followed by presales, and the release date would be set for April 15. By May 1, crops across the United States would be drenched in Spiker's sterilization cocktail, the effects of which would begin entering the food supply immediately and saturating it by May 31.

The timing was perfect. Menstruation rates would begin falling off for at least eight weeks, well into the beginning of the World Cup, which would run June 12 through July 13.

Spiker was prepared for that. He would release a study to mislead the public for a while—getting them off the scent. A team that was about to be very highly paid would suggest that global warming was starting to cause a certain kind of acid rain that could render menstruation temporarily dormant. Once the CDC had its first hundred cases, a scholarly article would be published in the prestigious *New England Journal of Medicine*, causing widespread concern—and the appropriation of new research funds.

What a plan! Spiker was giddy at the idea of a big, splashy announcement in front of the world, maybe even at the World Cup finals, if he could hold off that long. He loved the idea of mass hysteria, mayhem, and public outrage. The fantasy pervaded his thoughts.

Oh, he would send his message. Hitler would be rewritten as a small fry. His would be forever known as the loudest, clearest message in the history of humanity.

It was a beautiful thing: the single largest act of terrorism—ever.

30

SPIRITFEST was the sixth such global event in which the Spirit called forth many of the "spiritually aware" in a grand-scale union to lend assistance to the passing over of souls that for varying reasons had not yet crossed into the light. Like the previous events, it was to be another real-time webinar. In the past, these webinars were intended for psychics, mediums, clairvoyants, "lightworkers," healers, and other like-minded spirits.

This time, however, the invitation was broadened to all spiritual groups, including organized religions, though some of the invites would be received poorly and thrown into the trash.

Monisha had rescued one of these invitations from the garbage at her local church while volunteering at the front desk. "Now this is somethin' I jus' gotta see for myself," she said.

The date of the event was, in most places, October 9, depending on the time zone. The landing page of the webinar read, *"Quantum physics, organized religion, and spirituality each respect the great mystery."*

A voice came over the Internet: "Let us remember Saint Gregory of Nyssa, this great fourth-century theologian, who said that when considering the universe, we can easily believe that the divine spirit is present in everything; pervading, embracing, and penetrating it. According to Teilhard de Chardin, we live in a divine milieu in which energy permeates the entire universe. He considers energy the pulse of life. In his view, the Spirit is a channel of divine energy, evidenced by chaos, consciousness, and connection. We are here for this purpose as Teilhard de Chardin challenged us, 'to join forces and pool resources for the greater good.' In this setting linked spirits transcend limitations, joining that divine energy to liberate and bless. Welcome to Spiritfest."

Nearly two hundred thousand people had registered for this online celebration and all were tuning in to the message when a strange interference brought the webinar to a halt.

On computer screens throughout the world flashed an image of an F-35 Joint Strike Fighter. The image flickered and then became clear for about ten seconds. Later, it would be found that individuals throughout the world saw the F-35 Fighter leave the screen differently—some would claim it exited with a hard bank to the right, while others would claim it nose-dived down and still others would say the image turned and headed off the screen to the left.

Hackers? Webinar malfunction? No one was sure. Was it a sign of some sort? The viewers were largely open to the supernatural and the possibility was real to them that this appearance was not a mistake, but rather a specific message from the universe. Was it a warning? Was it a welcome?

One thing was sure. The F-35 Joint Strike Fighter was the new sweetheart powerhouse that had begun replacing the A-10 Warthog and the F-16 Fighting Falcon in the military's arsenal. Over the years, several tactical aircraft acquisition programs had attempted to deliver new war-fighting capabilities to the US Air Force, Navy, Marine Corps, and their allies. Most of those programs failed but the Joint Strike Fighter excelled. In recent years it had emerged as the world's most stealthy, supersonic, and powerfully lethal multirole fighter.

Monisha blinked her eyes and the image was still gone. Chatter from all over the world on the webinar's live-chat box confirmed that many thousands of people had seen the same thing, except for the way the plane left the screen. How odd.

They may all be woo-woo crackpots, she thought, *but sure as sugar they ain't all blind.*

The moderator, Tien, cut in and suspended the flurry of live chat. "I suspect we have received a sign from the universe. It is a warning or perhaps it is a welcome. Something to do with this plane is important for us to consider. Let us not be afraid; let us embrace the gift of this sign and meditate on what we need to do about the information we have received. Let us all be silent for the next twenty minutes and listen to the universe for clarity, and then we will resume the conference."

Monisha took the time to say a simple prayer: "Lord in heaven, please tell me, what are we supposed to do? Did you jus' send us a sign, or was it an accident to see a warplane? And please be clear 'cause you know I ain't too good with instructions anyway. If there's somethin' you need help with, you jus' let me know, but if you don't mind too much, be real clear 'bout it and don' go leavin' no guesswork in it 'cause you know how we humans are anyway, even when you are clear. Amen."

Getting impatient, she texted Miles: "You ain't gonna believe what I jus' now seen."

"Be quick, baby. Coach in a bad ol' mood today."

"Right. Me and, uh, well, my couple hundred thousand rather new, uh, spiritual friends— we have jus' seen a fighter jet!"

"You and who and what and where?"

"On the Internet."

"Girl, get off that Internet—darn viruses gonna blow up that computer."

She saw the group starting up again and resisted the urge to call CNN.

Tien began, "Thank you all for participating and being present with the Spirit. Thank you for taking the time to tune in and better clarify the message we are receiving. Please now take the time to write in the chat space your interpretations so that we may agree on actions."

Monisha read as many as she could. The messages seemed to be consistently saying that groups were feeling God was reaching out and speaking to them. She noticed that people were using the terms "God" and "the Spirit" and "the Universe."

People seemed excited, not afraid. Monisha decided not to chat; she certainly didn't want to get Miles upset by entering an online chat room. Poor man had never been on the Internet but had heard enough stories to scare him, and then after his buddy Mo had his identity stolen, Miles had no interest at all. Monisha, on the other hand, couldn't help herself. Life was a lot more interesting now, but she couldn't stay away from the darn thing.

When Miles came in for dinner she decided to abandon the group and check in later that night. In fact it would be twenty hours later that the chat would finally subside, setting a webinar record for the longest broadband conference in the history of the Internet; and in retrospect, a good thing she didn't try to stay with it the whole time.

At dinner, Monisha looked over at Lemar and said,

"Let me ask you somethin'. You ever heard of a JSF? It's a plane."

"Yes, ma'am."

"Well, would you min' tellin' your auntie all you know about that JSF?"

"Yes, ma'am. I mean no, ma'am. I don' mind at all."

After the plates were cleared, Monisha sat out on the porch with Miles as they listened to Lemar's description of the JSF and why it is important. The details went mostly over her head, but she asked a question she hoped would point her in the right direction: "So could the JSF be used for anything evil, like a weapon of mass destruction or somethin'?"

"No, ma'am." Lemar thought about his next words carefully. "I'll tell you this. If there ever was a WMD out there, one about to fire on us, let's jus' say, well, there in that moment you ain't never seen such a beautiful sight in your life as the F-35 JSF."

31

RABBI SHIRA ROSENBLATT of the Kesher group of liberal Jews at the University of Pennsylvania sat quietly, glued to her chair and captivated by what seemed to be an escalating debate, one she never thought she would hear. She had arrived more than an hour early due to a rare thing—almost no traffic on the Walt Whitman Bridge, a blessing from God, she was sure.

While she worked at the university, Shira commuted from the suburb of Cherry Hill, New Jersey, so she knew how slow traffic could be. She was attending the discussion at the invitation of her old friend Mandy Portman, now the eighth president of the university, and had been asked to lead a discussion and also serve as a panellist. The call from Mandy had been brief, but it seemed from her conversation with a colleague at Harvard recently that the university had been tipped off about an unorthodox group considering revising the Bible.

Mandy had finally tracked down Lisette, who was not only on her university's payroll but also a member of the group itself. After a brief and positive dialogue, Lisette readily agreed to present the project and be part of a panel. Harvard would not be the leading Ivy Leaguer on this one, no way. Other panellists from many Christian and Jewish denominations would be attending, along with more than five hundred students who would fill the lecture hall to capacity.

Shira had been asked to facilitate an inclusive discussion that would center on whether there would be enough interest and support in amending the Bible to reflect a more peaceful human purpose. At first she thought it was yet another intellectual exercise carried out in a large-group format—she was aware that academics are masterful at substituting thought for movement and movement for progress. Nonetheless, she set about to please her old friend in the high and lofty post.

Thoroughly prepared, she planned to use the extra time to catch up on e-mails and voice mails, but she happened upon a captivating conversation. There was only so much interest she had in listening to the Hillel rabbis debate the latest thinking on whether glatt kosher was truly the highest, purest way of keeping kosher, or whether—given current thinking—perhaps local organic, vegan glatt kosher was just a smidge safer. She had stumbled into a spirited live debate between two Christians and was going to do her best to be a fly on the wall so she could savor every point.

Lisette was explaining the group's project to Pastor Peter Billington, a conservative Presbyterian pastor from somewhere near Lubbock in west Texas. Peter was not only conservative, but also a true Calvinist, believing everything was predestined by God to happen. Born and raised in Collingswood, New Jersey, he came from a family that were proud members of the Faith Christian Church. His childhood church started an extreme movement of Presbyterians, deeming themselves "Bible Presbyterians," led by the late fire-and-brimstone-preaching Dr. Carl McIntire.

As extreme movements often do, this group predicted the Rapture and the end of the world by the turn of the millennium. Moreover, they were sure of it. All the signs were there. When the end of the world didn't come, the faction flatlined, and after years of spreading God's wrath and condemnation all over south Jersey, the church died in an ignoble, embarrassing, and quietly religious fashion. After a job transfer, Peter had been introduced to Sally, the daughter of the largest pig farmer in the Southwest. Since Sally had no intention of moving east, Peter felt the Lord intended him to relocate to west Texas. Peter did not believe women had the right to be leaders in his church and as a result, many Presbyterians in west Texas were being taught to think the very same way.

Peter, therefore, did not think highly of the project at hand, or of Lisette, the woman introducing it.

Lisette seemed uninterested in engaging with Peter in any kind of religious sparring but she had nowhere to hide. As she assembled her notes and handouts, he stated matter-of-factly, "What is the law according to God, man shall never question it or be condemned in His fury."

"I understand your perspective, Peter," Lisette said. "Tell me, what do you think of Ezekiel 20:25? You know the verse, right? The one in which God admits to intentionally giving out bad laws?"

"They are there for a reason, you see," said Peter.

"As a Calvinist, you must be thinking that maybe revising the Bible was predestined to happen at this time, right?" Lisette asked him, hoping that if only she could find a pleasant way to engage this guy for a while he might not be so offensive and actually walk away having learned something.

"Everything we need to learn is in the Bible, and we are to do exactly what it commands," said Peter, sounding sure of himself.

"You mentioned your wife's name is Sally, right?" said Lisette. "And her father's name?"

"Billy."

"So if Billy told you the only way you could marry Sally was to cut off the foreskins of one hundred men and bring them to him, would you do it? Would you perhaps try to show off by going all-out and killing two hundred men to collect their foreskins just to really impress him? I'm sure you knew that is what Saul told David to do in order to marry his daughter, Michal, in First Samuel 18:25–27. As I recall, he went all out and brought two hundred foreskins."

"I do not preach breaking any laws or killing anyone. The laws in the times of the Bible were the laws then," Peter said, realizing he might need to backpedal or he could very well lose some points with this woman.

"Peter, if the biblical laws do not apply to us, why do we continue to teach them to our children as though they should learn them and abide by them, too?" Lisette asked sincerely.

"We teach our children the Word as it is written, nothing more, nothing less," he said.

"Then have you taught your children the sweet story in Second Kings 2:23–24 in which Elisha is jeered while walking to Bethel, teased by children who called him a 'baldhead.'

Seems Elisha was really not in the mood for it, so he called a curse on them in the name of God and instantly two female bears came barrelling out of the woods, mauling forty-two children. Perhaps you pull that one out occasionally as a bedtime story?" Lisette asked sarcastically.

"Nonsense, children must be taught not to tease. That is the moral of the story," said Peter, clearly in a huff.

Shira was pretending to read countless e-mails on her cell phone in the back of the room, but not missing a single volley in this exchange.

"Do you teach children in your church to curse your fruit trees to death as Jesus did in Matthew 21:19?"

"Of course not," Peter said.

Lisette briefly caught Shira's eye and quickly threw her a look that could only mean "Would you please drive a nail through my skull and put me out of my misery?"

Shira shot back a look that could only mean "Oh, it's on, girlfriend."

But she calmly asked Peter, "Do you have any animals on your farm?"

"Why yes, we keep some livestock," he said.

"Do you teach your children that the animals can talk as in Balaam's talking donkey from Numbers 22:28?"

"No, of course not. That was the Lord's work, of course," Peter retorted, unwilling to bend.

Lisette added, "Peter, the others will be arriving any minute, and yes, I can go on all day. I hope you can contribute to the panel in a positive way. Now, if you will excuse me, I need to prepare my comments and test the equipment."

As she left, she thought she heard him say, "Darn women."

As mistakes go, this comment would go down as a rather big one, because nearby, Shira heard it, too.

Twelve minutes later the room was nearly full, the lights were dimming. Panellists took their seats at the front. University President Mandy Portman was seated front and center.

As Shira rose to welcome the group and introduce Lisette, a thought occurred to her. It was a radical departure from her planned approach, and she liked it very much.

"Welcome, everyone, and thank you all for coming out tonight for what promises to be an interesting exploration into some current thinking on the Bible and its teachings. In a moment, I will introduce our own researcher, Lisette Colliere, who will brief us on her group's very interesting efforts. I will also introduce our fine panel of eight leaders from many Christian and Jewish denominations. Lisette will present for the first twenty minutes, leaving forty minutes for a panel discussion. But first, I would like to call to the microphone Pastor Peter Billington of the Presbyterian Church of West Texas. Pastor, would you please kick off this session by reading from the King James Version of the Bible, book of Judges, chapter 19, verses 22–29."

A flash of red came over Peter as he walked to the microphone and read aloud the story of the Levite and his concubine:

> As they were making their hearts merry, behold, the men of the city, certain base fellows, surrounded the house, beating at the door; and they spoke to the master of the house, the old man, saying, "Bring out

> the man who came into your house, that we may have sex with him!" The man, the master of the house, went out to them, and said to them, "No, my brothers, please don't act so wickedly; since this man has come into my house, don't do this folly. Behold, here is my virgin daughter and his concubine. I will bring them out now. Humble them, and do with them what seems good to you; but to this man don't do any such folly." But the men wouldn't listen to him: so the man laid hold of his concubine, and brought her out to them; and they had sex with her, and abused her all night until the morning: and when the day began to dawn, they let her go. Then came the woman in the dawning of the day, and fell down at the door of the man's house where her lord was, until it was light. Her lord rose up in the morning, and opened the doors of the house, and went out to go his way; and behold, the woman his concubine was fallen down at the door of the house, with her hands on the threshold. He said to her, "Get up, and let us be going!" but no one answered. Then he took her up on the donkey; and the man rose up, and went to his place. When he had come into his house, he took a knife, and laid hold on his concubine, and divided her, limb by limb, into twelve pieces, and sent her throughout all the borders of Israel.

From a distance of about twenty feet, Lisette locked eyes with Shira in a powerful and sudden involuntary glance of gratitude. Well, the Jersey girl knows her stuff, she acknowledged. How perfect. From the looks of it, the room was filled with roughly half male and half female students. There was nothing right about that story and no moral to be found. A man travelling around with a concubine finally finds a place to sleep. The men of the village hear about the man, come to the house demanding to rape him. The owner of the house defends the male guest but offers the angry mob the man's concubine along with his own virgin daughter to rape. The angry mob refuses, still wanting to rape the man. Finally, the mob settles on gang-raping the concubine, which they do all night until it's not clear if she is still conscious. The man who brought her, whose life she has now just saved, gets angry with her and cuts her up into twelve pieces.

With a quick nod, Shira signalled, "Right back atcha, sister."

32

LISETTE AND LARRY tackled the task of finding out how to publish a new version of the Bible.

So far, they found that anyone could use or modify the King James Version. Published in 1611, it had no existing copyright, but the language was so antiquated that it would require substantial time and effort to revise into modern English. While antiquated and clunky to read, it was one option, but not a good one since they wanted their version to be accessible to everyone. It would be hard enough to comb through the Bible and make the language gender inclusive.

Although the Bible itself is not copyrighted, many translations are, such as the Phillips, NIV, Moffatt, NKJV, RSV, NRSV, Amplified, and NASB. Under US law, a work is automatically in the public domain if it was written pre-1923; therefore, the following Bible versions are considered public domain:

- KJV (King James Version; also known as Authorized Version)
- WEB (World English Bible)

- NET (The NET Bible)
- ASV (American Standard Bible of 1901)[47]

The NET Bible was recent (1996–2006) and deliberately has no copyright so that it is in the public domain and can reach as many people as possible. Intriguing, they thought. Did that mean they could edit and republish this version?

The US Copyright Office would not allow anyone to create a new version of the Bible unless there were enough substantial changes to the text to make it a new work. This would be a question they would have to answer: Was their new Bible a "version" of the old Bible or an entirely new work? Maybe they could get around copyright law that way. Maybe this task was all a big legal question.

They read and researched further. In order to get a copyright, a new version has to have substantial changes to the content, enough to make it a work that has never been published before and can therefore claim an original copyright. In short, that meant the new version had to be very different (legally speaking) from the King James Bible, which is recognized as the original Bible in the United States.

Yawning, Lisette read out loud, "US Copyright Office Circular 14: Derivative Works notes that 'a typical derivative work registered in the Copyright Office is a primarily new work but incorporates some previously published material. The previously published material makes the work a derivative work under copyright law . . . a derivative work must differ sufficiently from the original to be regarded as a new work or must contain a substantial amount of new material. Making minor changes or additions of little substance to a pre-existing work will not qualify a work as a new version for copyright purposes. The new material must be original and copyrightable in itself.'"

"What about the NIV? It seems everyone uses that these days," Larry said.

"Well, the New International Version—NIV—was a translation made by more than one hundred scholars working from sources in Hebrew, Aramaic, and Greek, which were the original texts they had. The work started in 1965 by committees from the Christian Reformed Church and the National Association of Evangelicals, which led a transdenominational and international group of scholars in an effort to bring a more contemporary translation into English.

"As far as usage, the NIV text can be quoted in written, visual, audio, and electronic forms it seems up to and inclusive of five hundred verses without permission of the publisher, as long as those verses don't add up to a one complete book of the Bible. The verses being quoted cannot add up to twenty-five percent or more of the total text from which they are quoted."[48]

"That won't help us much" Larry said.

"We could partner with them."

"What?"

"Well, there are no ways to get around the trademarks 'NIV' and 'New International Version.' Both are registered in the United States Patent and Trademark Office. Use of either trademark requires permission of the owner, which is Biblica. And there are strict rules regarding personal use, including no copying or reposting the scripture on the Internet. In addition, there are also strict rules for changing or altering scripture, since any commentary or other Biblical reference, work produced for commercial sale that uses the New International Version, must obtain written permission for the use of the NIV text . . . maybe we could just ask them nicely." Lisette muted her surge of optimism.

Larry pondered the idea. Ask them nicely. Why not? "Let's play this out: a company is the publisher, and publishers answer to stockholders. We have a viable business proposition. What's the worst they can do, laugh at us?"

The next hour was spent hammering out a draft of a letter to Good Book Works:

Mindy Jeffries
President & CEO
Good Book Works, Inc.
1200 Milk Street
Boston, Ma 02109

Dear Ms. Jeffries:

According to Susi Lee Maltman's report for *USA Today*, we have learned that soon Good Book Works plans to publish a new version of its copyrighted Bible.

Simultaneously we are about to announce that we are working on a project to publish a version of the Bible omitting references to violence, slavery, genocide, sexual and racial servitude, and gender bias. We are aware that your plans to revise the Bible in 1997 died when word got out that the new version would use "inclusive language," which would have eliminated masculine pronouns, and that you have faced other challenges from ultraconservative groups. We were sad to hear about that outcome and hope to propose an alternative to your modernization efforts.

We would like to partner with you to create an alternate version of the Bible for people who do not want to continue to promote violence and hate in God's world.

We are flexible in our approach to this partnership. Perhaps our nonviolent version could be called something other than a Bible. "The Good Book" might have been a nice title for our work but it might be confused with *The Good Book: Reading the Bible with Mind and Heart*, taken by our recently departed friend Peter J. Gomes at Harvard.

In an effort to explore collaboration with Good Book Works in which our work can leverage your superb translations of the Scriptures, we would like to set up an initial conversation to introduce our objectives, share market research, and identify ways in which we can work together toward our goals, which we believe are not mutually exclusive. We feel confident you will be astounded at our financial projections.

We will call you on Tuesday to determine a convenient time for a conversation. Thank you for your consideration; we hope to be able to collaborate on this important initiative.

The letter was signed by the founding members of the Sanctuary for Grace and Hope, followed by their credentials.

"Well that might at least get a response, but probably a ding." Lisette stared blankly.

"You never know. Let's be hopeful until we call Tuesday. Surely there is a way to do this—just look at this long list of Bible versions in existence."[49]

Lisette agreed. "There must be a way. Let me read what I found at www.biblegateway.com:

> The first English translations were spasmodic—paraphrases attributed to Cædmon (circa 680), Bede's translation of part of John's Gospel (673–735), and Middle English metrical versions. The first full versions were fourteenth-century New Testament translations from the Vulgate, made under Lollard influence. Illicit manuscript translations continued to appear, until a powerful impetus was provided by the printing of the Vulgate (1456), the Hebrew text (1488), and Erasmus's Greek New Testament (1516), which inspired Tyndale to make the first English New Testament translation from the original Greek (1526) and of the Pentateuch from the original Hebrew (1529–30). Coverdale, who's first complete English Bible (1535) was partly based on Tyndale, superintended publication of the Great Bible (1539–40). A new version (1557), issued in Geneva—the first with verse divisions—formed the basis of the so-called Geneva Bible, dedicated to Elizabeth (1560). Parker, however, authorized yet another, this time a more Latinate revision of the Great Bible, the Bishops' Bible (1568). Meanwhile, exiled English Catholics in Rheims translated their own New Testament from the

> Vulgate (1582), followed by the Old Testament at Douai (1609–10). At the Hampton Court conference (1604) James I commissioned a panel to produce the King James (or the so-called Authorized) Version of 1611, a comprehensive revision of previous translations. Its superb quality enabled it to supplant all previous versions, and for 250 years, it was the only one used. Though new scholarship led to a conservative Revised Version (1881–85), translations proliferated in the twentieth century: James Moffatt (1922, 1924), Ronald Knox (1945, 1949), followed by the Revised Standard Version (1952), the New English Bible (1961, 1970), Jerusalem Bible (1966), and others.[50]

"Hopefully Good Book Works will want to partner," Lisette concluded.

Larry agreed, "One way or another the Bible can be revised—it might just take a very long time and a whole lot of work."

33

FOCUS, JUST TRY TO FOCUS, Gil thought. Ron's old friend was pleased to get the call from Lisette just two nights earlier. Due to the many tasks assigned, Lisette was working alone on the topic of religious war and thought it would be helpful to hear directly from an expert.

Gil insisted on picking Lisette up at the tiny, upscale Nantucket Memorial Airport, which she readily accepted. Since the whole island was only eleven miles long, it wasn't exactly a hardship. His close buddy Ron was an odd combination of many things, but having known him his whole life, Gil knew he was never wrong about beautiful women.

At first sight, stepping off the island-hopping prop plane, she appeared stunning. From a distance, it was hard to tell if Lisette looked more like a fashion model or an anchorwoman about to appear on the evening news. Only one thing was certain—she needed no gym membership. Whatever she was doing was working.

She noticed something about him right away. He was six feet four inches tall. Since the time she grew above six feet, she made a habit of sizing every new man she met.

After the quick driving tour of the island, they got to work at Gil's family compound in Sconset, enjoying the hearth fire near the kitchen and spreading out some documents on the long wooden family dinner table.

"Has this place always belonged to your family?" She was genuinely interested.

"No, my grandmother bought it about fifty years ago to be able to vacation near her best friend."

"Oh, did that work out? Does the other family still have a house here, too?"

"Yes, right next door. We all grew up together; I was in the third generation. We spent all our summers here and then I became the official house sitter of sorts when I started researching. My older brother and sister are both married and have children now, and there are some fourth-generation kids next door, too, so that is really fun to see the tradition continuing. We are more like family than friends at this point. We've never dated each other, for example."

"Very interesting. Smart woman, your grandmother." Lisette had no idea what that kind of intergenerational family and friendship circle and bond could be like. She was an only child, and her mother died in a skiing accident in Innsbruck when Lisette was three. Her Parisian father hired a governess until Lisette was eleven, at which point he remarried and sent her to boarding schools in Switzerland until she was ready for university. Shortly after her acceptance, he died suddenly of a heart attack, leaving her without a parental guardian. But then in her early years, her grandmother tried to play an active role in her life, though slowly dementia set in, erasing even that bit of foundation. By all means possible, she would follow in this smart woman's footsteps and one day have a house surrounded by friends and family. One day.

"I guess we should get to work so I don't miss that last flight back tonight." Lisette wished she didn't have to work at all and that Gil had asked her here on a weekend date, which would then turn into a weeklong date, and ultimately never end.

Gil began, "A religious war is a war caused by differences in beliefs about God. Sometimes it can involve one state that has an established religion fighting against another state with a different religion; other times war can start between different sects within the same religion within a state. Certain leaders motivate groups to spread a faith by use of force and violence. Some leaders encourage followers to attack another religious group because of its religious beliefs or customs. Examples you might know about include the Muslim conquests, the French wars of religion, the Crusades, and the Reconquista.

"It is widely accepted that ninety percent of wars are fought in the name of God or religion or that God or religion plays a motivational part in the war."

"Wow. Does that make nonreligious people more peaceful than religious ones?"

"It can. Wars fought for pure power or greed of resources are few by comparison. Sometimes religions get a damaged identity due to their warring factions. Christianity has managed to emerge in our day and age with the outward appearance of a peaceful religion, which is quite a public relations victory given its bloody past. Islam is perceived to be radical and violent in our day and age, but in fact it may well be the most peaceful example of a religious people if one looks at the largest group of Muslims. Their culture is one of caring and kindness with more time spent in daily prayer and devotion than many other religions. A hundred years from now, when literacy rates improve and more Muslims can read and interpret the Koran for themselves and don't have to rely on the radical teachings of some of the misguided mullahs, Islam will evolve again and it will be interesting to see at that point which religions are seen as warring and which ones are peaceful. I often think we may all be surprised."

Lisette noticed Gil's wavy hair and tried not to appear distracted.

"Well, most world religions have found ways to justify wars. Historically, however, the concept started from what we can tell in the seventh century when Saint Augustine detailed a 'just war' theory for Christianity, in which war was justifiable on religious grounds. Saint Thomas Aquinas then elaborated on this in his own writings, which were used by the Roman Catholic Church in their efforts to establish regulations in European countries."[51]

He went to the fridge and offered her a soda. Lisette particularly loved natural sodas.

"We can still see examples today of wars that are not really religious but may include certain elements of religion, such as when priests bless battleships. Recently some sacred ancient Christian sites such as the Church of the Nativity in Bethlehem were damaged by Israeli and Palestinian cross fire; this was an inadvertent strike against Christians caught in the cross fire of other religions. Usually destroying sacred temples, mosques, or churches is done to break the morale of an opponent, no matter if the war had anything to do with religion to begin with.

"In Northern Ireland the situation is often misunderstood as a religious war because the Nationalists, who are predominantly Catholics, fight against the Unionists, who are mostly Protestants. Nevertheless, underlying the war is the issue of attaching Northern Ireland to either the Republic of Ireland or the United Kingdom. So in fact religion plays a role in the conflict but it is not a religious war at the core."

"Really? I always thought that was a good example of a religious war in which Christians were fighting Christians—a war of denominations."

"See? That's what I mean. No, Irish natives were for the most part Catholic, and then Britain sent in immigrants who were mainly Protestant. The war broke out between countries and cultures, but it is inaccurate to describe the conflict as a religious one.

"The doctrines of religion often were used to legitimize warfare. Sometimes religion gave certain armies a good excuse for their actions but their actions were more about territorial expansion or trade, and perhaps in some cases in the name of God tried for world dominance.

"Lisette, this can get really heavy, particularly when I start pulling out my list and maps, so tell me how much information is enough, and whether you need a break. I have been at this for a decade, staring at all this data, and it has become normal for me to spend my days and nights immersed in these topics. So you have to tell me when to stop, okay?"

"Okay, sure. Please keep going; I'm learning a lot already."

"The Crusades are grouped together as a succession of military campaigns which were planned and sanctioned by the pope that took place during the eleventh through the thirteenth centuries. The Crusades were in direct response to the Muslim conquests. Oddly enough, the goal of the Crusades was to recapture Jerusalem and the Holy Land from the Muslims. At the time, the Christian Byzantine Empire was under siege. Later Crusades were launched against others for religious reasons. Today, we think of the Crusades as a war of Catholics on anyone who refused to conform to its strict tenets, but they began with a different objective altogether.

"In sixteenth-century France there was a succession of wars between Roman Catholics and Protestants. These were known as the Wars of Religion. Later in the seventeenth century, the German states of Scandinavia and Poland were involved in religious wars. The Roman Catholics and Calvinists took opposite sides, for the most part. France, which was Catholic, did side with the Protestants for what may have been political reasons."

"In China there was an illegal Protestant missionary tract and the Taiping faith believed that their God, Shangdi, a high God of classical China, had chosen the Taiping leader to be Hong Xiuquan. His mission was to establish Shangdi's heavenly kingdom on earth. Naturally, Taiping rebels recruited many followers for the battle to restore the classical system of kingship. It was known as the bloodiest civil war with some twenty million estimated dead.

"Should I keep going?"

"But of course, keep going. This is good."

"Okay. Let's talk about the Hindus, who are thought of as very peaceful today. Many are even vegetarians, but we can't lose sight of the fact that they are remarkably proud of their nuclear power in India. Well, from the eleventh to the seventeenth century, Hindus fought against the Muslim invasions. In fact several times over the centuries, power moved into Hindu hands. Ultimately, after the loss of power to the Muslims, India was at peace, so long as the Muslim rulers did not attack the faith of the Hindus.

"But all that hard-earned peace came undone again in 1813 by Christianity. The East India Company charter was amended, paving the way for missionary work in India. What happened there in that delicate balance of peace was that well-intentioned missionaries soon spread almost everywhere and started denigrating Hinduism and Islam to promote Christianity, which of course caused a revolt. The revolt was started by a rumor that new British rifle cartridges were greased with pig and cow fat—can you imagine how awful that was for Muslim and Hindu soldiers, for religious reasons? That amounted to several hundred thousand killed."

He studied Lisette's face. "Keep going?"

"Keep going."

"We think of Buddhists as peaceful, right? Happiness-centered people. But anyone who carefully reads Buddhist texts, particularly the *Kalachakra Tantra* literature, can see battles that could easily be called 'holy wars.' Buddhists conquered the Cham people, as well as the Tamils in Sri Lanka.

"Buddhism emphasizes the principle of Ahinsa, which is the avoidance of violence, so most Buddhists try to resolve wars in nonviolent ways. But actually they have fought against Muslims as well as Hindus, especially from the eighth through the tenth centuries.

"In Judaism, the expression *Milhemet Mitzvah* means the 'Commanded War' and refers to a kind of war that all Jews are required to fight, but one that is limited within borders of Israel—the geographical limits of Israel, as written in the Hebrew Bible, especially Numbers 34:1–15 and Ezekiel 47:13–20. It is important to mention that modern Israel makes no reference to *Milhemet Mitzvah* in anything official for defense forces."[52]

Gil kept on track.

"In Sikhism, only after all peaceful means have failed is a holy war justifiable. The Sikhs seem pretty peaceful to me today, but the early Sikhs back in the sixteenth and seventeenth centuries had to fight off many Mughal Islamic invaders, as well as Hindu Rajputs. As stated by their tenth guru, Guru Gobind Singh, Sikhs are allowed to fight for the well-being of righteousness."

"So that's most of them, then?" Lisette asked, not sure of the range of answers that might come.

"Oh no, in fact we can go on and on. I have a list that you can review. I've never showed it to anyone. I've worked on it the past five winters and packed it up in the spring when the fun starts up again around here. It's starting to outgrow the house and may need its own museum someday."

"*Vraiment*—eh, honestly? No one has seen it, ever?"

"You will be the first."

"I'm honored. Why me?"

"Well, obviously you have all that long, wavy red hair, those long legs, the big marble green eyes, that intoxicating French accent—and so I am feeling like I don't have much to bring to the party. But I have my list and I'm counting on the fact that it will impress you."

Lisette blushed. "Good idea. Let's break. Over lunch we can have a light debate. Choose a topic: Was there actually a religious war against artists? Are mass suicides in the name of religion considered to be murders? You know, in France we are made up of sixty million Catholics and I was wondering, does the state or the church try to spread sexually transmitted diseases by prohibiting the use of condoms?"

"We could have a debate, or you could tell me a little about yourself . . ."

"Sure, but first, what are all these trellises around here?"

"Oh, those? They are actually for the roses. Sconset is known worldwide for its roses. Do you . . . happen to like roses?"

"Yes. When I was young I spent summers in my grandmother's garden. Smelling the roses is my favorite pastime."

Gil looked toward heaven. If he lacked anything in looks and charm, he could more than make up for it with his selection of roses. Sconset was truly rose heaven. It was actually hard to see some of the homes in the town because they were so overgrown with roses.

AT LUNCH they talked about their childhoods and dreams, and how each of them arrived at the course of their study. The hour flew by in what seemed like an instant. They returned to Gil's house for an afternoon of serious study.

He led her into his oversized living room, where all the furniture had been moved to the side and the art had been removed from the walls and replaced by paper charts taped in all directions. "Lisette, when I come in here, my head spins. Each name of a war represents real people—many hundreds of millions who have died. Many died for country, and many for God. I'm trying to sort them out. I am convinced that having our Bible promote violence adds to this problem, so your work is very important to me. What I have done here is very small in comparison to what you are working on. Please allow me to show you what I have done. This first section approximates deaths per war—it is a work in progress but here is what I have so far." He led her around the room quietly, allowing her time to digest the information.[53]

"I hate to ask, but have you added them up?"

"Yes, I keep a running total in my head. It's staggering; about four hundred million people by my very early count—and these you see here only include a fraction of all the wars. If it's true that ninety percent of people die for war in the name of God, then we can already assume some three hundred and sixty million lives have been lost in the name of religion. Here, come with me. I started another way to look at war chronologically." Gil walked into the boathouse, which was also cleared out and had the walls papered with charts.

Lisette stared at the first wall in astonishment and over the next several hours made her way through all the wars charted. She had to summon the strength to continue.[54]

Nearing the end of the extensive display of charts, diagrams, timelines, and maps, Lisette noticed the categorization of "1,000+ deaths." She read Gil's notes: "Conflicts in the following list are currently causing at least 1,000 violent deaths per year, a categorization used by the Uppsala Conflict Data Program and recognized by the United Nations. The UN also uses the term 'low-intensity conflict,' which can overlap with the 1,000 violent deaths per year categorization."

As Lisette finished her study of the room, she looked out the window to the dark sky. The absence of the lights from a nearby city allowed the stars to shine brightly against a midnight-blue backdrop. She let out a sigh for humanity.

"Gil, I must have missed the last flight hours ago."

"You're in luck. I have a vacancy. I actually made a dinner reservation at 21 Federal, just in case you decided to stay. Its a good place to unwind."

AT DINNER, Lisette had a hard time saying anything meaningful. Gil was in better shape, having had years to reflect on and digest the grim facts. Nonetheless, he could actually somewhat relate to what she was feeling. Once in Washington, D.C., Gil had decided to stay an extra day and take in some sights. It had seemed like a good idea at the time, but after spending the morning at both the Vietnam Memorial and the Holocaust Museum, he reworked his agenda to include a whole lot of nothing for a while. Quiet time is welcome following hard news or when presented with an unbearable amount of terrible facts.

Gil told Lisette about his childhood, his passion for golf, and his mother. He carried the whole conversation and tried to be engaging throughout the meal. He looked at her, recognizing the pain in the speechlessness, knowing the hopelessness that could set in. He knew only one thing for sure—he would find a way to bring her back.

After dinner, the two took a walk by the water. He held out his hand and she took it. As they walked they looked out at the boats in the harbor, from small fishing vessels to grand yachts.

There, amidst all things horrible, something wonderful began.

34

THE HEAT OF BANGKOK was only made worse by its filth and humidity. There was no way to escape it entirely. Two showers a day was the norm for Mongkut, who regularly started his workdays at three in the afternoon and ended sometime close to five in the morning, when all the "business" for the night that could be found was complete. Niran's number showed up on his private cell phone.

Mongkut answered. "Talk."

"Sir, I am very sorry to report that this week alone we have lost eighteen of our brothel girls. They disappeared from three different brothels in our network. We usually lose one or two to injuries or even death, but something new is under way."

"We continue to be on track with all the authorities who we need to pay in order to stay in business?"

"Of course. We pay them first. That's why they completely leave us alone."

"Competition?"

"No sir." Niran said confidently.

"Then what?" Mongkut demanded.

"I will find out at once and let you know, sir." Niran hung up the phone.

Mongkut punched the wall of his office then headed back out into the night.

35

AS JOE DROVE AWAY from the complex, he felt elated. Free. Clear-minded and balanced. He had really had some kind of breakthrough. It was a strange time for an epiphany, when he really hadn't set out in search of one. It just kind of grabbed him by surprise.

Some people probably go through all kinds of trouble to reach an "aha!" moment like that.

Joe thought back to his childhood. All that nonsense his dad went on about—with races mixing and the pure evil of it all, and how it was going to mess up the world—was a regular dinner discussion topic. He often threw in Bible verses to strengthen his points.

His father wasn't a dumb man. He was well educated and thanks to his great grandfather's fortune, he lived in great luxury with a heightened amount of respect.

But was his respect earned? What had his father really done in his lifetime?

His mother just rolled her eyes when his father started up about the races mixing. She put up with a lot, but then, her own parents shared the same kind of sentiments.

Maybe it was the times they lived in that influenced them that way. He could not figure out how people who had so much to give could be so filled with hate. What was the sense in it?

His brother, Troy, was the family diplomat; never making waves, but never agreeing, either. Joe was surprised, he remembered, when as a boy he passed a local park and saw Troy picking up a game of basketball with some black guys. Maybe Troy never bought into all that nonsense anyway. Why had he? And why had he influenced Spiker so much?

36

JOE FOUND HIMSELF WRESTLING several times a day with the fear of being a hypocrite. He couldn't help but face the truth: he didn't want to know.

Joe wanted to believe that his ancestors were better, smarter, and more pure overall than anyone else's. And he also knew why this was so important to him. At the age of six he overheard his mother talking to a friend about the secret little Joey and Troy would never have to know: that his father wasn't really his father. Maybe even his father didn't know the truth. Joe had blocked that thought out for years, but the memory of the conversation had found its way back recently.

Who was he? Which, if any, pure people did he really belong to? That afternoon, after much contemplation, he called the phone number on the letter and made an appointment for a genetic screening. The results would be quick.

With that information, he only had one question left: To bail or not to bail?

He decided to gather the last piece of information he needed to make a balanced decision. Then he got on the next flight to LaGuardia Airport in New York City.

AFTER HAVING MICHELLE FOLLOWED for two weeks, he knew her routine. His flight landed at 7:35 a.m., and he was at the Sweets and Treats bakery in the Flatbush section of Brooklyn by 8:30, just before Michelle walked in.

"Hey there, sunshine!" said a woman in her eighties to Michelle as she burst through the door.

"Hey there yourself, hot stuff."

"Same old?"

"Same old."

Joe jumped in line behind Michelle and slipped her a short note that read, "Michelle, I am a friend and colleague of Tommy Williams. We never met at the time but I was his Harvard roommate. Would you please join me for a cup of coffee over in the corner?"

Michelle didn't react at all but headed directly to the corner table with her coffee and muffin.

A few old men were speaking Arabic at a table nearby.

Joe pulled up a chair and said, "I didn't expect to see Arabs in this neighborhood."

"They're not Arabs. They're old Jews who grew up in Syria. They never bothered to learn English when they got here. Since they never leave Flatbush, they will never need it."

"Michelle, I finance most of Tommy's research. His focus and dedication to this project is not unlike the commitment that a person makes to a top-secret government position, although it is a private company. Tommy is immersed in a project. I know you tried to reach out to him. I am under strict orders not to disturb him for a while. In order to determine if I can assist you, can you tell me a little about your time together in Boston?"

"He's okay, right? Not in the hospital or anything?"

"No, he's fine—just very busy with something big."

"Oh, gosh, I don't even know what he does these days. We lost touch a long time ago. Well, you are a stranger, but I don't mind telling you that we were crazy in love for two years, and stupidly, very stupidly, I ended it to come back here, at which point I was suicidal for the next three years, bulimic for five years after that, and finally became a cutter, you know—self-mutilation—so I was a regular at the Bellevue Hospital for fifteen years and then—"

"And then?"

"I left this place. Left my parents, my childhood friends, six thousand years of Jewish tradition; turned my back on all this to save my own life. I only come by to say hi to my parents once a day, then back into Manhattan."

"So, you never married?"

"Married? Who would have married me? I was completely out of my mind in love with Tommy and everyone knew it, there was no way to hide it. There really was no point in marrying, so I stayed single—but at least my parents weren't shunned."

"What have you been doing these past five years?"

"Oh, just more along the lines of strange. I never much liked animals but I started finding all these stray cats, you know, starving, neglected, abandoned, and injured. I was taking them in. After a while I started New York's first cat rescue squad and orphanage. I take them in, rehabilitate them, and give them to old people. They are pretty low maintenance and old people do well with them. Kind of therapy, I guess, since I could never help myself."

"You help cats."

"Yep." Michelle leaned in. "Did Tommy ever . . . marry?"

"No, actually he just focused on his work. He's not the same guy you remember, Michelle. I suspect whatever you two had, and then lost, sent him off the deep end in a way."

"I believe that. After wishing I were dead for so long, and knowing what I put him through, that makes sense. I had nothing to compare love to and thought we would move on, but I guess there are some loves so strong we should know better than deny them their chance. I didn't know better. But now I do. I wonder if there's still a chance we could be together . . ."

"That's really hard to imagine. He's just . . . and well . . . you wouldn't even recognize him."

"So why are you here?"

"I needed to find this out for myself in order to make a big decision. I appreciate your honesty and wish you well."

"Please tell him, sometime, that I still . . . that I'm still . . . no, don't tell him anything. Thanks."

Michelle left the bakery, waving briefly to Joe. The expression on her face was pure anguish. In an instant she disappeared into a subway station stairway, leaving Joe to contemplate his next move.

37

SPIKER TWITCHED only slightly at the unexpected intrusion. Over the years he had mastered a calm response so that his surprise or outrage was barely noticeable.

Joe stood by silently as Spiker took a moment to compose himself and appear in control. He had come to expect complete subordination and never tolerated interruptions or unscheduled meetings.

"This better be urgent," Spiker said.

"You're a huge fraud and I'm out of here," Joe replied.

"Fraud?"

"Your intentions were never pure. There's no such thing as pure. You're just Tommy, the jilted lover. I know the whole story. Even if your aim was pure, it turns out there is no such thing. Look at this. I just got my DNA results back from a lab and guess what? I'm not pure, either. No one is pure anything. Look at this—part Russian, part Chinese. Chinese! You know what that means? That means that Genghis Khan or someone raped my German ancestors in some conquest. No one in this project is pure white. Pure white doesn't really exist."

Spiker's face could not conceal his shock. "What's this about? We've worked together for so long planning the perfect solution. We're so close. I have it all worked out. Now in the eleventh hour you want to pull the plug?"

"No, I want *you* to pull the plug—this is your deal. I just financed it and stupidly believed all our supremacy babble."

"What? Where—where do you think you're going?"

"Surfing."

"Are you flippin' kidding me? Are you on something, man?"

"Get this. I woke up calm, having stayed up last night writing my good-byes in letters to people and redirecting all my assets, making sure the trust fund has a new beneficiary. I woke up with my Glock ready to catapult me into a new place or no place. I didn't even care. My gorgeous, powerful, seventeen-round Glock, with all three safeties off, and I was ready to blow my useless, miserable, self-hating self to smithereens."

"And?"

"And I thought I should take you with me, so I started heading over here."

"That's why you came? To kill me and then yourself?"

"Not as it turns out. I hate hypocrites and so I would be willing to blow your brains out. Favorite Glock is right here in my left pocket so say the word, but hear me out. So I had this calm come over me and it had to do with how you conduct your experiments on cats, which is pretty much torturing them for a reason, and how Michelle rescues and helps cats. Cats. I met with her. She has a cat orphanage and everything—treats them like gold—the neglected, abused, injured, mangled cats all over New York City. And I thought to myself, *I don't even like cats and why should I care if they live or if they suffer or if they die.* I mean, think about it. Why should I be spending my last few minutes on earth thinking about cats? But I was crystal clear about one thing. That is no coincidence. What are the odds?"

"What are you talking about?"

"Listen, I don't believe anything. I used to believe in God, I even used to believe in you. Now I don't believe anything. I don't believe in humanity, but I wouldn't sterilize a lot of humans for impurity when I myself am impure. That makes no sense. Either I'm better than most or not, and it seems not. But something, someone, some force or some power, is at work in this world.

"You know, I spent my life in the shadow of my identical twin, who was always a little smarter, a little faster, a little more charming. We were identical, but he got the pretty girls. I never had the courage to hate him. We were supposed to be natural lifelong best friends, and everyone thought that's how we were. Even when we flew in the air force, he got the promotions first. I was a damn smokin' hot fighter pilot, probably better than he was, but he always moved up first."

"Joe—" Spiker tried to cut in.

"He never had much fun, though. Always consumed in the competition, always too focused on the finish line to enjoy the race, and you know what? I could win that race. Now it's time for some fun."

"Fun?"

"Yeah, pretty much. I guess you haven't heard that word in about twenty years. And I don't care if you sterilize all seven billion of us. I guess I just don't care anymore. I wish I cared, but right now there are only ten things on my new bucket list, maybe eleven, if I get the chance to fly again.

"I'm thinking maybe a month in each place, starting with Old Man's at San Onofre State Beach, California. I'll finally end up at Supertubes, Jeffreys Bay, South Africa; the finest right-hand point breaks in the world. That's the plan."

"You're out of your mind."

"Let's be clear. One of us wants to sterilize a third of humanity because a Syrian Jewess dumped him. The other of us wants to surf his way around the world in search of happiness."

"Happiness?"

Joe smiled broadly and stared at Spiker. "Look carefully. Ever seen that before? Didn't think so, but remember it. Remember that smile on my face. And now that I'm Chinese, let me give you some ancient Chinese wisdom from another ancestor of mine, Confucius: 'They must often change, who would be constant in happiness or wisdom.'

"One more thing. She wants you back. Now tell me, was that a yes or no to my offer to blow your twisted brains out? Well?"

"Why now?" Spiker asked in a puzzled tone.

"Dude, surf's up."

38

IN MEDFORD, Massachusetts, the end of March still felt a lot like winter. People were timidly sporting brighter colors in expectation of the Boston spring that would be short and sweet. Larry always thought that summer was the most glorious season there, but fall was pretty great as well. Somehow, every year the last few weeks of winter lasted too long and the people who were eagerly awaiting spring were almost exhausted by the time it finally arrived.

By nature, Larry was always hopeful, but for a few weeks he had been feeling down. Not so much depressed from winter, but he just wasn't feeling very useful. Everyone knew he was an excellent attorney and a world-class musician, but he hadn't been able to contribute much on the group project.

He had been chosen to assist the group on an as-needed basis because he had another specialty in addition to immigration law. There was a busy intersection between religion and law that Larry had become fascinated with early in his immigration law career. Abdul Bin Hassan had been working as a pediatric neurologist in Boston at Children's Hospital. One day Abdul, having heard about Larry and his compassion for immigrants, stopped in to see if the lawyer could help him bring over his four wives and many children from Oman. The project opened a new doorway through which Larry stepped, blogging about various issues related to religious persecution and how to decide who is afforded asylum in the United States, and laws related to parents refusing to medicate children due to religious beliefs. He exposed the horrors of female genital mutilation, something that happened even in Boston. Soon he was the most widely read author on the subject of religiously ambiguous legal messes. But that was just his hobby and a way of keeping himself from feeling like the empty nester he had recently become.

Not that he was completely alone; he had what amounted to a "pet" one-legged seagull. Although it wasn't much, Larry had companionship.

The group had decided their next meeting would be in Jerusalem, during the week of both Easter and Passover. Most of the members had never been to Israel, a spectacular place in the spring, and would enjoy sightseeing and learning about some of the places discussed in the Bible. Pilgrims from all over the world would bring the spiritual histories of biblical peoples to life. In addition, it seemed fitting to meet there amid the turmoil in search of peace.

Most of the members were booking travel and looking forward to their stay at the prominent King David Hotel in Jerusalem. Larry hadn't decided if he was really needed there and was beginning to wonder if perhaps he should skip this session and go surprise his daughter with an Easter visit.

As he noticed some crocus popping up outside his

window, his phone rang. It was Courtney! At least something to brighten his day.

"Dad! Check Grandpa's e-mail—that Gmail account I set up. Quick!"

"Courtney, are you okay? Where are you? Your Grandpa has been dead over a year."

"Dad, hurry! Now. Head over to Widener. I'm at work, can't talk. Found something odd—horrible, I think. Need you to check this out. Fast. Bye!"

Before Larry could reply, she was gone. Courtney rarely called with anything other than bright news about her new career as executive assistant to some science bigwig. A beautiful blonde Boston-Irish bombshell, complete with freckles and blue eyes; she was easily mistaken for a ditz by more than a few men. Over the years she refined the blonde-ditz routine by developing killer listening skills. While smiling politely and never saying too much, she studied people, their expressions, listening carefully to tone and cadence, noticing nearly inaudible voice inflections. She read every memo that passed her desk. Courtney didn't miss much. More than a few times since her childhood, Larry had been delighted as he witnessed her "pounce"—it was total shock and awe to those around when she did. She never opened her mouth until the moment was perfect, then BOOM! With clarity and precision, she had no trouble setting the record straight. It was her way of saying, "Gotcha! And oh yeah, I am all that. Blonde, gorgeous, *and* smart." He always thought his daughter would be a powerful trial attorney, but she never expressed much interest in law. Science was her thing, and while her first job was as a high-level assistant, she felt she was on her way to a good career.

What was all this about? Grandpa's e-mail? Widener Library. Holy cow. He didn't mind making the trek over to Harvard and knew he could use his alumni credentials to get in and use the resources, but what on earth had she been upset by? Widener was Harvard's main library. It was also bigger than the Library of Congress.

As he hopped on the MBTA's Red Line over to Cambridge, Larry enjoyed an old article from 2010 by Jerold Aust that might be worth sharing with the group:

> Easter or Passover: Which Is Christian?
> Many believe that God's endorsement of Passover ended with Christ's death—and that He has since replaced it with the observance of Easter as a celebration of Christ's resurrection. But is that so?
>
> On April 4 of this year, a billion or more people who identify themselves as Christian will celebrate Easter. The week before, a far smaller number will observe Passover. How do these two scenarios compare? On the one hand, we have a fun-filled Easter egg hunt, Easter bunnies galore and an Easter Sunday sunrise service. On the other, a solemn Passover service that typically includes participants washing one another's feet and partaking of unleavened bread and wine.
>
> Easter seems more fun, more joyous; Passover seems old-fashioned and more serious. These are some differences that are obvious on the surface. Many other differences aren't so obvious.

He read on.

You can check in nearly any Bible help or encyclopedia to verify several fundamental facts:

- Easter cannot be found in Scripture.
- Easter was never instituted by God.
- Easter was never sanctioned by Jesus Christ.
- Easter was never taught by Christ's apostles.
- Easter was never observed by the early New Testament Church.

The article went on but his stop was approaching. *Fascinating stuff,* Larry thought as he folded his paper and stepped off into the damp wind.

As he approached the stairs up to Widener, he remembered his days as a student, even as a freshman in the Harvard Yard. By the time Courtney was accepted at the college, she was the fourth generation to attend. He was proud of his daughter. He remembered his father being proud of him, too. Huffing and puffing his way up the stairs, he first greeted the security guard, opened his backpack for inspection, showed his alumni ID, and then heard, "Sorry, sir, we are actually closed today."

"Closed for what?"

"Upgrades to the digitized data—or some important stuff," the hefty woman behind a safety glass counter said.

"Man, they still haven't perfected that system yet? Well, I need you to help me out. I'm not married—dumped a long time ago for a younger model. But my daughter is one fire-breathing dragon if I don't do as she says, and since she is the only woman left in my life, and she told me to get on the Red

Line and get myself over here today, I think I'd better not blow it. What if I don't do any work in the stacks—I won't touch a single volume. I will just sit and research on the computer. I can be out in one hour, I promise."

"Um-hmmmm. Now, is that your only daughter?"

"Yes, ma'am."

"And she told you to come on down here. And you did that for her?"

"Yes, ma'am."

"Well. You are a fine example of a father, and for that reason, you deserve one hour at the computer. Now hurry in and make yourself scarce."

"Yes, ma'am!"

Larry got to work immediately. He logged in to his deceased father's Gmail account, remembering the passwords they always used as a secret code: dumbblonde123 (username), Einstein (password). It took just over an hour but Larry was able to download and print out all seventeen documents Courtney had sent to him. As they were printing, he reviewed the content: chemical compositions, lists of production facilities, distribution lists, product lists having to do with the FIFA World Cup tournament, all kinds of pesticide information, and corn. He couldn't put it all together in just an hour, but right there in the stacks of Widener he had all the source information he needed.

Over the course of the weekend, he would piece together what Courtney had found. Working tirelessly and pulling his first all-nighter in thirty years, he did see an incredibly horrible scenario shaping up. If what he read was true, the company his daughter was working for was about to launch a full-scale bioterror attack. Could it be true? He feared for his daughter—his only daughter. Was she okay? How did she figure this out? Would she get caught and killed by whoever was behind all this?

BACK AT WORK, Courtney sat up straight at her desk as Spiker finally emerged from his office.

"You're here early, aren't you?" he said with a steely cold undertone, looking suspiciously over at her monitor.

Courtney stood to greet him. "No, sir, it appears you were here quite late. I took the time to make you some fresh coffee and grab a change of clothes for you. Better hurry. Your 9:00 a.m. is here in the lobby. Go change quickly and you can grab a shower later at lunch. I'll keep him busy. Go. Go!"

Well, thank goodness for a strong assistant, Spiker thought. *At least I have that going for me.*

What he didn't know was that Joe had intentionally left himself logged in on Courtney's computer before leaving to tip her off to the plot. When Courtney had arrived for work and noticed her boss asleep in his chair, she quietly closed the door and started scouring Joe's files, rapidly absorbing all she could and sending out files from Joe's account so that she could not be caught. Smart guy—Joe knew her well. Joe was long gone, that news was out. Some kind of dispute. And if Spiker ever learned that Joe had sent out confidential files, they could certainly never be traced to her. Still, she had to be careful. Something was amiss. Something smelled foul.

39

SPIKER SAT ALONE in his old leather armchair for several hours. He never imagined mutiny. He never suspected Joe of uncovering his true motivations. His thoughts were interrupted by thoughts of Michelle. He finally reached over to his bookshelf and pulled out a book Rabbi Milner had given him years earlier, *The Kabbala*, an ancient book of Jewish mysticism, now a modern trend thanks to the pop star Madonna.

As he contemplated Confucius's words about happiness and change, Spiker vaguely remembered that the science of Kabbala is supposed to explain how everything occurs in us. For that reason, it is believed by the Kabbalists that in order to change the world, one needs to focus on change within oneself. Gandhi's famous advice to be the change you want to see in the world came to mind and resonated with him. Briefly. He was still in shock, ripped open, confused, and trying to make sense of the day.

He read on that Kabbalists believed the challenge for most people is that the feeling of being distant from each other creates desire and hatred. Other problems in returning to "infinity" include ego, pain, or the threat or feeling of rejection; and lastly, the hunger for power.

Spiker sat back. That hit home—hard. *The feeling of rejection*. The sting of rejection was still present after all these years.

He let that resonate for a while.

He felt tired, drained. He settled into a section of the book and read that if people understand by uniting with others they will return to the state of infinity, in spite of difficult conditions. He learned that in spite of the pain of rejection, a person could begin to create a connection with another. Unable to destroy the ego, a person doesn't do anything with the ego at all—he or she simply builds a connection with others above it. In the Kabbala, this bridge is called building a screen over the desire. The rejection between the souls may remain at a low level, but at a new, higher level, a stronger bridge connects their souls.

Above the evil. Was that possible? Was he evil or was he good? He wondered why he wasn't sure anymore.

Spiker fell asleep in his office with the Kabbala, and all this new information, in his lap.

40

A WELL-RESEARCHED MEMO went out to all group members informing them of the weeklong itinerary set for their upcoming meeting in Jerusalem. There would be specific agenda topics and project updates as well as plenty of Christian and Jewish cultural events and scheduled site visits.

The memo said that in the Christian tradition, the week before Easter is called Holy Week. It begins with Palm Sunday and includes the days from Monday through Thursday; the Great Triduum begins on Thursday, which consists of Maundy Thursday, Good Friday, and Holy Saturday. This leads up to the Great Vigil of Easter after sundown on Saturday, and the Sunday of the Resurrection, Easter Sunday.

However, to the surprise of many, they learned that the earliest Christians observed a Christian Passover in the early spring. Adapted from the Jewish Passover, it was a festival of remembrance and redemption, commemorating events leading up to the crucifixion and resurrection of Jesus.

Around AD 381, a woman named Egeria wrote a detailed description of the worship services of Christians going on throughout Egypt, Palestine, and Asia Minor. She also described in detail the worship of religious pilgrims to Jerusalem during the week before the annual festival and the Sunday of the Resurrection. Five centuries later, Holy Week worship services were flourishing in Spain, and a couple hundred years after that they had spread to churches in France and England.

But as the weeklong holiday celebration spread, it took on new forms and meanings, gradually departing from a Passover celebration of the Jews' exodus from Egypt to what we have today. Many current Easter customs are adapted from pagan worship symbols and practices, mostly pre-Christian European and Middle Eastern springtime fertility celebrations. Eggs and rabbits in particular were widely used as pagan symbols of fertility, which is why there is a focus on Easter eggs—truly pagan practices.

The objectives for this task force session were to provide research updates and discuss the topic of "God Within" or the "Spark of the Divine" and what that meant for their project.

Various biblical texts alluded to a certain amount of power that people own from within; however, many of the churches and synagogues discount personal power, unwittingly disempowering their people to act; conversely teaching that only God has power and humans are powerless and completely at God's mercy. This point would be explored. And they would explore the power of people to bring about miracles, and study the examples of Jesus and his disciples' own miracles. A list was provided for prework. Verses related to miracles were distributed.[55]

These examples and other contemporary examples would be discussed. Miracles—no one could resist studying the examples.

Guest speakers were invited to discuss links to modern religion; the power of prayer; the impact of remote prayer, such as the Noetic Sciences; and the overall link to the power of intention/attention in quantum physics—that is, thoughts become things; individuals are each powerful beyond measure, and combined, are exponentially more powerful.

"The essential stuff of the universe is nonstuff," Rahul Patel had told them. He was kind enough to agree to attend their upcoming meeting to add his quantum insights.

Even in the powerful project known as "One," Father Thomas Keating of the Roman Catholic Church described the highest level of spiritual awareness as no separation of a God *out there* and a God *in here*. According to him, we are one and the same. The feeling of separation from God is one learned from religion but perhaps is not real.

The group was given some heavy reworks to study, including examples of prayer and its impact on battle, prayer's impact on sick patients individually and in groups, and prayer's impact on violence in cities. What was particularly interesting was the example of the Institute of Noetic Sciences' experiment in which a large group prayed or meditated on lowering violence in cities for a period, and its incredible results that showed there was indeed lower violence during those periods.

There was a lot of reading on field mechanics, quantum physics, and wave-particle duality—which, for most people in the group meant finding a lot of patience to carefully read and study scientific data. But they found that all quantum physics breaks down to something easy to understand. Think of the smallest amount of something as an atom, and what makes up the atom is either a "wave," which is a current of energy, or a "particle," which is something hard and real that can be seen. The unusual thing is that what is expected to be seen with complex optic sensors *is* what the atom becomes. The observer influences the potential of the wave. So, if a particle is expected, then that is what is seen. Thus, everyone influences the world with their very thoughts and expectations. It turns out that humans are powerful.

Therefore, Jesus was right about that; after all, that is what he said.

The group members would figure out what to do with this information.

However, maybe the real questions were: Where was Jesus headed with his message before his death, and was there a way to continue and extend that?

They would soon find out.

41

LARRY COULDN'T WAIT any longer. It had been four days since Courtney's call and he had pretty much figured out what she was trying to say. She was somehow involved in a bioterrorism plot that would be launched soon—if it hadn't been already. He was about to alert Homeland Security when he remembered the name of the place she was working and tracked down a phone number of a holding company, then some of its subsidiaries, and finally a location somewhere near Death Valley, California. He thought she mentioned that they moved the headquarters to the desert. This must be the place.

Fighting the urge to bolt in the middle of the night, Courtney knew her chances of survival were slim on her own outside the complex, which was guarded like Fort Knox these days. It was hundreds of miles from the nearest airport, and her chances of being caught were extremely high since there was only one road in and one road out. She thought as fast as she could and planned her escape. In three days she had all the documentation she needed. She was reasonably sure Spiker wasn't on to her yet.

What she needed was a big distraction on the way out, and she thought long and hard about how to create one. *What about that woman? Michelle! From New York?*

As Spiker was walking into his office, Courtney asked for a brief moment with him.

"I realize my timing is bad for this request, but my sister has been in a terrible accident in Boston."

"Your sister?"

Yes, sir. She needs surgery and I need to get back to be with her for a while. Do you mind if I hire a temp for a few days?"

He stood and listened as she explained her request. She needed to go back to Boston to get some tests run. Her sister needed a kidney, and she might be a match. She needed to leave that afternoon.

"Sister? Temp?" Surprised, he sighed, "Be back quick. Things are busy here and with Joe leaving. I need your help. E. coli won't go away without us. E. coli is not taking any vacations."

"Yes, sir," she managed quietly, knowing that a week would be enough time to fly to Washington, present her incriminating data, and have the place shut down.

Behind her a phone rang, and she recognized the number on caller ID—her dad. How did he track her down here? Spiker noticed it, too. She grabbed the phone and dramatically answered, "Dad, is she all right? Is she hanging in there? I'm getting in on Delta flight three-twenty-three, landing at nine twenty-five p.m. at Logan. Keep praying, Dad—I'll be there soon." She looked at Spiker as she hung up the phone.

A few hours later, Spiker randomly remembered something from Courtney's job interview before he hired her. She had said she was an only child. He walked to her desk but the temp was already sitting with her back to him at the computer. Dark curly hair. Black suit. He began, "Excuse me, do you know where . . ."

Michelle swung the desk chair around and stood up.

Spiker froze in place and felt stunned with high voltage. "Michelle? What are you doing here?"

Exasperated, she replied in a no-nonsense tone, "Great question. I thought you were in trouble so I showed up. I got a call, so I got out of bed at three a.m. to catch a plane. Anyway, when I got here, there were all these credentials to get me in and instructions to sit at this computer and await further guidance. Now what am I supposed to be—your secretary?"

"Whoa! You look, I mean, really great."

"Yeah, well you look like crap. Don't you shower or get any food or sleep around here? And what kind of crazy hot and dry place is this, anyway? By the way, you don't appear to be in danger, so good-bye."

"Um."

"Um? First, I go to hell and back because of my love for you. Leave my family. Leave my religion. Leave my community. In and out of mental hospitals. Needles, drugs, alcohol, twelve-step programs. You don't call or write me back in years, and then you send your spy to New York to meet with me. Now I get a crazy, urgent call in the middle of the night to get on a flight to save your life and all you can say is *um*?"

"Okay, this is not going well. I need to stop someone, then I will be back to talk with you."

But Courtney was long gone. She got in the taxi that had dropped off Michelle; the second taxi on its way was just a diversion hired to drive to a different airport in the event she was followed. Her USB drive went undetected through the security checkpoint on the way out of the complex. Amazing what a stick drive could hold. More amazing was what the female body could hold, inside of her via tampon insertion; it was the first time she had transported data *that* way. But there was always a first time for everything.

Spiker was steaming. So was Michelle. Of the two it would have been hard to tell who was more infuriated. Probably Spiker, since he was also so terribly embarrassed.

"Michelle, I'm sorry. I didn't know you were trying to reach me. I was involved in a big project."

"What kind of project?"

"You—you—you really wouldn't understand."

"Because I'm a moron? Try me. I'm not so dense."

"No, of course not. I didn't mean—"

"What the hell is your problem?" She was fuming.

"*My* problem . . . what the hell is *your* problem? You dumped me years ago. *My* problem is you and your religion and your community and the savage way you ripped out my heart."

"Tommy, I left them years ago. I know I was wrong. I always wanted to say I was sorry and—"

"And?"

"And now look at me yelling at you. I guess I was really freaked that you might be near death and I could never tell you how sorry I was or that I always did and always will love you."

He flushed, looking straight into her eyes.

"Okay, that said, I gotta go—can you please get me out of here—Death Valley or wherever we are?"

Tommy nearly collapsed. "I . . . I . . . I . . ."

"Well, what?"

"Please. Please. You have to help me. I made a huge mistake. Maybe it's not too late."

"What's not too late? Too late for what?"

"The unthinkable."

42

"YOU DID *WHAT*?" Michelle could not believe her ears.

"I thought I was doing the right thing. I guess I wanted revenge. I just don't know anymore, I mean, who I am, where I belong. I don't know what is right and what is wrong."

"Oh, I got this one. Look at me, Tommy Williams. You are a good man who took a very, very, very wrong turn. You are going to do an about-face and turn this thing around, and I mean NOW. We will fix this and then you will figure the rest of this out. Am I clear?"

"Yes, okay. I agree. I just don't know how…" His voice trailed off.

"How to what?"

"Stop it," he said, with a baffled look that defied his senses.

"You don't know how to stop it?"

"Joe was the operations guy. I mostly did research and production."

"Where's Joe? Get him on the phone."

"We can't. He's gone. I'll have to find a way, alone I guess."

"Oh, no, Tommy Williams, you may be in deep trouble but you are not alone. If it is the last thing I do, I will help you fix this nightmare. What were you thinking? No, don't bother telling me. You were so off course I don't even care. Is that what fanatics do, they convince themselves they are right?"

"You tell me, Michelle."

"Listen, my community is seriously misguided. I wasn't mature enough to know that when we were young. But I figured that out a long time ago."

"How did you figure it out, that they were wrong?"

"I overheard a child reciting a poem."

"A poem."

"It was like a bell went off in my head. Do you know "Outwitted" by Edwin Markham?

> He drew a circle that shut me out—
> Heretic, rebel, a thing to flout.
> But Love and I had the wit to win:
> We drew a circle that took him in!

"You always were witty. But, I don't know how you can help. I really think I am alone now."

"Not in this lifetime. You were meant for me and I was meant for you, and I will walk this earth with you, and if it takes until the end of time we will undo this mess together." Michelle kicked into high gear and began searching Joe's computer for details.

"You read the letter." Tommy buried his face in his hands and sobbed uncontrollably.

"A million times, maybe more."

43

"OKAY, I GET IT. Not looking good. Distribution already under way, ahead of schedule. No way to slow down the trucks from being loaded—oh I see, that has been done." Tommy put his phone down.

It seemed like the day flew by. It was already nearing 4:00 p.m. As Tommy reviewed the distribution matrix, he realized that as of a few hours earlier, probably four major US locations were already in possession of the sterilant, but possibly had not yet loaded it onto their trucks. With Easter weekend, the schedule was sketchy.

Michelle looked on, stunned at the implications. Tommy had described the whole plot and the whole logic train that got him there as well. She felt partly to blame. In the name of religion she destroyed a man and set him loose on society. She didn't have time to contemplate the gravity of the situation. She knew minutes counted. She looked at papers that described the plan to quickly penetrate the top twenty-five retail outlets in the country through a variety of products, foods, and beverages.

He hung up the phone, desperation written all over his face. "No way to stop it. Done, they tell me. It seems we were a week ahead of schedule, and with the EPA fast-tracked on this, they went ahead with the distribution. We have no way to know if the trucks will leave in the morning. Since tomorrow is Easter, some union drivers got the long weekend off and there is no real communication with the regular crew until Monday. I'm catching the next flight over to St. Louis."

"What can I do? How can I help?" Michelle asked.

"I don't know. We have to stop them. Shut it down. Kill the project. Let me think . . ."

Indeed some trucks had been loaded with the new E. coli-killing pesticide sterilant. Drivers would report in about 4:00 a.m. to begin the process of hauling the formula, which included somewhat of an arduous paperwork process to document anything that required hazardous materials.

Late that night Tommy and Michelle were still in the office trying frantically to reverse the nightmare he had set in motion. So many parts of the plan were already under way; it was unclear if there was any possible way to contain it.

"Michelle, I thought it was the right thing to do. What happened to me? Who did I become? Who am I now—I mean what is going on? I feel like some schizophrenic Jekyll and Hyde."

"I don't know, had my own dragons to slay and instead of taking out my anger on humanity I just took it all out on myself. Look at me, I'm nothing to anyone."

"You still have your mind. And you actually look really great."

"Come on, get it together. Lets undo this thing and then we can catch up."

Just after eleven, Spiker remembered that Courtney's father had called her at work. He searched the incoming call logs and found a Boston number. Bingo.

"Mr. Conihan, I'm Sp . . . Tom. Tom Williams, Courtney's boss. Sir, may I speak with her?"

Larry couldn't believe his ears. "You need to halt this thing! Its Easter weekend and Courtney was just about to call Homeland Security. You need to turn yourself in now and turn this ship around!"

"I know. I won't waste your time with apologies. It was a crazy, bad idea. We need all the help we can get. Right now, I'm trying to stop the whole thing—it may not be possible. Maybe Courtney can help. Maybe she knows the delivery schedules. Get her on the phone, please!"

Courtney was both relieved and outraged at the same time. "Dad, hand me that phone."

She got on the line. "You listen to me, you slimy, low-crawling sycophantic, toady, parasitic fawner . . . you damn well deserve the deranged global citizen of the year award. How dare you lure me into a ploy to 'save the world' from E. coli when you planned to totally annihilate a huge segment of humanity. Now, stop wasting time and tell me why you want my help."

"It's clear I made a huge mistake. Please help me stop it. They're telling me the trucks may be loaded and the first run will go out before Monday morning. After that it's only a matter of hours until those supplies are delivered and used, some directly into the food stream. Anyone in contact with it will be sterilized. It will all start to snowball."

"Are you telling me that Joe was the only one with the

exact rollout plan? We need help quick! Look, we can try, but we do need to call the FBI and Homeland Security."

Michelle addressed Courtney directly: "Courtney, this is Michelle Mizrahi. We met earlier."

"You! Beware. This man is a risk, a menace, a danger."

"Fair enough. But he didn't used to be and maybe I helped somehow send him round the bend—off the edge—if you will. We were in love, and I wasn't allowed to marry him. He became unhinged, it appears. Anyway, we need your help."

"What?"

"Please, there is not much time to reverse what's been staged for months. Please, in this urgent moment, help us."

"But how? There's really nothing I can do, everything is already staged for delivery," Courtney said.

Larry cut in. "I'm going make some calls. You keep working and update us in two hours."

His next call was to the group members assembling in Jerusalem.

He reached Pumpkin, who told Hala, who told Lisette.

Rahul was hearing bits and pieces and picked up Larry's next call. He listened as Larry asked, "What should we do, Rahul? We have to act fast. Before Monday, today if possible, please."

Rahul took out his laptop and began typing something. "Give me a minute. I have an idea."

As Rahul explained the plan, he activated his own network of resources. Larry King, Madonna, Bono, Oprah, and various celebrities immediately volunteered their help.

Larry only knew one famous, powerful person on the

planet, but he knew him well. His next call was to his old jamming buddy, his musician friend, Will Starr.

"Will, I know it's late. It's Larry. I have an emergency."

Courtney looked at her dad's phone ID—"Starr" came up. "*The* Will Starr," she wondered as she looked at her dad in surprise. He nodded.

Courtney never put two and two together. Will Starr and her dad attended prep school together—then Will went off to Princeton and her dad went to Harvard but they kept the close bond as musicians. Before Will became an acclaimed author, he was a decent musician.

"What can I do?" Will asked.

"I don't know—there's not much time. Remember all that Noetic stuff? Is it real or were you making that up?"

"No, it's real. Why?"

"If a whole bunch of people prayed or meditated at the same time to prevent a certain outcome, would it help?"

"Maybe."

"Will, Easter is this Sunday around the world—tomorrow morning; in some places in the world it has already begun. The entire Christian world will be attending churches. If the pope and every other church leader was made aware of a grave threat to humanity and asked their people to pray, would it possibly help on a grand scale?"

"Hey, I don't really know—I mean I'm a humble musician who makes a living as a writer. What is this about, anyway? If I hadn't known you for so long I would think you were nuts."

"Will, could you, I mean would you, uh, call the pope? I mean, are you *that* famous?"

"Ha! Good one! Really, you are nuts! The pope. He's not my biggest fan, you know."

"Do you have a minute—are you sitting down? I have a story to tell you."

"This oughta be good."

44

AFTER DISCUSSING the situation at length with the FBI, Tommy and Michelle worked late into the night, feverishly exhausting options. They had no way to reach Joe, who was probably the only person who knew the exact deployment schedule for the agent. When he left, the first thing Joe did was chuck his cell phone out of the car window. Following that, he tried out his newfound smile for a good long time, at the feeling of freedom from everyone and everything.

Courtney knew some of the distribution details and thought that there would be three or four US centers concurrently beginning distribution, followed closely by three European centers, but she couldn't remember which ones. She agreed with the recollection that St. Louis would be first. She thought the others were possibly Newark, Atlanta, and Cleveland.

Tommy paced the office, racking his brain for a solution, but none came. His blood pressure was sky-high, he was unable to eat or drink, and started feeling dizzy. The first flight to St. Louis on Easter Sunday morning was a 10:35 arriving in at 12:30 p.m. The soonest he could be at the distribution center was 1:15 p.m. It wasn't clear that any deliveries would go out on the holiday, but there was a chance.

Who was he kidding? Even if the loaded trucks were still at the facility, he would have no chance of talking the center management out of delaying their schedule. They were carefully graded and measured on their timeline and rewarded or punished for efficiency. A late shipment could cost a manager a bonus check—so he had no idea how he would persuade them to delay.

Even if he spoke to someone who was willing to hear him out, which would be nearly impossible since he had gone to great lengths to prevent anyone in supply chain management to know his real identity, carefully hiding behind a long list of subsidiaries with executive props, what could he say? The truth was too bizarre to be believed. He would be carted off in a straitjacket—after being arrested.

Even if they believed the truth, they had no authority to stop the run. Imagine a room filled with truck drivers who were willing to work Easter for more pay being told to go home. Surely he would be escorted, removed, or even thrown out of the building.

As he and Michelle left the complex to start driving to Las Vegas, which was the closest airport that had a flight the next morning, he felt hopeless.

"Seems there is no stopping what I've done. Maybe there are ways to slow it down; maybe tens or hundreds of thousands instead of millions and billions will be affected, but I can't see any way to reverse this nightmare."

"Come on. We can't give up. Maybe an idea will come along."

They called Courtney's father, right on time, two hours later.

"What's the update?"

"Abysmal progress, none to be exact. We are trying to head out to one of the distribution centers to see if we can persuade them, but we don't know the precise plan and we can't get there until after one p.m. It will likely be too late. Please tell me you've thought of something."

"Not really, but we're praying."

"Praying . . ."

"Actually, a group I'm in is fairly well-connected with world religions and we are praying on a global scale, all faiths, all times of the day and night around the world until Monday. There's some evidence to suggest it may have an impact in big numbers like that."

"That sounds useless. I'm useless. I want to throw myself off a bridge but I can't stop trying to help fix this before I do. Oh, God," Spiker said. "What have I done?"

"Listen, I'm going to patch in Rahul Patel, who has a few words for you."

"Namaste, Rahul speaking."

"This is Sp— Tom. Tom Williams. Sir, thank you for offering to speak to me but I'm in a huge hurry and have really little time right now." He hit the speaker so he could drive. Michelle was tuned in completely.

"Time is a construct. If you ask a quantum physicist, and I mean a really top one, she will tell you there is no such thing as time, no fourth dimension, so I guess we both have no time."

"What is this about? Please, I have to hurry."

"We each have within us the divine and the diabolical. Under the right conditions, the divine begins to shine through. Under the wrong conditions, the reverse happens. When I was a smoking, drinking, stressed-out lawyer, I was trying to move toward the divine but it wasn't working. I was spinning in circles like a squirrel in a box. Now, having meditated for over thirty years, I am experiencing the shift. You, Tom, are rare in that you have crossed back into divine pursuit from the far reaches of the diabolical grip. Most people, having veered that far off, cannot make their way back. Once they take a wrong turn, they just keep going."

"So?"

"The ones who make it back tend to go on to greatness. Something about seeing the edges of the worst enables one to conceive new things."

"I don't know, Rahul. I'm really just trying to fix what trouble I caused and then I'll turn myself in, or better yet hang myself to spare the public the cost of my care in prison."

"Long ago, Emperor Constantine was exposed as a child to Christianity by his mother, Helena, but for years he tortured Christians. Then one day, in writing to Christians, Constantine made clear that he owed his successes to the protection of a High God alone.

"Tom, it was Constantine's endorsement of the Christian tradition that was the critical turning point for early Christianity. In 313, Constantine issued the Edict of Milan, legalizing Christian worship, and so Constantine, the Roman emperor, became a great patron of the Church. After decades of persecuting Christians, he did an about-face.

"What I'm saying, Tom, is that Christianity didn't stand a chance without a certain savage lunatic far out into the diabolical reaches who crossed back into the divine realm.

"You know, I hear a lot of complaining about Christianity, but I'll tell you this— considering all that was in place in the world before Christianity, Constantine did us all a huge favor."[56]

"Okay. I didn't know that. I guess I learned something new. So what's this about praying in big groups around the world? I mean, could that even possibly work?"

"It could most certainly work. You can be praying, too."

"What is it that you're all saying to God in order to fix this disaster?"

"Oh, we're not saying anything to God, we're asking."

"Asking for what?"

"How. When we invoke the 'how' in our prayers and we listen to the responses, the intelligence, the answers that come; we access solutions from God."

"You've got people all around the world asking God how to fix this?"

"Indeed. Trust me, nothing ever goes wrong. There is a reason for all this. Namaste."

Rahul hung up.

Tommy and Michelle quietly pulled their car over to the side of the road. Holding hands, they looked toward the sky and asked aloud, "How?"

45

THE DRIVE from Death Valley to San Diego took only six hours, but Joe allowed himself to enjoy his first Saturday off in years, taking in many sights and staying the night in a lovely seaside hotel. Sunday morning, as Joe started the drive north to San Onofre State Park to begin the first of his monthlong surfing sprees, he remembered that his twin brother, Troy—an Air Force general now—who was usually based at Eglin Air Force Base in Florida, was temporarily working at Marine Corps Air Station Miramar. It was perhaps only about fifteen minutes from where he currently was.

He hadn't seen Troy in years and had no real sense of urgency about reconnecting now. But, after a moment he concluded for the sake of convenience he should stop by for a few minutes to say hello. Troy would be thrilled, on Easter, no less! What was the harm in a detour?

He wouldn't know that Troy was at that same moment discussing his possible whereabouts with Homeland Security. As Troy listened to the situation and tried to be of assistance, Joe was being waved in at the MCAS North Gate, smiling broadly. It was clearly a case of mistaken identity; they had mixed him up with his identical twin, but he saw no reason not to take advantage of a friendly welcome.

As Joe got out of his car, Bret Larson, the Lockheed Martin Vice President of F-35 test and verification, walked up to him and said, "Loaner, General? Better hurry. Briefing time."

Joe looked at him calmly, waiting for the man to take a breath so he could explain.

"Come on, I'll catch you up on the way over. You'll remember that the first successful vertical landings have been meeting our test objectives and fully demonstrate the F-35B's capacity to operate from a very small area at sea or onshore—a unique capability for a supersonic, stealth fighter. As you know, sir, this is only the first of many such tests to fully define the short takeoff and vertical landing characteristics—called STOVLs for short—of the world's most capable fifth-generation fighter. We routinely conduct vertical landings and short takeoffs to further expand the operational flight envelope for the F-35B. Today you'll be viewing one of our F-35B STOVL jets as it is undergoing flight trials. Now I know what you're wondering, sir. It's powered by a single Pratt & Whitney F135 turbo-fan engine, which drives a counter rotating Rolls-Royce Lift Fan. Of course the shaft-driven Lift Fan system includes a Rolls-Royce three-bearing swivel duct that vectors engine thrust and underwing roll ducts that provide lateral stability, and not to brag, but they produce more than forty-one thousand pounds of vertical lift."

Joe was stunned at the man's nonstop aero babble. He was about to cut in with a heavy dose of honesty when Bret continued: "For the last few years the F-35 program has been using Lockheed Martin's Autonomic Logistics Information

System—ALIS—for maintenance actions, spares tracking, and technical data support. Sir, the F-35 Lightning II is a fifth-generation fighter, combining advanced stealth with fighter speed and agility, fully fused sensor information, network-enabled operations, advanced sustainment, and lower operational and support costs. And of course we didn't build it alone, it was a joint effort, sir. Lockheed Martin developed the F-35 with its principal industrial partners, Northrop Grumman and BAE Systems. These two interchangeable F-35 engines are hot—combined effort with Pratt & Whitney F135 and the GE Rolls-Royce Fighter Engine Team F136. Okay, that's all the briefing we have time for. Easter morning, open skies. Suit up, General. Up you go."

Of the 140,000 or so Lockheed Martin employees, Joe hadn't met their brightest one.

"Did you say—"

"Come on, don't look surprised, General. You boys are paying us to the tune of $42.2 billion annually and we like to keep you happy. Take her out for a test flight."

As Joe looked out on the sun-drenched tarmac, he saw the F-35 Joint Strike Fighter sitting alone.

"Sweet."

46

COULD IT POSSIBLY WORK? Was this some kind of gift from the universe? Joe had been thinking as he drove away from Death Valley that, given all the new information, he should halt the run of chemicals and spare humanity. But he had no idea about how to do that.

Was this really happening? He looked up to heaven.

Joe had a thought. What were the odds of a skilled fighter pilot gaining access to one of the most powerful warplanes on the planet just in time to save the world from a disaster? Must be a sign. *Good enough for me,* he thought. *I'm in.* "God, if you can, help me. Help us all."

47

RAHUL WAITED QUIETLY as the thirteen powerful Christian leaders of Jerusalem delivered their Easter message. The leaders were from many global churches. They were seated in a panel being broadcast around the world.

> Alleluia! Christ is Risen. He is Risen Indeed. Alleluia!
>
> . . . We know the power of despair. We know the power of evil. We know the power of the 'principalities and powers' of this world which promote agendas of division and oppression to bring harm to God's people throughout God's creation. We, with you, know the power of sin and death.
>
> We also know the power of the Resurrection. We know the power of God to bring hope out of despair. We know the power of God in Christ Jesus, our Lord and Savior, to use forgiveness and love to conquer evil. We know the power of God in Christ to confront those same 'principalities and powers' to promote faith, mutual respect, compassion, and courage to speak the truth to benefit all of God's people. We know the power

> of the forgiveness of sins to redeem relationships in families and among the family of nations. We know the power of the gift of eternal life for all who believe.
>
> . . . May the one and living God, the Father, the Son, and the Holy Spirit, bless, preserve, and keep you, now and always. Amen.[57]

AS THE LEADERS EXITED, some recognized and immediately greeted Rahul. He drew the attention of all the others. Rahul asked for a moment with the group on an urgent matter. Within thirty minutes he had the commitment each of the leaders: prayers would commence immediately across the globe.

AFTER COUNTLESS ATTEMPTS, Will Starr was finally successful in getting through to someone high enough to ultimately get five minutes with high enough cardinals to finally get one minute by phone with the pope himself. One minute. Fortunately that's all it took. Prayers and fasting began throughout the Catholic Church, with all 1.2 billion members instructed to pray and ask God how to prevent this disaster.

TWO WEEKS BEFORE there had been a historic meeting between Jews and Arabs. At the meeting, both sides expressed a desire to reduce tensions in the city. Said an Israeli journalist afterward, "There has never been a meeting like this . . . if the rabbis and sheiks ran the state, there would have been peace a long time ago." Having read about this, Rahul next went to the journalist and requested a meeting with both leaders together. Interfaith cooperation was imperative. They were already leading the way, and forward momentum was key.

Next he worked on getting an audience with the most powerful rabbis in Israel. However, getting them all in the room together would be an incredible feat—many insiders thought that if Israel hadn't been under constant attack by the outside world it would have imploded by now. The list was rough but included leaders of the Orthodox, Conservative, and Reform movements as well as some ultraorthodox, who had the allegiance of hundreds of thousands of followers, and also controlled political parties and whole government coalitions.

Each leader was briefed and asked to personally call every other leader they knew of every faith and denomination. It would be a matter for God, the God of all.

No one knew how to approach Muhammad Khalid Hussein, the Grand Mufti of Jerusalem since July 2006, who had been appointed by the president of the Palestinian National Authority. Rahul led the group over to the Al-Aqsa Mosque in hopes of reaching out to him directly. Arriving at the mosque just after prayer time, they washed their hands and feet and waited to be greeted by a guard. As the guard approached, Hala came forward.

"Sir, these distinguished scholars and teachers, including Dr. Rahul Patel, request an immediate meeting with the Grand Mufti. Please use these words from the Koran when asking him: 'It is righteousness to give of yourself and your substance, out of love for Allah, to your kin, to orphans, to the needy, to the stranger, to those who ask . . .' Thank you."

They waited. And waited. And waited. They were there for nearly two hours and spoke among themselves about the many advances their task force was making. Just as they were about to give up and head back to the drawing board, the Grand Mufti appeared.

"My guests, you are welcome here. Please, come with me to the garden for tea."

As they described the situation and the incredible response by the Christian and Jewish faith communities, the Grand Mufti agreed to make some calls. It was not his decision. "My guests, inshallah—God willing—support will be quick," he said, departing.

Quick it was. By Saturday-evening prayers, every madrasa and mosque in the East had orders to pray a specific prayer—to ask God how to prevent this catastrophe from happening.

Prayers were sent to heaven in record numbers.

Was anyone up there listening?

48

FOLLOWING A TWENTY-FIVE-MINUTE orientation to the F-35 Joint Strike Fighter, which Joe learned was also being called the Lightning II, he was amazed that the single-engine stealth multirole fighter could perform close-air support, tactical bombing, and air-defense missions.

Each F-35 Fighter costs $112 million, and Joe braced himself to hear about its bells and whistles. As Bret rambled on, he studied the advanced, powerful sensor suite and more importantly, the weapons. The F-35 Joint Strike Fighter carried more weapons payload than any fighter jet in history.

Before taking off, Joe reviewed the list of firepower one more time, which included: guns: 1 × GAU-22/A 25 mm (0.984 in) cannon internally with 180 rounds; hardpoints: 6 × external pylons on wings with a capacity of 15,000 pounds and 2 × internal bays with two pylons each for a total weapons payload of 18,000 pounds; missiles, both air-to-air: AIM-120 AMRAAM, AIM-132 ASRAAM, AIM-9X Sidewinder, IRIS-T; and air-to-ground: AGM-154 JSOW, AGM-158 JASSM; bombs including: Mark 84, Mark 83, and Mark 82 GP bombs;

Mk.20 Rockeye II cluster bomb; Wind Corrected Munitions Dispenser capable; Paveway-series laser-guided bombs; Small Diameter Bomb; JDAM-series, and what appeared to be a possible nuclear weapon.

Holy crap. Remember not to touch that last button.

In the years since Joe had flown a fighter jet, they had figured out how to get nukes onboard these birds.

Finally, Joe took time to calculate his route. At the supersonic speeds, perhaps reaching Mach 1.05 at 30,000 feet, he would make four transitions through the sound barrier.

If he hit all five of his targets, he would return in under two hours. His goal was to take out the headquarters in Death Valley, and the four distribution centers—while harming no one in the four locations.

If.

Lifting off with a loud roar, Joe said one simple prayer: "God, I'm sorry for my misguided efforts. If you're there, talk me through this flight. Help me do the right thing and get this done."

IN JERUSALEM, it was Easter evening. Monisha checked in with Miles to tell him what was happening and asked that he and Lemar start praying. She also updated her new virtual spiritual friends around the globe and asked for their prayers or thoughts or meditations.

Pumpkin and the others tried reaching the president but it was nearly impossible.

"Miles, you and Lemar get down on your knees and keep prayin' until I call again! We got to do what we can to help in this situation."

"Yes, baby. We'll be doin' that. Call when you can. We love you, baby."

"And I love you, too, now you boys start prayin'!"

Fifteen minutes later, Miles called back. "Baby, you won't believe this! There's been a bomb in California near Nevada. Something about that same JSF you been talkin' about. Death Valley. Complex destroyed . . ."

Monisha thought long and hard, and then she used a trump card she rarely pulled out. She made a phone call.

"Ms. Adams, this here's Monisha Ray. You may remember, the late Reverend Montel Ray's niece. We've met several times. Yes, well. I know it's Easter Sunday but I need to speak to the president. This cannot wait, it is a matter of—"

"Mrs. Ray. There's just been a second bomb. St. Louis this time. I can't possibly get his attention at a time like this."

"Ms. Adams, now I know who's flyin' that JSF plane and I know what he's doin'. He's aimin' to save this country from a bioterror attack. Now, and I mean NOW, go get me the president."

The president had just heard the most unthinkable scenario—stuff a best-selling fiction writer couldn't even make up—that our armed forces had no way of stopping the JSF from its attack on the country. The JSF was in fact the strongest fighter in the world and nothing would stand up to it. He picked up the phone.

"Mrs. Ray, what do you know?"

"Sir, there was about to be a bioterror attack. Some kind of sterilant would have been out by tomorrow, enterin' our food supply. This man flyin' the plane up there, he knew, sir.

He acted fast. He's the only person who knew the locations of distribution and he's taking them out one by one, including the place in Death Valley. That's what I know."

"Anything else?"

"Yes, sir. I need to be patched in to him in that plane. I'm askin' you to put me through right now. Actually I'm tellin' you, sir, put me on with him *now*."

"Mrs. Ray—"

"Son, don't go there. You know what this country was like before my uncle laid down his life; he paved that path to the White House for all races of presidents. Now you put me through."

As Monisha held, CNN blaring in the background, the whole country held its breath. Was this worse than 9/11? Every news network was buzzing. People were scrambling. Easter services were halted. Nearly every person with a cell phone was using it. Countless more prayers were going up to God. Faith groups around the world held vigils. Side by side, all races and religions prayed wherever they were on Easter Sunday. Many fell to their knees to ask the higher power for help. No one knew or could fathom what was unfolding.

"Go ahead, Mrs. Ray. You're live with the pilot."

The connection was bad. There was a lot of noise in the cockpit. Joe thought he heard something coming over but hadn't tested his headset.

Monisha started. "Joe Kleiner. You're doin' fine. My name is Mrs. Ray."

Unfortunately, all Joe heard was "Joe Kleiner. You're doin' fine."

As Joe smiled that big smile, he headed to target three.

He said to himself, "Newark, you're looking gorgeous this morning."

BOOM!

Soaring through the skies at supersonic speeds, he hit Atlanta almost twenty minutes later.

Now there was one last target, Cleveland. The other centers had looked abandoned since it was Easter, and he was hoping Cleveland was no different.

As he locked onto his target, he couldn't be sure. He circled the target again. Still unsure, he heard the voice again on the speaker.

Monisha had been talking the whole time but he only caught "Now boy, you get this done."

BOOM!

It was done. Joe had successfully blasted the daylights out of all four threats and the headquarters, after verifying that it had been abandoned. There was no more threat. All the other distribution channels had time to halt their runs.

Joe smiled all the way back to Miramar, noticing there was no company up in the sky. All flights must have been grounded due to the perceived threat. No fighter jets would have gone up against him; he knew that. Commercial flights had obviously been grounded. He was alone in the sky except for God. That felt pretty good.

And God only knew what trouble awaited him upon landing, but he smiled. Whatever it was, it was worth it. He hadn't done a good deed in a long time and it felt awesome. Would he get life in prison? Would he be shot as he stepped off the plane? Would he be water-boarded and tortured at an undisclosed location? He didn't care.

That moment was forever his, with God Almighty as his co-pilot.

Upon landing, Joe saw the huge crowd of service members, first responders, fire trucks, police, and every imaginable news reporter, all waiting for his arrest, hoping to catch the moment on camera.

But, something totally unexpected happened as he deplaned. The crowd went wild. Cheers erupted from everywhere, cameras flashed. Service members saluted. And out walked Troy.

"Hey, bro. Welcome back. We're proud. The whole country knows what you did. How's it feel to be a hero?"

"Hero?"

"Joe, hold this line for the president."

"Joe, you gave us quite a scare until we figured out what you were up to," the president said. "Next time, clear your plans first, okay? And just so my people know, on whose authority did you act?"

"Well, sir, you might say it was on God's authority."

"Really. Joe, you heard God tell you to do that? What did He sound like?"

"I can't be a hundred percent sure, sir, there was very poor sound."

"Well, then make an educated guess. I need to tell the people something."

"Okay. Sir, to me she sounded like a powerful black woman from the South."

49

IMMEDIATELY FOLLOWING the news confirmation of the successful bombing of the distribution centers in the United States, lining up outside the King David Hotel in Jerusalem were top reporters eager for their chance to interview members of the task force. Word spread around the world like telepathy that some kind of focused, global-prayer initiative with a single purpose had been set in motion to help deter a bioterrorism plot—and moreover—that it *had worked*. The world and its inhabitants had dodged a huge bullet.

If true, the implications were incredible.

Henry Goldfarb, the BBC's long-time Jerusalem correspondent, would be the first to learn of the press conference shaping up on the hotel's South Garden Veranda, so he quietly exited the front lobby crowd and starting making his way across the hotel. Knowing the wait would be long, he stopped at the men's room where he caught a glimpse of a scene altogether out of place. There in the men's room, it appeared that a couple of guys from Thailand were putting on orange Buddhist robes over their clothes.

Go figure, he thought, as he resumed his walk across the lobby. He always thought monks wore nothing under those robes. *Hey, but who knew?* Just by habit he took note of their appearance. Maybe these guys were becoming more religious as they heard the news of the global prayer impact. Weird . . . Henry also thought monks were bald or shaved their heads. *Oh, well, maybe some new modern offshoot.*

As he settled himself in for the long wait on the veranda, Henry continued to amuse himself with this thought of a Superman-like group of Buddhists blending in like Clark Kent by day but secretly in place to protect Jerusalem with peace. It was a beautiful spring evening in Jerusalem, the sun's glow just right on the city.

After what seemed like an hour or so, Pumpkin was first to take her place on the platform. Next came Monisha, Ron, Hala, and Anneke. Lisette would be delayed by an urgent call from Gil.

Applause and joyous shouts in all languages rang out across the garden at the sight of the task force.

Henry turned to survey the crowd and noticed that the Buddhist monks were oddly positioned at corners and in high perches, kind of like . . .

"E-VVV-RRRYYY-OOO-NNN-GGGETTT-DDDOWN!!!!" The words left his mouth before his brain finished connecting the dots. *Terrorists.* In a moment of unification and global celebration, other terrorists had made their way through. Just when there had been peace.

Lisette, who was just approaching the platform, ducked behind a pillar and held her breath. She remained perfectly still, taking only shallow breaths and holding her eyes closed completely shut as long as she could.

Before the group members had time to react, they felt the hot, splintering burn of bullets ripping through their flesh. Some managed to make eye contact with each other as they fell hard against the limestone. Within seconds a melded stream of their diverse, mixed blood began running down the white steps of Jerusalem.

HOLIDAY OR NOT, celebration or not, the King David Hotel was never without its secret service. Boaz Rivkin, the on-duty Israeli Secret Service officer, not only caught the whole shooting on video, he activated a powerful electronic network very few suspected: the Israeli public. These men would get nowhere. And fast.

SIMULTANEOUSLY watching the men move into a Muay Thai stance, two Israeli women in the hotel's north parking lot instinctively pulled out an ace. Most Asian forms of martial arts are defensive, contrary to the Israeli form of Krav Maga, an offensive martial art that was developed in Czechoslovakia as a means of attacking anti-Semites. Pretty much shock and awe from an offensive point of view. They quickly took the Thai thugs down with a combination of striking, grappling, and wrestling moves.

Within the next hour Israeli interrogation methods that no one would ever reveal would quickly uncover their motivation: the group of scholars and their work on revising the Bible, along with their activism, was perceived as a direct threat to Bangkok's sex-slave trade.

Larry watched the shooting again and again on CNN. Courtney screamed in shock.

It sunk in. They were gone. Everyone was dead, except Larry and Lisette.

News broadcasts around the world would hail them as heroes, listing their names and photos in a silent slideshow at the end of their evening broadcasts: Ron Goodman, *Senior Researcher, Institute for Philosophy and Religion, Yale University;* T. Pumpkin Rowe, *Author, Maternal Aunt of the President of the Unites States of America;* Hala El Feddak, *CEO, Muslim Women's Global Leadership Initiative;* Monisha Ray, *Board Member, The Civil Rights Museum, Memphis, Tennessee;* Anneke Lebner, *Chief Art Conservationist, The National Gallery of Art, Washington, D.C. Two surviving members of the team include* Lisette Colliere, *Faculty, University of Pennsylvania Department of Religious Studies;* and Larry Conihan, *Esq., Jazz Musician, Mathematician and Professor at MIT.*

BACK IN WASHINGTON, members of a powerful right-wing lobby breathed a sigh of relief: someone else had taken it upon themselves to wipe out the threat the task force represented. Their worries were over. No one would be able to revise the Bible, and they reasoned the whole thing would fade out with a whimper. It was a very lucky Easter evening for them because their lobby stood to lose it all—its power base. The Bible was an extremely convenient tool for their purposes. In fact, the task force had made many enemies they never knew existed.

But, as the slave trade celebrated and the lobbyists secretly delighted in the demise of the team, clarity arrived to some others. Before the day was done, a pact was made. Via Skype, Larry, Courtney, Lisette, and Gil committed to finish the work, joined by one powerful blogging fan: Jane Alton, the Midwestern Sunday school teacher with the widely read weekly blog. And while they felt the crushing blow of their loss, they discovered they were stronger in numbers than they ever dreamed. Their project website indicated over sixty thousand new supporters in one day alone.

And the group had secured a powerful new leader. Jane Alton stepped up and assumed the role. Over the months that the group had been working together, Jane had already started a grassroots movement in support of the work. Her followers added the support base they needed to make the revised Bible a reality, available to all religions.

The pact they agreed to was simple: In the name of all things good and in the name of all things right; in the name of something higher than religion; in the name of humanity itself; in the name of their devoted friends and colleagues; and, in the name of all those who died for "heresy," the Bible would be revised.

50

Camp David, Maryland

"MR. PRESIDENT, we appreciate the opportunity to present our recommendations to you and this esteemed group of leaders from around the world." Lisette rose and walked to the front of the walnut-panelled conference room. She spoke confidently despite her accent.

"When you first took office we were tasked with isolating the troubling teachings of the Bible, both Old Testament and New, that were at cross-purposes with the ideals of our country: equality, liberty, fairness, goodness, kindness, respect for human dignity, and peace." Making eye contact with every leader, she confirmed: "At great cost we completed that task, and presented our early findings last year. Today we are pleased to share our findings with this unique global forum of leaders, who hold the power to call for change. History will remember this day."

Handing out the first binder, she continued. "There exist Bible verses that are truly reprehensible, teaching violence, hatred, rape, slavery, genocide, and other horrifying, demeaning, and demoralizing behavior. These specific verses contradict most of what is in the Bible and do not correlate with the overwhelming majority of good and worthwhile teachings in the Bible. The Bible has been and can be revised; it just hasn't been revised recently."

Passing around a draft copy of the new Bible, she said, "Based on this precise knowledge, we are recommending that a new edition of the Bible be published as an option for all to study, with these specific, questionable, and objectionable verses omitted. We have a draft version awaiting approval at a major publisher. Readers will need the opportunity to upgrade and we have a gradual transition plan mapped out for this.

"Grassroots movements within churches and synagogues will begin immediately to offer the new version as an alternative to the current versions in use. We feel confident this approach will work with the right set of incentives and disincentives. Change will be compelling and quick."

Standing perfectly still, she captured every eye of the sixteen leaders in attendance. "We were asked to step back from what we thought we knew. Never before in humanity has a group done this. We dove deep into the text itself, without all the commentary, and saw the Bible for what it is. We tested its moral fiber. Sir, we have determined where the Bible's true north is in relation to the guideposts we use as Americans, and there is not currently a direct correlation. Sir, you ran on a platform of change, with the backdrop of hope. What you asked for, and what we are here to deliver, is the how."

Walking very close to the group of leaders, she leaned forward. "We are not experts in other holy texts. Nevertheless, perhaps by this task we set the example of modern leadership in a modern world. Maybe even the kind of leadership that could be called courageous and that could one day prompt other countries to sponsor such undertakings within their own faith communities toward global progress and peace."

As Lisette concluded the leaders rose in acknowledgment and clapped.

THE GROUP of world leaders stayed on for a lengthy discussion in the expansive room. Questions were directed to the president about how and why he chose to undertake this mission and what kinds of reactions he might expect from the public.

He quietly answered, "Many people don't know this. Some, perhaps many, of our founding fathers took exception with certain verses in the Bible. None of them wished to diminish faith but rather hoped to bring about more productive forms of worship and action. Washington, Jefferson, and Franklin are included in these. In their time, progress in this realm was nearly impossible. Questioning the Bible would have earned them the label 'infidels,' a term we rarely hear in Christian circles these days.

"Thomas Jefferson actually wrote his own version of the Bible. He never spoke about religion, and certainly never wrote about his views, but he did some of this work early on.

"At the encouragement of my aunt, T. Pumpkin Rowe, who wound up dying for this cause, I set out to try to understand what problems they had with the Bible and whether anything could be done in our day and age to make better progress on peace in our country and in the world. Perhaps our founding fathers are still leading us today."

"Mr. President, may I ask, if everyone will have to buy a new Bible, won't that change be rather slow?" asked the German chancellor.

"May I answer that, Mr. President?" asked Larry.

"Certainly."

"The president's aunt had a keen ability to calculate risk. She left nothing to chance. In her will, which I had the privilege of drafting, she donated the proceeds of her substantial estate to underwrite the cost of development for the new Bible. And, by executive order of the president, anyone anywhere in the world can now download the new Bible free of cost in electronic form. It is not translated into many languages yet, but that will come. Her estate also provided funds for approximately three hundred million print copies as requested by the American public. Certainly courts, hotels, schools, and many faith institutions will require them in print form. Any remaining funds in her estate are to provide capital for a think tank of experts on other religious texts. Obviously in our diverse country we have many religions to study."

As the group dispersed, the researchers of the president's task force were quietly escorted to a reception area where they were presented with presidential commendations written to each of them, and posthumously to each of their departed colleagues, for their "Contributions to world peace and outstanding support of the values to which we subscribe."

EPILOGUE

Washington, D.C.

"MR. VERNACK will see you now." The executive assistant to the secretary of the US Department of Agriculture indicated Special Adviser Tom Williams to follow her down a long marble corridor.

Tom Williams and Joe Kleiner had spent an intense month at Guantanamo Bay prison, undergoing various forms of interrogations and psychological evaluations. In the end they were given only two options: either serve a life sentence or serve their country by being advisers to Homeland Security on the prevention of bioterror attacks.

It was an easy decision. Both would live out their days making the country a safer place.

Tom took his new responsibilities seriously. With twins on the way, he had something to live for. His life was on a much better course and humanity would benefit, he would make sure.

During the course of his work he had recently come across something interesting, but not specifically bioterror related. Realizing its value, he used all his connections to schedule this meeting and could only hope the secretary would hear what he was saying and take him seriously.

"Thank you for seeing me, Mr. Vernack. I'm Tom Williams."

"I know who you are."

"In my research I ran across something unusual, so I've spent a number of months testing and confirming my theory. It took a while but I am reasonably certain and brought with me empirical data for you: six double-blind tests and a score of results logs."

"Please cut to the chase, Mr. Williams."

"Yes, sir. As you know, our country has had a mysterious four-year-old crisis of disappearing honeybees and the situation is worsening. We expect a heavy bee die-off this winter; it seems the hives are laden with pesticides."

"Ah, the bee problem."

"Einstein said if the bee disappeared off the surface of the earth, people would only have four years of life left."

"Einstein said that?"

"Yes, sir. Anyway, the bee population is down by fifty percent and declining. All your agencies are trying to get to the bottom of it. They are ordering new research on pesticides. Federal courts are even weighing in, ruling that the US Environmental Protection Agency did overlook a requirement in allowing a pesticide on the market.

"The big concern for humans is of course is that bees play such an incredibly important role in our food supply. People eat about thirty percent plant foods that require pollination from honeybees. Also, sir, since 2006 we've seen 'colony collapse disorder,' in which large groups are dying en masse inexplicably. This disorder causes adult bees to abandon their hives and fly off to die.

"Due to this year's harsh winter, bees seem to be in bigger trouble, according to an internal USDA document. One-third of those surveyed had trouble finding enough hives to pollinate California's blossoming nut trees, which grow the bulk of the world's almonds.

"To cut to the chase, sir, I think I have found the root cause of the decline: certain types of pesticides—systemic pesticides that are designed to address the whole plant."

"What can we do?"

"Sir, imagine someone who enjoys an occasional drink of alcohol. If that person drank three bottles of gin over a two-week period, their system would need a rest, some good food, and lots of water before it could handle any more alcohol, right?"

"I suppose."

"Our bees have been on a bender of pesticides and their bodies are stressed and chemically hung over. I recommend no pesticides for two years straight. Some crops will be lost, but the bees will recover. Look this chart. See right here? One of my studies found 121 different types of pesticides within 887 wax, pollen, bee, and hive samples. That's 121 pesticides—imagine all that in your system, sir. Now, let's go back to the gin analogy. So in two weeks, add vodka, wine, Jack Daniel's, and rum. You get the point, right?

"After the two years we need to rotate crops and pesticides—farmers will need to be flexible with their land. We might need government incentives for that . . ."

Mr. Vernack picked up his phone before his visitor had even concluded. "Get me an immediate audience with the EPA and every single pesticide company out there we buy from. Today begins the Great Bee Revival."

"Mr. Williams, fine work." He hung up the phone and looked up.

"Thank you, sir."

"What's next, son?"

"Algae. Amazing stuff. It cleans the air, cools the planet, and produces cheap natural fuel."

"Don't waste a second. You get to work on that and report to me on it directly, you understand? Anything you need, just say the word. Glad to have you working with us."

"It is an honor to be of service to my country, sir."

References

Backman, Clifford. *The Worlds of Medieval Europe*. New York: Oxford University Press, 2003.

British Broadcasting Corporation. *Jesus in India?* 2009. Retrieved from http://krishnatube.com/video/293/Jesus-in-India--BBC-Documentary

Burr, William Henry. *Self-Contradictions of the Bible*. 1859.

Caner, Ergun Mehmet, and Emir Fethi Caner. *Christian Jihad: Two Former Muslims Look at the Crusades and Killing in the Name of Christ*. Kregel Publications, 2004.

Chand, Hukum. *History of Medieval India*. Anmol Publications Pvt. Ltd., pp. 424, 433.

Chittlister, Joan D., OSB. *Discipleship for a Priestly People in a Priestless Period*. Dublin, Ireland, 2001.

David, Saul. *The Indian Mutiny*. New York: Penguin Books, 2003, p. 398.

Esposito, John. *Islam: The Straight Path*. Oxford University Press, 2004, p. 93.

——. *Unholy War: Terror in the Name of Islam*. Oxford University Press, 2002, p. 26.

Gabriel, Mark A. *Islam and Terrorism*. Charisma House, 2002.

GenocideIntervention.net. *Genocide Intervention*. Retrieved December 2011 from http://www.genocideintervention.net

Girer, Nick. *Buddhist Nationalism and Religious Violence in Sri Lanka*. University of Idaho, 2006.

Hitchens, Christopher. *God is Not Great: How Religion Poisons Everything*. New York: Twelve Books, 2007, ch. 14.

Holdren, John. *Ecoscience*. 1977. Retrieved from http://zombietime.com/john_holdren/

Janssen, Michel. *The Transition from Newtonian Particle Mechanics to Relativistic Field Mechanics*. 2003. Retrieved from http://www.tc.umn.edu/~janss011/pdf%20files/copenhagen1.pdf

Jeurgensmeyer, Mark. *Terror in the Mind of God: The Global Rise of Religious Violence*. Berkeley, CA: University of California Press, 2003.

List of Christian Denominations. Retrieved December 2011 from http://www.wikipedia.org/wiki/List of Christian denominations

List of Wars. Retrieved December 2011 from http://www.wikipedia.org/wiki/List of wars

Mahajan, V. D. *Modern Indian History*. India: S. Chand, 1980, p. 188.

McGarry, John, and Brendan O'Leary. *Explaining Northern Ireland: Broken Images*. Oxford: Blackwell, 1995.

National Underground Railroad Freedom Center. *Historic Timeline of Slavery and the Underground Railway*. 2010. Retrieved from http://www.freedomcenter.org/underground-railroad/timeline/

Neill, Stephen. *A History of Christianity in India*. Cambridge University Press, 2002, p. 471.

Ontario Consultants on Religious Tolerance. *Religious Tolerance.org*. 2009. Retrieved from http://www.religioustolerance.org/god_cana.htm

Peters, Ralph. *Endless War*. Stackpole Books, 2010.

Pryor, Francis (2004). *Britain A.D.: A Quest for Arthur,*

England and the Anglo-Saxons. London: HarperCollins, 2006.

Raid on Deerfield. Retrieved December 2011 from http://www.wikipedia.org/wiki/Raid on Deerfield

Ramesh, Randeep. *Millions died in Indian Mutiny of 1857.* 2007. Retrieved from http://www.kuwaittimes.net/read_news

Appendix A

NAMES OF NATIVE AMERICAN PEOPLES

Ababco
Abenaki
Aberginian
Abittibi
Abnaki / Abenaki
Absentee
Accohanoc
Accominta
Achiligonan
Achomawi
Acolapissa
Acquintanacsnak
Acuera
Adai
Adshusheer
Agawam
Agua Caliente
Ahantchuyuk
Akonapi
Ais
Alabama
Alchedoma
Aleut
Algonquian
Algonquin
Alibamu
Allakaweah
Alliklik
Alsea / Alsi
Amacano
Amahami
Amaseconti
Amikwa
Anadarko
Ancient Puebloans
Anishinaabe (Ojibwe)
Ani-Stohini / Unami
Aondironon
Apache
Apalachee
Apalachicola
Appomattoc
Aquackanonk
Aranama
Arapaho
Arawak
Arendahronon
Arikara (Arikaree, Ree)
Arivaipa
Arkokisa
Armouchiquois
Arosaguntacook
Asa
Ascahcutoner
Assegun
Assiniboine (Stoney)
Assuti
Atanumlema
Atchatchakangouen
Atfaiati
Athapascan
Atikameks
Atquanachuke
Atsina
Atsugewi
Attacapa
Aucocisco
Avavares
Avoyel
Awani / Awanichi
Awatobi
Axion

Bahacecha
Bankalachi
Bannock
Basawunena
Bayougoula
Bear River
Bellabella
Beothuks
Bersiamite
Bidai
Bigiopa
Big Swamp Indians
Biloxi
Blackfoot/Siksika
Blewmouths
Bocootawwonauke
Brotherton
Buena Vista
Caddo
Cahokia
Cahuilla
Cajuenche
Calapooya
Callam
Calusa
Canarsee
Caparaz
Cape Fear Indians
Capinans
Catawba
Cathlacomatup
Cathlacumup
Cathlakaheckit
Cathlamet
Cathlanahquiah
Cathlapotle
Cathlathlalas
Caughnawaga
Cayuga
Cayuse
Chactoo
Chakankni
Chakchiuma
Chastacasta
Chatot
Chaui
Chaushila
Chawasha
Chehalis
Chelamela
Chelan
Chemehuevi
Chepenafa
Cheraw
Cherokee
Chesapeake
Chetco
Cheyenne
Chiaha
Chickahominy
Chickamauga
Chickasaw
Chilliwack
Chilluckittequaw
Chilula
Chimakiun
Chimakum
Chimariko
Chine
Chinook
Chippewa (Ojibwe)
Chiricahua
Chitimacha
Choctaw
Choula
Chowanoc
Chumash
Chumashan
Clackama
Clallam
Clatskanie
Clatsop
Clowwewalla
Coahuiltecan
Coaque
Cochimi
Cochiti
Cocopa
Columbians
Colville
Comanche
Conestoga
Congaree
Conoy
Coos
Copalis
Coree
Costanoan
Coushatta (Koasati)

Cowichan
Cowlitz
Cree
Creek
Croatan
Crow
Cuñeil
Cupeño
Dakota
Dakubetede
Deadose
Delaware
Diegueño
Diné
Dotame
Doustioni
Dwamish
Eno
Erie
Eskimo—See Inuit
Esselen
Etchaottine
Etchareottine
Etheneldeli
Eyak
Eyeish
Fernandeño
Five Civilized Tribes
Flathead
Fox
Fremont
Fresh Water
Gabrieleno
Grigra
Gros Ventre
Guacata
Guale
Guasas
Haida
Hainai
Halchidhoma
Halyikwamai
Hanis
Hathawekela
Hatteras
Havasupai
Hidatsa
Hitchiti
Hoh
Hohokams
Honniasontkeronon
Hopi
Houma
Housatonic
Hualupai
Huchnom
Humptulips
Hupa
Huron
Ibitoupa
Icafui
Illinois
Innu
Inuit
Inupiat
Iowa
Iroquois
Isleta del Sur
Jeags
Juaneño
Kadohadacho
Kalapooian
Kalispel
Kamia
Kanza/Kaw
Karankawa
Karok
Kaska
Kaskaskia
Kaskinampo
Kato
Kawaiisu
Kawchodinne
Kawia
Kawia
Keresan
Keyauwee
Kichai
Kickapoo
Kiowa
Kitanemuk
Kitksan
Klamath
Klickitat
Koasati—See Coushatta
Kohuana
Konomihu
Kootenai/Kutenai
Koroa

Koso
Kosotshe
Koyeti
Kuitsh
Kusan
Kutchin
Ktunaxa
Kwaiailk
Kwakiutl
Kwalhioqua
Lakmiut
Lakota
Lassik
Latgawa
Lenape
Lillooet
Lohim
Luckeamute
Luiseño
Lumbees
Lummi
Lutuamian
Macapiras
Machapunga
Mahican
Maidu
Makah
Maliseets
Manahoac
Mandan
Manhattan
Manso
Marameg
Maricopa
Mariposan
Mascouten
Mashpee
Maskegon
Massachusett
Matchoctic
Matinecoc
Mattabesic
Mattole
Meherrin
Meits
Menominee
Methow
Metoac
Miami
Mical
Michigamea
Michilimackinac
Micmac
Mikasuki
Miluk
Mishikhwutmetunne
Missouri
Miwok
Mobile
Mocogo
Moctobi
Modoc
Mogollon
Mohawk
Mohegan
Mojave
Molala
Monacan
Mono
Mono
Montagnais
Montauk
Moratoc
Moravians
Mosepolea
Muckleshoot
Mucogo
Mugulasha
Muklasa
Multnomah
Muskogean
Munsee
Nabedache
Nacisi
Nacogdoche
Nahane
Nakota
Nakotchokutchin
Naltunnetunne
Nanaimo
Nanatsoho
Nanticoke
Napissa
Napochi
Narragansett
Natchez
Natchitoch
Natchitoches
Nauset

Navajo
Neketemeuk
Nemalquinner
Nespelem
Neusiok
Neutrals
Nez Percé
Niantic
Nipmuc
Nippissing
Nisqualli
Nongatl
Nooksak
Nootka
Noquet
Nottoway
Ntlakyapamuk
Occaneechi
Oçita
Oconee
Ofo
Ojibwe/Ojibway
Okanagon
Okelousa
Okwanuchu
Omaha
Onathaqua
Onatheaqua
Oneida
Oneota
Ononchataronon
Onondaga
Ontonagon
Opelousa
Osage
Osoche
Oto
Ottawa
Ouachita
Ozette
Paiute
Paloos
Palouse
Panamint
Papago
Pascagoula
Passamaquoddy
Patiti
Patwin
Pawnee
Pawokti
Pecos
Pedee
Pennacook
Penobscot
Pensacola
Peoria
Pepikokia
Pequawket
Pequot
Piankashaw
Piegan
Pima
Pinal Coyotero
Piro Pueblo
Pit River
Pocomtuc
Pohoy, Pooy, Posoy
Pomo
Ponca
Poosepatuck
Potano
Pottawatomie
Powhatan
Pshwanwapam
Pueblo
Puntatsh
Puyllup
Quahatika
Quapaw
Queets
Quileute
Quinaielt
Quinault
Quinipissa
Rappahannock
Ree
Rouge River
Saconnet
Sahehwamish
Salinan
Salish
Saluda
Samish
Sanpoil
Santee
Santiam
Saponi
Satsop

Saturiba
Saturiwa
Sauk
Sauk and Fox
Sawoki
Secwepemc
Seechelt
Sekani
Semiahmoo
Seminole
Seneca
Senijextee
Serrano
Sewee
Shahala
Shakori
Shasta
Shawnee
Shinnecock
Shoshone
Shuswap
Siksika
Siletz
Sinkakoius
Sinkiuse/Sinkyone
Sioux
Sissipahaw
Siuslaw
Skaddal
Skagit
Skidi
Skilloot
Snake
Snohomish
Snoqualime/Snoqualmie
Soacatino
Sobaipuri
Souchitioni
Spokan
Squuaxon
Stehtsasamish
Stillaquamish
Stockbridge
Stony—See Assiniboine
Sugeree
Suislaw
Suquamish
Surruque
Susquehanna
Susquehannock
Sutaio
Swallah/Swalash
Swinomish
Tacatacuru
Tachi
Taensa
Taidnapam
Takelma
Tali
Taltushtuntude
Tangipahoa
Tano Pueblo
Taposa
Tatlitkutchin
Tawakon
Tawasa
Tawehash
Tekesta, Tequesta
Tenino
Tewa/Tano
Tillamook
Timucuan
Tionontati
Tiou
Tiwa/Tigua
Tlingit
Tocobaga
Tohome
Tolowa
Tongva
Tonkawa
Tsattine
Tschantoga
Tsilkotin
Tsimshian
Tübatulabal
Tukkuthkutchin
Tulalip
Tunica
Tunxis
Tuscarora
Tuskegee
Tutchonekutchin
Tutelo
Tututni
Twana
Tyigh
Ucita
Umatilla

Umpqua
Unalachtigo
Unami
Ute
Utina
Wabanaki
Waccamaw
Waco
Wailaki
Walapai
Walla Walla
Wampanoag
Wanapan
Wappinger
Wappo
Wasco
Washa
Washoe
Wateree
Watlala
Wauyukma
Waxhaw
Wea
Weanoc
Weapemeoc
Wenatchee
Wenrohronon
Whilkut
Wichita
Winnebago
Wintu
Wintun
Winyaw
Wishram
Wiyot/Wiyat
Woccon
Wyandot
Wynoochee
Yahi
Yahooskin
Yahuskin
Yakama
Yakonan
Yamasee
Yamel
Yampa
Yana
Yankton
Yaquina
Yatasi
Yavapai
Yazoo
Yodok
Yojuane
Yokuts
Yonkalla
Yscanis
Yuchi
Yufera
Yui
Yuki
Yuma
Yurok
Yustaga
Zuni

Appendix B

WHITE SUPREMACIST GROUPS IN CALIFORNIA

American National Socialist Workers Party	Neo-Nazi	CA
American Renaissance/ New Century Foundation	White Nationalist	CA
American Thule Society	Neo-Nazi	CA
Aryan Nations Youth Action Corps	Neo-Nazi	CA
Council of Conservative Citizens	White Nationalist	CA
Golden State Skinheads	Racist Skinhead	CA
Golden State Skinheads	Racist Skinhead	CA
Jewish Defense League	General Hate	CA
Knights of the Nordic Order	Neo-Nazi	CA
National Socialist Movement	Neo-Nazi	CA
New Black Panther Party	Black Separatist	CA
San Fernando Valley Skins	Racist Skinhead	CA
United Southern Brotherhood	Ku Klux Klan	CA
White Revolution	Neo-Nazi	CA
Traditional Values Coalition	Anti-Gay	Anaheim CA
Aryan Militia	Neo-Nazi	Bakersfield CA
Coors Family Skinheads	Racist Skinhead	Big Bear Lake CA
Camarillo Storm Skinheads	Racist Skinhead	Camarillo CA
Tony Alamo Christian Ministries	General Hate	Canyon Country CA
Aryan Nations	Neo-Nazi	Chino CA
Nation of Islam	Black Separatist	Compton CA
Volksfront	Racist Skinhead	Concord CA
Brotherhood of Klans Knights of the Ku Klux Klan	Ku Klux Klan	Crescent City CA

Aryan Nations	Neo-Nazi	Dulzura CA
California Skinheads	Racist Skinhead	Fresno CA
National Socialist Movement—NSM	Neo-Nazi	Fresno CA
National Socialist Movement—NSM	Neo-Nazi	Glendale CA
California Coalition for Immigration Reform	Anti-Immigrant	Huntington Beach CA
United Society of Aryan Skinheads	Racist Skinhead	Lakeside CA
United Society of Aryan Skinheads	Racist Skinhead	Lancaster CA
Jewish Defense League	General Hate	Los Angeles CA
Nation of Islam	Black Separatist	Los Angeles CA
Tradition in Action	Radical Traditionalist Catholic	Los Angeles CA
Volksfront	Racist Skinhead	Los Angeles CA
Odium Books	General Hate	Montecito CA
Institute for Historical Review	Holocaust Denial	Newport Beach CA
Noontide Press	Holocaust Denial	Newport Beach CA
Chick Publications	General Hate	Ontario CA
Blood and Honour	Racist Skinhead	Orange County CA
Orange County Skins	Racist Skinhead	Orange County CA
United Society of Aryan Skinheads	Racist Skinhead	Orange County CA
OMNI Christian Book Club	Radical Traditionalist Catholic	Palmdale CA
Skinheads of the Rahowa	Racist Skinhead	Porterville CA
Nation of Islam	Black Separatist	Rialto CA
Nation of Islam	Black Separatist	Richmond CA
Inland Empire Skinheads	Racist Skinhead	Riverside CA
National Socialist Movement	Neo-Nazi	Riverside CA
Western Hammerskins	Racist Skinhead	Riverside CA
American Front	Racist Skinhead	Sacramento CA
European Americans United	White Nationalist	Sacramento CA
Jewish Defense League	General Hate	Sacramento CA
National Alliance	Neo-Nazi	Sacramento CA
National Socialist Movement—NSM	Neo-Nazi	Sacramento CA
Sacramaniacs	Racist Skinhead	Sacramento CA
Sacto Skinheads	Racist Skinhead	Sacramento CA
United Society of Aryan Skinheads	Racist Skinhead	Sacramento CA
Berdoo Skinhead Family	Racist Skinhead	San Bernardino CA
Save Our State	Anti-Immigrant	San Bernardino CA

WAR Skins	Racist Skinhead	San Bernardino CA
Western Hammerskins	Racist Skinhead	San Bernardino CA
European American Issues Forum	White Nationalist	San Bruno CA
Nation of Islam	Black Separatist	San Diego CA
United Society of Aryan Skinheads	Racist Skinhead	San Diego CA
American Renaissance/ New Century Foundation	White Nationalist	San Francisco CA
Bay Area Skinheads	Racist Skinhead	San Francisco CA
Council of Conservative Citizens	White Nationalist	San Francisco CA
Nor Cal San Jose Skins	Racist Skinhead	San Jose CA
Brotherhood of Klans Knights of the Ku Klux Klan	Ku Klux Klan	San Luis Obispo CA
Golden State Skinheads	Racist Skinhead	San Luis Obispo CA
National Socialist Skinhead Front	Racist Skinhead	San Luis Obispo CA
Brotherhood of Klans Knights of the Ku Klux Klan	Ku Klux Klan	Santa Ana CA
League of the South	Neo-Confederate	Scotts Valley CA
American Patrol/Voice of Citizens Together	Anti-Immigrant	Sherman Oaks CA
Brotherhood of Klans Knights of the Ku Klux Klan	Ku Klux Klan	Soledad CA
Volksfront	Racist Skinhead	Sunset Beach CA
United Northern and Southern Knights of the Ku Klux Klan	Ku Klux Klan	Susanville CA
Abiding Truth Ministries	Anti-Gay	Temecula CA
United Realms of America Knights of the Ku Klux Klan	Ku Klux Klan	Ukiah CA
Chalcedon Foundation	Anti-Gay	Vallecito CA
White Devil Industries	Racist Music	Ventura CA
Voz de Aztlan	General Hate	Whittier CA
Hardcore Skins	Racist Skinhead	Yuba County CA

Appendix C

TIMELINE OF WOMEN IN LEADERSHIP ROLES IN CHRISTIAN CHURCHES

Early 1800s: A fundamental belief of the Society of Friends (Quakers) has always been the existence of an element of God's spirit in every human soul. Thus all persons are considered to have inherent and equal worth, independent of their gender. This led naturally to an acceptance of female ministers. In 1660, Margaret Fell (1614–1702) published a famous pamphlet to justify equal roles for men and women in the denomination. It was titled: *Women's Speaking Justified, Proved and Allowed of by the Scriptures, All Such as Speak by the Spirit and Power of the Lord Jesus And How Women Were the First That Preached the Tidings of the Resurrection of Jesus, and Were Sent by Christ's Own Command Before He Ascended to the Father (John 20:17)*. In the United States, in contrast with almost every other organized religion, the Society of Friends (Quakers) has allowed women to serve as ministers since the early 1800s.

1853: Antoinette Brown is ordained by the Congregationalist Church. However, her ordination is not recognized by the denomination. She quits the church and later becomes a Unitarian. The Congregationalists later merge with others to create the United Church of Christ.

1861: Mary A. Will is the first woman ordained in the Wesleyan Methodist Connection by the Illinois Conference. The Wesleyan Methodist Connection eventually becomes The Wesleyan Church.

1863: Olympia Brown is ordained by the Universalist denomination in 1863, in spite of a last-moment case of cold feet by her seminary, which fears adverse publicity. After a decade and a half of service as a full-time minister, she becomes a part-time minister in order to devote more time to the fight for women's rights and universal suffrage. In 1961, the Universalists and Unitarians join to form the Unitarian Universalist Association (UUA). The UUA becomes the first large denomination to have a majority of female ministers.

1865: Salvation Army is founded, which ordains both men and women. However, there are initially rules that prohibit a woman from marrying a man who has a lower rank.

1879: Church of Christ, Scientist is founded by a woman, Mary Baker Eddy.

1880: Anna Howard Shaw is the first woman ordained in the Methodist Protestant Church, which later merges with other denominations to form the United Methodist Church.

1888: Fidelia Gillette might be the first woman ordained in Canada. She serves the Universalist congregation in Bloomfield, Ontario, during 1888 and 1889. She is presumably ordained in 1888 or earlier.

1889: The Nolin Presbytery of the Cumberland Presbyterian Church ordains Louisa Woosley.

1889: Ella Niswonger is the first woman ordained in the United Brethren Church, which later merges with other denominations to form the United Methodist Church.

1892: Anna Hanscombe is believed to be the first woman ordained by the parent bodies, which form the Church of the Nazarene in 1919.

1909: The Church of God (Cleveland, Tennessee) begins ordaining women.

1911: Ann Allebach is the first Mennonite woman to be ordained. This occurrs at the First Mennonite Church of Philadelphia.

1914: Assemblies of God is founded and ordains its first woman clergy.

1917: The Church of England appoints female Bishop's Messengers to preach, teach, and take missions in the absence of men.

1917: The Congregationalist Church (England and Wales) ordains their first woman, Constance Coltman (née Todd) at the King's Weigh House, London. Its successor is the United Reformed Church (a union of the Congregational Church in England and Wales and the Presbyterian Church of England) in 1972. Since then, two more denominations have joined the union: The Reformed Churches of Christ (1982) and the Congregational Church of Scotland (2000). All of these denominations ordained women at the time of union and continue to do so. The first woman to be appointed General Secretary of the United Reformed Church was Roberta Rominger in 2008.

1920s: Some Baptist denominations start ordaining women.

1922: The Jewish Reform movement's Central Conference of American Rabbis state that "Woman cannot justly be denied the privilege of ordination." However, Reform Judaism takes a few more decades to actually ordain women.

1922: The Annual Conference of the Church of the Brethren grants women the right to be licensed into the ministry, but not to be ordained with the same status as men.

1929: Izabela Wiłucka is ordained in Old Catholic Mariavite Church in Poland.

1935: Regina Ronas is ordained privately by a German rabbi.

1936: United Church of Canada starts ordaining women.

1944: Anglican Communion, Hong Kong. Florence Li Tim Oi is ordained on an emergency basis.

1947: Czechoslovak Hussite Church starts ordaining women.

1948: Evangelical Lutheran Church of Denmark starts ordaining women.

1949: Old Catholic Church (in the United States) starts ordaining women.

1956: Maud K. Jensen is the first woman in a Protestant denomination to receive full clergy rights and conference membership in the Methodist Church.

1956: A predecessor church of the Presbyterian Church (USA) ordains its first woman minister.

1958: Women ministers in the Church of the Brethren are given full ordination with the same status as men.

1960: Evangelical Lutheran Church in Sweden starts ordaining women.

1967: Presbyterian Church in Canada starts ordaining women.

1971: Anglican Communion, Hong Kong. Joyce Bennett and Jane Hwang are the first regularly ordained priests.

1972: Reform Judaism starts ordaining women.

1972: Swedenborgian Church starts ordaining women.

1972: Sally Priesand becomes the first woman rabbi to be ordained by a theological seminary. She is ordained in the Reform tradition.

1974: Methodist Church in the United Kingdom starts ordaining women.

1974: Sandy Eisenberg Sasso becomes the first woman rabbi to be ordained within the Jewish Reconstructionist Movement.

1976: Episcopal Church—eleven women are ordained in Philadelphia before church laws are changed to permit ordination.

1976: Anglican Church in Canada ordains six female priests.

1976: The Reverend Pamela McGee is the first female ordained to the Lutheran ministry in Canada.

1977: Anglican Church of New Zealand ordains five female priests.

1979: The Reformed Church in America admits women to the offices of deacon and elder.

1983: An Anglican woman is ordained in Kenya.

1983: Three Anglican women are ordained in Uganda.

1984: Community of Christ (known at the time as the Reorganized Church of Jesus Christ of Latter Day Saints) authorizes the ordination of women. This is the second largest Latter-Day Saint denomination.

1985: According to the *New York Times*, February 14, 1985, "After years of debate, the worldwide governing body of Conservative Judaism has decided to admit women as rabbis. The group, the Rabbinical Assembly, plans to announce its decision at a news conference . . . at the Jewish Theological Seminary . . ." Amy Eilberg becomes the first female rabbi.

1985: The first women deacons are ordained by the Scottish Episcopal Church.

1988: Evangelical Lutheran Church of Finland starts ordaining women.

1988: Episcopal Church chooses Barbara Harris as the first female bishop.

1990: Anglican women are ordained in Ireland.

1992: The Church of England passes a measure to allow women to be ordained priests.

1992: Anglican Church of South Africa starts ordaining women.

1994: The first women priests are ordained by the Scottish Episcopal Church.

1994: The first women priests are ordained by the Church of England.

1995: Seventh-Day Adventists. Sligo Seventh-Day Adventist Church in Takoma Park, Maryland, ordains three women in violation of the denomination's rules.

1995: The Christian Reformed Church votes to allow women ministers, elders, and evangelists. In November 1998, the North American Presbyterian and Reformed Council (NAPARC) suspends the CRC's membership because of this decision.

1998: General Assembly of the Nippon Sei Ko Kai (Anglican Church in Japan) starts ordaining women.

1998: Guatemalan Presbyterian Synod starts ordaining women.

1998: Old Catholic Church in the Netherlands starts ordaining women.

1998: Some Orthodox Jewish congregations start to employ female "congregational interns." Although these "interns" do not lead worship services, they perform some tasks usually reserved for rabbis, such as preaching, teaching, and consulting on Jewish legal matters.

1999: Independent Presbyterian Church of Brazil begins ordaining women (ordination as either clergy or elders).

2000: The Baptist Union of Scotland votes to allow their churches to either allow or prohibit the ordination of women.

2000: The Mombasa diocese of the Anglican Church of Kenya starts ordaining women.

2000: The Church of Pakistan ordains its first women deacons.

2005: The Lutheran Evangelical Protestant Church (LEPC) (GCEPC) in the United States elects Nancy Kinard Drew first female presiding bishop.

2006: The Episcopal Church elects Katharine Jefferts Schori first woman presiding bishop, or primate.

Appendix D

TIMELINE OF SLAVERY IN NORTH AMERICA

Date	Event
1585	First Africans brought to North America and enslaved at St. Augustine, Florida
Shortly after this	Underground Railroad begins when someone unknown aids first freedom seeker
February 18, 1688	Mennonites in North America oppose slavery, aid freedom seekers (disputed)
1754	Quakers in North America condemn slavery, require manumission among Quakers
1775	First abolition society formed in Philadelphia
1780	Methodist Church in America states that slavery contradicts laws of God and man
1780 to 1786	Nine northern states abolish slavery and/or legislate emancipation
November 20, 1786	George Washington writes of his acting as a slave catcher
1787	Rev. Absalom Rones and Rev. Richard Allen form Independent Free African Society
July 13, 1787	Northwest Ordinance bans slavery in Ohio, Indiana, Illinois, Michigan, Wisconsin
1787	Presbyterian Church of America condemns slavery, begins promoting abolition

June 21, 1788	United States Constitution ratified, fails to deal with slavery
November 1788	George Washington, an enslaver from Virginia, elected President
1789	Baptist Church of Virginia condemns slavery, urges abolition
November 1796	John Adams, only abolitionist among main Founders, elected President
1808	United States outlaws further importation of slaves
June 14, 1811	Harriet Beecher Stowe, future author of *Uncle Tom's Cabin*, born in Connecticut
1816	African Methodist Episcopal Church founded, opposes slavery, aids fugitives
February 1818	Frederick Douglass, national hero, born enslaved on the Maryland eastern shore
Probably 1822	Harriet Tubman, national heroine, born enslaved on the Maryland eastern shore
1827	John Russworm and Samuel Cornish, black journalists, publish *Freedom's Journal*
1828	Russworm and Cornish publish *The Rights of All*, first black abolitionist periodical
1830	James and Lucretia Mott form Pennsylvania Anti-Slavery Society
January 1, 1831	Twenty-six-year-old William Lloyd Garrison publishes first issue of his antislavery newspaper, *The Liberator*. Continues publication until Thirteenth Amendment is passed in 1865
August 21, 1831	Nat Turner Rebellion in North Carolina alarms South, emboldens abolitionists
1831	William Lloyd Garrison, others, form New England Anti-Slavery Society

1831	Arthur and Lewis Tappan form the National Anti-Slavery Society in New York
1830s	Vigilance committees formed in northern cities to prevent return of fugitive slaves
1830s	Network aiding freedom seekers first takes on the name Underground Railroad
June 17, 1833	Detroit Riots rescue Lucie and Thornton Blackburn from jail and slave catchers
August 1, 1833	Great Britain abolishes slavery throughout its worldwide Commonwealth. Canada becomes magnet for U.S. freedom seekers
1830s, 1840s	Some other European powers abolish slavery at home and in their colonies
1849	Harriet Tubman escapes enslavement
Beginning in 1850s	Philadelphia businessman and safe-house operator William Still begins recording accounts of those freedom seekers he assists
1850–1859	Harriet Tubman makes at least nine successful rescues of Maryland freedom seekers. "Never lost a passenger"
September 18, 1850	Fugitive Slave Act passed requiring U.S. citizens to aid in capturing freedom seekers
April 1, 1852	*Uncle Tom's Cabin* by Harriet Beecher Stowe published, sells a record 500,000 copies in months, same number abroad in two years. First international bestseller
September 11, 1851	Blacks in Christiana, Pennsylvania, run off slave catchers, kill leader, alarm South
Between 1831 and 1865	Baltimore & Ohio Railroad Company sued for aiding freedom seekers
March 6, 1857	Dred Scott decision, authored by Supreme Court Chief Justice Roger Taney, strips blacks free and enslaved of citizenship

October 16, 1859	Abolitionist John Brown seizes federal armory at Harpers Ferry, West Virginia
December 2, 1859	John Brown hanged in Charlestown, West Virginia (then Virginia)
By 1860	Of the thirty-three states, eighteen no longer permit slavery
March 1861	Abraham Lincoln inaugurated as sixteenth President. Southern states begin seceding
April 12, 1861	Fort Sumter fired on, Civil War begins
January 1, 1863	Emancipation Proclamation promulgated abolishing slavery in Confederate states
July 1863	Working as a Union scout, Harriet Tubman in a single week frees more than 750 enslaved people along Combahee River in South Carolina
May 26, 1865	Civil War ends
December 6, 1865	Thirteenth Amendment outlaws slavery, with Mississippi the only dissenting state
1872	William Still authors *The Underground Railroad* recounting 190 accounts of over 900 freedom seekers he had aided
February 20, 1895	Frederick Douglass dies
July 1, 1896	Harriet Beecher Stowe dies
1898	Wilbur Siebert authors *The Underground Railroad from Slavery to Freedom*, the first extensive cataloging of Underground Railroad safe houses, routes, and people
March 10, 1913	Harriet Tubman, national heroine, dies at her home in Auburn, New York
1961	Larry Gara authors *The Liberty Line: The Legend of the Underground Railroad*, which recasts the Underground Railroad into the experience of the freedom seeker

May 4 to July 6, 1996	Anthony Goodman walks Maryland-to- Canada route of his freedom seeker ancestor. October 1996, *Smithsonian* article on walk sparks Underground Railroad interest
1998	Congress authorizes creation of Network to Freedom, an Underground Railroad program within the National Park Service
August 2004	The National Underground Railroad Freedom Center, a $110,000,000 museum on the Underground Railroad, opens in Cincinnati
September 17, 2004	Friends of the Underground Railroad, Inc., a private international organization promoting Underground Railroad history and restoration, is incorporated
January 2006	Bethesda, Maryland, cabin where Josiah Henson was enslaved and which lent itself to the title of *Uncle Tom's Cabin* saved from developers by public purchase
July 15, 2006	*Underground Railroad Free Press*, first independent news outlet, first publishes
2007	The National Underground Railroad Freedom Center launches extensive nationwide education programs for students, teachers, and the general public
July 15, 2007	Results of the first-ever survey of the international Underground Railroad community announced by *Underground Railroad Free Press*
September 2007	Friends of the Network to Freedom Association, a private-sector support group for the National Park Service's Network to Freedom program, is formed
2008	Congress authorizes funding for the National Museum of African-American History and Culture to include the federal government's second Underground Railroad program

January 15, 2008	*Underground Railroad Free Press* announces annual prizes for contemporary Underground Railroad leadership, preservation, and advancement of knowledge
September 15, 2008	*First Underground Railroad Free Press* Prizes awarded

Appendix E

COMMON PRODUCTS CONTAINING CORN

Acetic acid
Alcohol
Alpha tocopherol
Artificial flavorings
Artificial sweeteners
Ascorbates
Ascorbic acid
Astaxanthin
Baking powder
Barley malt
Bleached flour
Blended sugar
Brown sugar
Calcium citrate
Calcium fumarate
Calcium gluconate
Calcium lactate
Calcium magnesium acetate
Calcium stearate
Calcium stearoyl lactylate
Caramel and caramel color
Carbonmethylcellulose sodium
Cellulose microcrystalline
Cellulose, methyl
Cellulose, powdered
Cetearyl glucoside
Choline chloride
Citric acid
Citrus cloud emulsion
Coco glycerides
Confectioners' sugar
Corn alcohol, corn gluten
Corn extract
Corn flour
Corn oil
Corn oil margarine
Corn sweetener, corn sugar
Corn syrup
Corn syrup solids
Corn, popcorn, cornmeal

Crosscarmellose sodium
Crystalline dextrose
Crystalline fructose
Cyclodextrin
DATUM Decyl glucoside
Decyl polyglucose
Dextrin
Dextrose
Dextrose anything
Gluconic acid
Distilled white vinegar
Drying agent
Erythorbic acid
Erythritol
Ethanol
Ethocel 20
Ethylcellulose
Ethylene
Ethyl acetate
Ethyl alcohol
Ethyl lactate
Ethyl maltol
Fibersol-2
Flavorings
Food starch
Fructose
Fruit juice concentrate
Fumaric acid
Germ/germ meal
Gluconate
Gluconic acid
Glucono delta-lactone
Gluconolactone
Glucosamine
Glucose
Glucose syrup
Glutamate
Gluten
Gluten feed/meal
Glycerides
Glycerin
Glycerol
Golden syrup
Grits
High-fructose corn syrup
Hominy
Honey
Hydrolyzed corn
Hydrolyzed corn protein
Olestra/Olean
Polenta
Polydextrose
Polylactic acid
Polysorbates

Polyvinyl acetate
Potassium citrate
Potassium fumarate
Potassium gluconate
Powdered sugar
Pregelatinized starch
Propionic acid
Propylene glycol
Prop. glycol monostearate
Saccharin
Salt
Semolina
Simethicone
Sodium carboxymethylcellulose
Sodium citrate
Sodium erythorbate
Sodium fumarate
Sodium lactate
Sodium starch glycolate
Sodium stearoyl fumarate
Sorbate
Sorbic acid
Sorbitan
Sorbitan monooleate
Sorbitan tri-oleate
Sorbitol
Sorghum* (not all is bad; the syrup and / or grain *can* be mixed with corn)
Starch
Stearic acid
Stearoyls
Sucrose
Sugar
Threonine
Tocopherol
Treacle
Triethyl citrate
Unmodified starch
Vanilla, natural flavoring
Vanilla, pure or extract
Vanillin
Vinyl acetate
Vitamin C
Vitamin E
Vitamins
Xanthan gum
Xylitol
Yeast
Zea mays
Zein

Appendix F

KNOWN DENOMINATIONS OF CHRISTIANITY

Catholicism—1.2 billion

Catholic Church—1,147 million

Roman Catholic Church (Latin Rite)—1,125.5 million

Eastern Catholic Churches (Eastern Rite)—21.5 million

Alexandrian

Ethiopian Catholic Church—0.21 million

Coptic Catholic Church—0.17 million

Antiochian (Antiochene or West Syrian)

Maronite Catholic Church—3.1 million

Syro-Malankara Catholic Church—0.5 million

Syriac Catholic Church—0.17 million

Armenian

Armenian Catholic Church—0.54 million

Chaldean (Eastern Syrian)

Syro-Malabar Catholic Church—4.0 million

Chaldean Catholic Church—0.65 million

Byzantine (Constantinopolitan)

Ukrainian Greek Catholic Church—4.3 million

Melkite Greek Catholic Church—1.6 million

Romanian Church United with Rome, Greek-Catholic—0.8 million

Ruthenian Catholic Church—0.65 million

Slovak Greek Catholic Church—0.37 million

Hungarian Greek Catholic Church—0.27 million

Italo-Greek Catholic Church—0.07 million

Croatian Greek Catholic Church—0.06 million

Belarusian Greek Catholic Church—0.01 million

Bulgarian Greek Catholic Church—0.01 million
Georgian Byzantine Catholic Church—0.01 million
Macedonian Greek Catholic Church—0.01 million
Albanian Greek-Catholic Church—0.01 million
Greek Byzantine Catholic Church—0.01 million
Russian Catholic Church—0.01 million
Breakaway Catholic Churches—28 million
Apostolic Catholic Church—5 million
Chinese Patriotic Catholic Association—4 million
Philippine Independent Church—3 million
Brazilian Catholic Apostolic Church—1 million
Old Catholic Church—0.6 million
Mariavite Church—0.03 million

Protestantism—670 million

Historical Protestantism—350 million
Baptist Churches—105 million
Southern Baptist Convention—16.3 million
National Baptist Convention, USA, Inc.—7.5 million
National Baptist Convention of America, Inc.—5 million
Nigerian Baptist Convention—3 million
Progressive National Baptist Convention—2.5 million
American Baptist Churches USA—1.4 million
Brazilian Baptist Convention—1.4 million
Baptist Bible Fellowship International—1.2 million
Myanmar Baptist Convention—1.1 million
Baptist Community of the Congo River—1 million
National Baptist Convention, Brazil—1 million
National Primitive Baptist Convention of the USA—1 million
National Missionary Baptist Convention of America—1 million
Samavesam of Telugu Baptist Churches—0.8 million
Baptist Convention of Kenya—0.7 million
Union of Evangelical Christians-Baptists of Russia—0.6 million

Lutheranism—87 million

Evangelical Church in Germany—26.9 million
Church of Sweden—6.9 million

Evangelical Lutheran Church in America—4.8 million
Ethiopian Evangelical Church Mekane Yesus—4.7 million
Evangelical Lutheran Church in Tanzania—4.6 million
Danish National Church—4.5 million
Evangelical Lutheran Church of Finland—4.3 million
Batak Christian Protestant Church—4 million
Church of Norway—3.9 million
Malagasy Lutheran Church—3 million
Lutheran Church–Missouri Synod—2 million
Lutheran Church of Christ in Nigeria—1.7 million
United Evangelical Lutheran Church in India—1.5 million
Evangelical Lutheran Church in Papua New Guinea—0.9 million
Andhra Evangelical Lutheran Church—0.8 million
Evangelical Church of the Lutheran
Confession in Brazil—0.7 million
Evangelical Lutheran Church in Namibia—0.6 million
Evangelical Lutheran Church in Southern Africa—0.6 million

Methodism—75 million

United Methodist Church—12 million
African Methodist Episcopal Church—3 million
Methodist Church Nigeria—2 million
African Methodist Episcopal Zion Church—1.5 million
Church of the Nazarene—1.8 million
Methodist Church of Southern Africa—1.7 million
Korean Methodist Church—1.5 million
Christian Methodist Episcopal Church—0.9 million
Methodist Church Ghana—0.8 million
Free Methodist Church—0.7 million
Methodist Church in India—0.6 million

Reformed Churches—75 million

Church of Jesus Christ in Madagascar—3.5 million
United Church of Zambia—3.0 million
Protestant Church in the Netherlands—2.5 million
Swiss Reformed Church—2.4 million
Evangelical Church of Cameroon—2 million

Protestant Evangelical Church in Timor—2 million
Christian Evangelical Church in Minahasa—0.7 million
United Church in Papua New Guinea—0.6 million
United Church of Christ in the Philippines—0.6 million
Protestant Church in Western Indonesia—0.6 million
Evangelical Christian Church in Tanah Papua—0.6 million
Protestant Church in the Moluccas—0.6 million
Reformed Church in Hungary—0.6 million
Reformed Church in Romania—0.6 million
Uniting Reformed Church in Southern Africa—0.5 million

Presbyterianism

Presbyterian Church of East Africa—4 million
Presbyterian Church of Africa—3.4 million
Presbyterian Church (USA) —3.0 million
United Church of Canada—2.5 million
Church of Christ in Congo/
Presbyterian Community of Congo—2.5 million
Presbyterian Church of Korea—2.4 million
Presbyterian Church of Cameroon—1.8 million
Church of Scotland—1.1 million
Presbyterian Church of the Sudan—1 million
Presbyterian Church in Cameroon—0.7 million
Presbyterian Church of Ghana—0.6 million
Presbyterian Church of Nigeria—0.5 million
Uniting Presbyterian Church in Southern Africa—0.5 million

Congregationalism

United Church of Christ—1.2 million
Evangelical Congregational Church in Angola—0.9 million
United Congregational Church of Southern Africa—0.5 million
Anabaptism—5 million
Brethren—1.5 million
Mennonites—1.5 million
Plymouth Brethren—1 million
Moravians—0.7 million
Amish—0.2 million

Hutterites—0.2 million
Quakers—0.4 million
Waldensians—0.05 million

Modern Protestantism—588 million
Pentecostalism—130 million
Assemblies of God—60 million
New Apostolic Church—11 million
International Circle of Faith—11 million
The Pentecostal Mission—10 million
Church of God (Cleveland) —9 million
International Church of the Foursquare Gospel—8 million
Apostolic Church—6 million
Church of God in Christ—5.5 million
Christian Congregation of Brazil—2.5 million
Universal Church of the Kingdom of God—2 million
Church of God of Prophecy—1 million
God is Love Pentecostal Church—0.8 million
Indian Pentecostal Church of God—NA

Nondenominational Evangelicalism—80 million
Calvary Chapel—25 million
Born Again Movement—20 million
Association of Vineyard Churches—15 million
New Life Fellowship—10 million
True Jesus Church—2.5 million
Charismatic Episcopal Church—NA

African-Initiated Churches—40 million
Zion Christian Church—15 million
Eternal Sacred Order of Cherubim and Seraphim—10 million
Kimbanguist Church—5.5 million
Church of the Lord (Aladura) —3.6 million
Council of African Instituted Churches—3 million
Church of Christ Light of the Holy Spirit—1.4 million
African Church of the Holy Spirit—0.7 million
Seventh-Day Adventist Church—17 million

Restoration Movement—7 million
Churches of Christ—5 million
Christian Churches and Churches of Christ—1.1 million
Christian Church (Disciples of Christ)—0.7 million
Church of Christ/Community
of Disciples of Christ Congo—0.7 million

Eastern Orthodoxy—210 million
Autocephalous churches
Russian Orthodox Church—125 million
Romanian Orthodox Church—18 million
Serbian Orthodox Church—15 million
Orthodox Church of Greece—11 million
Bulgarian Orthodox Church—10 million
Georgian Orthodox and Apostolic Church—5 million
Greek Orthodox Church of Constantinople—3.5 million
Greek Orthodox Church of Antioch—2.5 million
Greek Orthodox Church of Alexandria—1.5 million
Orthodox Church in America—1.2 million
Polish Orthodox Church—1 million
Albanian Orthodox Church—0.8 million
Cypriot Orthodox Church—0.7 million
Greek Orthodox Church of Jerusalem—0.14 million
Czech and Slovak Orthodox Church—0.07 million
Autonomous churches
Ukrainian Orthodox Church (Moscow Patriarchate)—7.2 million
Moldovan Orthodox Church—3.2 million
Russian Orthodox Church outside Russia—1.25 million
Metropolitan Church of Bessarabia—0.62 million
Orthodox Ohrid Archbishopric—0.34 million
Estonian Orthodox Church—0.3 million
Patriarchal Exarchate in Western Europe—0.15 million
Finnish Orthodox Church—0.08 million
Chinese Orthodox Church—0.03 million
Japanese Orthodox Church—0.02 million
Latvian Orthodox Church—0.02 million
Churches in resistance/Not universally recognized churches

Ukrainian Orthodox Church (Kyiv Patriarchate)—5.5 million
Belarusian Autocephalous Orthodox Church—2.4 million
Macedonian Orthodox Church—2 million
Orthodox Church of Greece (Holy Synod in Resistance)—0.75 million
Old Calendar Romanian Orthodox Church—0.50 million
Old Calendar Bulgarian Orthodox Church—0.45 million
Croatian Orthodox Church—0.36 million
Montenegrin Orthodox Church—0.05 million
Orthodox Church in Italy—0.12 million
Churches that opted out
Ukrainian Autocephalous Orthodox Church—5.5 million
Old Believers—1.8 million
Greek Old Calendarists - 0.86 million
Russian True Orthodox Church—0.85 million

Oriental Orthodoxy—75 million
Autocephalous churches in communion
Ethiopian Orthodox Tewahedo Church—45 million
Coptic Orthodox Church of Alexandria—15.5 million
Syriac Orthodox Church—10 million
Armenian Orthodox Church—8 million
Eritrean Orthodox Tewahedo Church—2.5 million
Indian (Malankara) Orthodox Church—2 million
Armenian Orthodox Church of Cilicia—1.5 million
Autonomous churches in communion
Jacobite Syrian Orthodox Church—2.5 million
Armenian Patriarchate of Constantinople—0.42 million
Armenian Patriarchate of Jerusalem—0.34 million
French Coptic Orthodox Church—0.01 million
British Orthodox Church—0.01 million
Churches not in communion
Malabar Independent Syrian Church—0.06 million

Anglicanism
Anglican Communion—80 million
Church of Nigeria—18 million
Church of England—13.4 million

Church of Uganda—8.8 million
Church of South India—3.8 million
Anglican Church of Australia—3.7 million
Episcopal Church in the Philippines—3.0 million
Anglican Church in Aotearoa, New Zealand, and Polynesia—2.5 million
Anglican Church of Tanzania—2.5 million
Anglican Church of Southern Africa—2.4 million
Episcopal Church of the United States—2.2 million
Anglican Church of Canada—2.0 million
Anglican Church of Kenya—1.5 million
Church of North India—1.3 million
Church of the Province of Rwanda—1 million
Church of Pakistan—0.8 million
Anglican Church of Burundi—0.8 million
Church of the Province of Central Africa—0.6 million
Church of Christ in Congo / Anglican Community of Congo—0.5 million
Scottish Episcopal Church—0.4 million
Church of Ireland—0.4 million
Continuing Anglican Movement—1.5 million

Nontrinitarianism—

Latter-Day Saint Movement (Mormonism)—14 million
The Church of Jesus Christ of Latter-Day Saints—13.5 million
Jehovah's Witnesses—7.1 million
Iglesia ni Cristo—6 million
Oneness Pentecostalism—6 million
United Pentecostal Church International—4 million
Pentecostal Assemblies of the World—1.5 million
Church of Christ, Scientist—0.4 million
Community of Christ—0.25 million
Friends of Man—0.07 million
Christadelphians—0.05 million

Nestorianism

Assyrian Church of the East—0.5 million
Ancient Church of the East—0.3 million

Appendix G

VERSIONS OF THE BIBLE

Amharic Ebook Bible

Amuzgo de Guerrero

Arabic Ebook Bible

Arabic Life Application Bible

1940 Bulgarian Bible

Bulgarian Bible

Chinanteco de Comaltepec

Cebuano New Testament

Cakchiquel Occidental

Haitian Creole Version

Slovo na cestu

Dette er Biblen Dansk

Hoffnung für Alle

Luther Bibel 1545

21st Century King James Version

American Standard Version

Amplified Bible

Bible in Basic English

Contemporary English Version

Darby Translation

Douay-Rheims 1899 American Edition

English Standard Version

Good News Translation

Holman Christian Standard Bible

James Moffatt Translation (Moffatt Bible)

King James Version

New American Standard Bible

New Century Version

New English Translation

New International Reader's Version

New International Version

New International Version—UK

New King James Version

New Living Translation

New Revised Standard Version

New Testament in Modern English (Phillips Bible)

Revised Standard Version

The Message

Today's New International Version

World English Bible

Worldwide English (New Testament)

Wycliffe New Testament

Young's Literal Translation

Biblia en Lenguaje Sencillo

Castilian

Dios Habla Hoy

La Biblia de las Américas

Nueva Versión Internacional

Reina-Valera 1960

Reina-Valera 1995

Reina-Valera Antigua

Farsi Ebook Bible

Farsi New Testament

La Bible du Semeur

Louis Segond

1550 Stephanus New Testament

1881 Westcott-Hort New Testament

1894 Scrivener New Testament

The Westminster Leningrad Codex

Hiligaynon Bible

Hiligaynon Ebook Bible

Croatian Bible

Hungarian KÃ¡roli

Icelandic Bible

Conferenza Episcopale Italiana

La Nuova Diodati

La Parola è Vita

Japanese Ebook Bible

Jacalteco, Oriental

Kekchi

Korean Bible

Korean Living New Testament

Kurdish-Sorani Ebook Bible

Biblia Sacra Vulgata

Luo New Testament

Maori Bible

Macedonian New Testament

Malayalam Ebook Bible

Mam, Central

Mam de Todos Santos Chuchumatán

Reimer 2001

Náhuatl de Guerrero

Het Boek

Det Norsk Bibelselskap 1930

Levande Bibeln

Ndebele Ebook Bible

Oromo Bible

João Ferreira de Almeida Atualizada

Nova Versão Internacional

O Livro

Quiché, Centro Occidental

Romanian

Russian Ebook Bible

Russian Synodal Version

Slovo Zhizny

1979 Slovak Bible

Nádej pre kazdého

Albanian Bible

Levande Bibeln

Svenska 1917

Swahili New Testament

Thai Contemporary Bible

Ang Salita ng Diyos

Ukrainian Bible

Uspanteco

1934 Vietnamese Bible

Chinese Ebook Bible

Chinese Union Version (Simplified)

Chinese Union Version (Traditional)

Appendix H

WARS BY NUMBER OF DEATHS

60,000,000–72,000,000—World War II	(1939–1945)
36,000,000—An Shi Rebellion	(China, 755–763)
30,000,000–60,000,000—Mongol Conquests	(13th century)
25,000,000—Qing Dynasty Conquest of Ming Dynasty	(1616–1662)
20,000,000—World War I	(1914–1918)
20,000,000—Taiping Rebellion	(China, 1851–1864)
20,000,000—Second Sino-Japanese War	(1937–1945)
10,000,000—Warring States Era	(China, 475–221 BC)
7,000,000–20,000,000—Conquests of Tamerlane	(1360–1405)
5,000,000–9,000,000—Russian Civil War	(1917–1921)
5,000,000—Conquests of Menelik II of Ethiopia	(1882–1898)
3,800,000–5,400,000—Second Congo War	(1998–2007)
3,500,000–6,000,000—Napoleonic Wars	(1804–1815)
3,000,000–11,500,000—Thirty Years' War	(1618–1648)
3,000,000–7,000,000—Yellow Turban Rebellion	(China, 184–205)
2,500,000–3,500,000—Korean War	(1950–1953)
2,300,000–3,800,000—Vietnam War	(1945–1975)
300,000–1,300,000—First Indochina War	(1945–1954)
100,000–300,000—Vietnamese Civil War	(1954–1960)
1,750,000–2,100,000—Vietnam-American phase	(1960–1973)
170,000—Vietnam final phase	(1973–1975)
175,000–1,150,000—Secret War	(1962–1975)
2,000,000–4,000,000—Huguenot Wars	(1562-1598)
2,000,000—Shaka's Conquests	(1816–1828)

2,000,000—Mahmud of Ghazni's Invasions of India (1000–1027)
300,000–3,000,000—Bangladesh Liberation War (1971)
1,500,000–2,000,000—Afghan Civil War (1979–present)
1,000,000–1,500,000—Soviet Intervention (1979–1989)
1,300,000–6,100,000—Chinese Civil War (1928–1949)
300,000–3,100,000—Chinese Civil War (before 1937)
1,000,000–3,000,000—Chinese Civil War (after World War II)
1,000,000–2,000,000—Mexican Revolution (1910–1920)
1,000,000—Iran-Iraq War (1980–1988)
1,000,000—Japanese Invasions of Korea (1592–1598)
1,000,000—Second Sudanese Civil War (1983–2005)
1,000,000—Nigerian Civil War (1967–1970)
618,000–970,000—American Civil War (1861–1865)
900,000–1,000,000—Mozambique Civil War (1976–1993)
868,000–1,400,000—Seven Years' War (1756–1763)
800,000–1,000,000—Rwandan Civil War (1990–1994)
800,000—Congo Civil War (1991–1997)
600,000–1,300,000—First Jewish-Roman War (AD 66-73)
580,000—Bar Kokhba's Revolt (AD 132–135)
570,000—Eritrean War of Independence (1961–1991)
550,000—Somali Civil War (1991–present)
500,000–1,000,000—Spanish Civil War (1936–1939)
500,000—Angolan Civil War (1975–2002)
500,000—Ugandan Civil War (1979–1986)
400,000–1,000,000—War of Triple Alliance in Paraguay (1864–1870)
400,000—War of the Spanish Succession (1701–1714)
371,000—Continuation War (1941–1944)
350,000—Great Northern War (1700–1721)
315,000–735,000—Wars of the Three Kingdoms (1639–1651)
English campaign—40,000
Scottish campaign—73,000
Irish campaign—200,000–620,000
300,000—Russian-Circassian War (1763–1864)

300,000—First Burundi Civil War (1972)

300,000—Darfur Conflict (2003–present)

230,000–2,000,000—Eighty Years' War (1568–1648)

270,000–300,000—Crimean War (1854–1856)

234,000—Philippine-American War (1898–1913)

230,000–1,400,000—Ethiopian Civil War (1974–1991)

224,000—Balkan Wars, includes both wars (1912–1913)

220,000—Liberian Civil War (1989–present)

217,000–1,124,303—War on Terror (9/11/2001–present)

200,000–1,000,000—Albigensian Crusade (1208–1259)

200,000–800,000—Warlord Era in China (1917–1928)

200,000–400,000—Indonesian War of Independence (1946–1949)

200,000—Second Punic War (218–204 BC)

200,000—Sierra Leone Civil War (1991–2000)

200,000—Algerian Civil War (1991–present)

200,000—Guatemalan Civil War (1960–1996)

190,000—Franco-Prussian War (1870–1871)

180,000–300,000—La Violencia (1948–1958)

170,000—Greek War of Independence (1821–1829)

150,000—Lebanese Civil War (1975–1990)

150,000—North Yemen Civil War (1962–1970)

150,000—Russo-Japanese War (1904–1905)

148,000–1,000,000—Winter War (1939)

125,000—Eritrean-Ethiopian War (1998–2000)

120,000–384,000—Great Turkish War (1683–1699)

120,000—Third Servile War (73–71 BC)

117,000–500,000—Revolt in the Vendée (1793–1796)

103,359–1,136,920—Invasion and Occupation of Iraq (2003–present)

101,000–115,000—Arab-Israeli Conflict (1929–present)

100,500—Chaco War (1932–1935)

100,000–1,000,000—War of the Two Brothers (1531–1532)

100,000–400,000—Western New Guinea (1984–present)

100,000–200,000—Indonesian Invasion of East Timor (1975–1978)

100,000—Persian Gulf War (1991)
100,000–1,000,000—Algerian War of Independence (1954–1962)
100,000—Thousand Days War (1899–1901)
100,000—Peasants' War (1524–1525)
97,207—Bosnian War (1992–1995)
80,000—Third Punic War (149–146 BC)
75,000–200,000—Conquests of Alexander the Great (336–323 BC)
75,000—El Salvador Civil War (1980–1992)
75,000—Second Boer War (1898–1902)
70,000—Boudica's Uprising (AD 60–61)
69,000—Internal Conflict in Peru (1980–present)
60,000—Sri Lanka / Tamil Conflict (1983–2009)
60,000—Nicaraguan Rebellion (1972–1991)
55,000—War of the Pacific (1879–1885)
50,000–200,000—First Chechen War (1994–1996)
50,000–100,000—Tajikistan Civil War (1992–1997)
50,000—Wars of the Roses (1455–1485)
45,000—Greek Civil War (1945–1949)
41,000–100,000—Kashmiri Insurgency (1989–present)
36,000—Finnish Civil War (1918)
35,000–40,000—War of the Pacific (1879–1884)
35,000–45,000—Siege of Malta (1565)
30,000—Turkey / PKK Conflict (1984–present)
30,000—Sino-Vietnamese War (1979)
28,000—1982 Lebanon War (1982)
25,000—Second Chechen War (1999–present)
25,000—American Revolutionary War (1775–1783)
23,384—Indo-Pakistani War of 1971 (1971)
23,000—Nagorno-Karabakh War (1988–1994)
20,000–49,600—US Invasion of Afghanistan (2001–2002)
19,000+—Mexican-American War (1846–1848)
14,000+—Six-Day War (1967)
15,000–20,000—Croatian War of Independence (1991–1995)

11,053—Malayan Emergency	(1948–1960)
11,000—Spanish-American War	(1898)
10,000—Amadu's Jihad	(1810–1818)
10,000—Halabja Poison Gas Attack	(1988)
7,264–10,000—Indo-Pakistani War of 1965	(1965)
7,000–24,000—American War of 1812	(1812–1815)
7,000—Kosovo War	(1996–1999)
5,000—Turkish Invasion of Cyprus	(1974)
4,600—Sino-Indian War	(1962)
4,000—Waziristan War	(2004–2006)
4,000—Irish Civil War	(1922–1923)
3,500—The Troubles	(1969–1998)
3,000—Civil War in Côte d'Ivoire	(2002–2007)
2,899—New Zealand Land Wars	(1845–1872)
2,604–7,000—Indo-Pakistani War of 1947	(1947–1948)
2,000—Football War	(1969)
2,000—Irish War of Independence	(1919–1921)
1,975–4,500+—Israeli-Palestinian Conflict	(2000–present)
1,724—War of Lapland	(1945)
1,500—Romanian Revolution	(December 1989)
1,500—Lebanon War	(2006)
1,000—Zapatista Uprising in Chiapas	(1994)
907—Falklands War	(1982)
62—Slovenian Independence War	(1991)

Appendix I

WARS BY DATE

Kurukshetra War, based on warfare in the Kuru Kingdom of ancient India, ca. 3000–900 BC
Battle of Magh Ithe in Ireland ca. 2530 BC
Battle of Zhuolu, ca. 2500 BC
Border Wars between Umma and Lagash ca. 2500–2450 BC
Battle between Haik and Nimrod ca. 2492 BC
Conquest of Sumer by Lugalzagesi ca. 2330 BC
2300 BC: Conquests of Sargon of Akkad
Kassite attacks on Babylon ca. 1720 BC
1650–1600 BC: Conquests of Hattusili I and Mursili I
1600 BC: Hyksos Conquest of Egypt
1600 BC: Xia-Shang War in China
1430–1350 BC: Kaska Invasions of Hatti
Trojan War, based on events of ca. 1200 BC
1100 BC: Sea Peoples harrying the Mediterranean; Dorian Invasion
1046 BC: Shang-Zhou War in China
740–720 BC: First Messenian War
722–481 BC: Wars of the Chinese Spring and Autumn Period
710–650 BC: Lelantine War
701 BC: Sennacherib's Campaigns in the Near East
685–668 BC: Second Messenian War
595–585 BC: First Sacred War
499–448 BC: Persian Wars
499–494 BC: Ionian Revolt

492–490 BC: First Persian Invasion of Greece
480–479 BC: Second Persian Invasion of Greece
478–477 BC: Greek Counterattack
476–449 BC: Wars of the Delian League
475–221 BC: Wars of Warring States Period in China
464–455 BC: Third Messenian War
460–445 BC: First Peloponnesian War
449–448 BC: Second Sacred War
431–404 BC: Second Peloponnesian War
410–340 BC: Second Sicilian War
395–387 BC: Corinthian War
358–338 BC: Wars of the Rise of Macedon
357–355 BC: Social War
356–346 BC: Third Sacred War
343–290 BC: Samnite Wars between Rome and Samnium
343–341 BC: First Samnite War
327–304 BC: Second Samnite War
298–290 BC: Third Samnite War
334–323 BC: Wars of Alexander the Great
323–322 BC: Lamian War
323–280 BC: Wars of the Diadochi
315–307 BC: Third Sicilian War
274–200 BC: Syrian Wars
274–271 BC: First Syrian War
260 BC: Battle of Changping
260–255 BC: Second Syrian War
245–241 BC: Third Syrian War
219–217 BC: Fourth Syrian War
202–200 BC: Fifth Syrian War
267–261 BC: Chremonidean War
265–263 BC: Kalinga War
264–146 BC: Punic Wars between Rome and Carthage
264–241 BC: First Punic War

218–202 BC: Second Punic War
149–146 BC: Third Punic War
215–168 BC: Macedonian Wars
215–205 BC: First Macedonian War
200–196 BC: Second Macedonian War
171–168 BC: Third Macedonian War
209–88 BC: Parthian-Seleucid Wars
206–202 BC: Chu-Han Contention in China
191–188 BC: Roman-Syrian War
135–71 BC: Roman Servile Wars
135–132 BC: First Servile War
104–100 BC: Second Servile War
73–71 BC: Third Servile War or Spartacist Rebellion
133–89 BC: Sino-Xiongnu War
122–105 BC: Jugurthine War
113–101 BC: Cimbrian War
109–108 BC: Gojoseon-Han War
91–88 BC: Social War
89–63 BC: Mithridatic Wars
89–85 BC: First Mithridatic War
83–82 BC: Second Mithridatic War
74–63 BC: Third Mithridatic War
88–87 BC: Sulla's First Civil War
82–81 BC: Sulla's Second Civil War
58–50 BC: Julius Caesar's Gallic Wars
55–54 BC: Julius Caesar's Roman Invasion of Britain
53–51 BC: Parthian War of Marcus Licinius Crassus
49–45 BC: Caesar's Civil War
44–30 BC: Roman Civil War
44 BC: Post-Caesarian Civil War
44–42 BC: The Liberators' Civil War
44–36 BC: Sicilian Revolt
41–40 BC: Fulvia's Civil War

32–30 BC: Antony's Civil War
40–37 BC: Parthian Invasion on Syria and Asia Minor
36–33 BC: Marc Anthony's Invasion of Parthian Empire
34–22 BC: Chinese War
43: Aulus Plautius' Roman Occupation of Britain
58–63: Roman-Parthian War over Armenia
60–61: Boudica's Uprising
66–70: The First Jewish-Roman War
68: Year of the Four Emperors, Roman Civil War
101–106: Trajan's Dacian Wars
115–117: Trajan's Invasion on Parthian Empire
115–117: Second Jewish-Roman War
132–135: Third Jewish-Roman War (aka Bar Kokhba's Revolt)
161–166: Parthian War of Lucius Verus
166–180: Marcomannic Wars
184–205: Yellow Turban Rebellion in China
190–191: Campaign against Dong Zhuo in China—A War of the Three Kingdoms
193–199: Parthian War of Septimius Severus
194–199: Sun Ce's Conquest of Wu in China—A War of the Three Kingdoms
215–217: Parthian War of Caracalla
220–265: War of Three Kingdoms in China
228–234: Northern Expeditions of Zhuge Liang in China
247–262: Jiang Wei's Northern Expeditions in China—A War of the Three Kingdoms
272–274: Palmyrene War of Aurelian
291–306: War of the Eight Princes in China
316–589: Civil Wars in China triggered by Wu Hu Invasion,
lasted until 589 by Southern and Northern Dynasties
376–382: Gothic War in the Balkans
502–506: Anastasian War against the Persians
526–532: Iberian War between East Romans and Persians over Caucasian Iberia

527–528: Iwai Rebellion in Japan

533–534: Vandalic War in North Africa

534–547: Wars against the Moors in North Africa

535–553: Gothic War in Italy

541–562: Lazic War between East Romans and Persians over Lazica

572–591: Roman-Persian War

588: First Perso-Turkic War

588–589: Chen-Sui Wars in China

598–614: Goguryeo-Sui Wars in Korea

600–793: Frisian-Frankish Wars

613–628: Transition from Sui to Tang in China

619: Second Perso-Turkic War

627: Battle of Nineveh

630: Tang-Göktürks War

632–633: Ridda Wars

632–677: Byzantine-Arab Wars

633–651: Islamic Conquest of Sassanid Empire

634–635: Tang-Tuyuhun War

638: Battle of Songzhou, Tang-Tufan War

639–641: Islamic Conquest of Egypt

640–648: Tang-Xiyu States War

645–668: Goguryeo-Tang Wars in Korea

645–646: Tang-Xueyantuo Wars

656–661: First Islamic Civil War

650s–737: Khazar-Arab Wars

670–676: Silla-Tang War in Korea

663: Battle of Baekgang

672: Jinshin War

680–1355: Byzantine-Bulgarian Wars

711–718: Islamic Conquest of Hispania

715–718: Frankish Civil War

717–718: Siege of Constantinople by the Arabs

718–1492: Spanish Reconquista

732: Balhae Expedition to Tang China
721–737: Arab-Frankish Wars
751: Arab-Chinese War
756–763: An Shi Rebellion China
772–804: Saxon Wars
793–1066: Viking Raids across Europe
827–902: Arab Conquest of Sicily
868–883: Zanj Rebellion in southern Iraq
892–936: War of Later Three Kingdoms in Korea
894–970: Magyar Raids in Germany, France, Italy, and Byzantine
907–960: Chinese Civil War
927: Croatian-Bulgarian War
941: Siege of Constantinople by the Igor of Kyiv
977–978: War of the Three Henries
993: First Goryeo-Khitan War
999: Viking Civil War
1010: Second Goryeo-Khitan War
1014: The Battle of Clontarf, Ireland leading to the expulsion of the Vikings by Irish forces under King Brian Boru
1015–1016: Canute the Great's Conquest of England
1018: Kiev Expedition
1019: Toi Invasion
1019: Third Goryeo-Khitan War
1021–1042: Byzantine-Georgian Wars
1030: Ladejarl-Fairhair Succession Wars
1043–1044: Rus'-Byzantine War
1051–1063: Early Nine Years' War
1064–1308: Byzantine-Seljuk Wars
1066: Norman Conquest
1067–1068: War of the Three Sanchos
1081–1180: Restoration of the Byzantine Empire
1081–1492: Spanish Reconquista
1095–1291: The Crusades

1095–1099: First Crusade
1101: Crusade of 1101
1147–1149: Second Crusade
1187–1191: Third Crusade
1122–1127: Jurchen-Sung War
1147–1242: Northern Crusades Conflicts, distinct
from those of the Crusades
1159–1176: War of the Lombard League
1160–1184: Danish-Slavic Wars
1169: The English-backed Norman Invasion of Ireland
1170–1203: Khmer-Cham War
1180–1185: Genpei War
1185–1186: Vlach-Bulgarian Rebellion
1202–1204: Fourth Crusade
1209–1229: Albigensian Crusade
1212: Children's Crusade
1217–1221: Fifth Crusade
1228: Sixth Crusade
1248–1254: Seventh Crusade
1270: Eighth Crusade
1271–1291: Ninth Crusade
1208–1227: Estonian Crusade
1211–1276: Mongol Invasion of China
1213–1214: Angevin-Flanders War
1215–1217: First Barons' War
1218–1222: Mongol Invasion of Central Asia
1220–1264: The Age of the Sturlungs
1223–1480: Mongol Invasion of Rus
1223–1236: Mongol Invasion of Volga Bulgaria
1231–1273: Mongol Invasions of Korea
1240: Russo-Swedish War
1241–1242: Mongol Invasion of Europe
1242: Teutonic-Novogorod War

1260–1274: The Great Prussian Uprising

1262–1267: Berke-Hulagu War

1264–1267: Second Barons' War

1266–1268: French Conquest of Sicily

1274–1281: Mongol Invasion of Japan

1284–1302: War of the Sicilian Vespers

1287: Mongol Invasion of Poland

1288: Mongol Invasion of Vietnam

1296–1328: First War of Scottish Independence

1301–1453: Byzantine-Ottoman Wars

1302: French-Flemish War

1308: Teutonic takeover of Danzig (Gdańsk)

1315: Swiss War of Independence

1315–1318: Irish War of Independence

1321–1322: Kexholms War

1323–1328: Peasant Revolt in Flanders

1325–1330: Hungarian-Wallachian Wars

1326–1332: Polish-Teutonic War

1332–1333: Second War of Scottish Independence

1336–1392: Nanboku-chō Period

1337–1453: Hundred Years' War

1341–1364: Breton War of Succession

1358: Jacquerie Popular Revolt

1375–1378: War of the Eight Saints

1380: Muscovite-Mongol War

1383–1385: Crisis in Portugal

1385–1399: Tokhtamysh-Timur War

1386–1389: Ottoman-Serbian War

1386–1404: Timur's Invasions of Georgia

1400–1402: Ottoman-Timurid War

1405–1427: Chinese Conquest of Vietnam

1409–1410: Polish-Lithuanian-Teutonic War

1410 or 1411: Ming-Kotte War

1414: Hunger War
1422: Oei Invasion
1420–1436: Hussite Wars
1422: Ottoman Siege of Constantinople
1422: Gollub War
1425–1454: Wars in Lombardy
1431–1435: Polish-Teutonic War
1443–1468: Albanian Resistance against the invading Ottomans
1453: Fall of Constantinople
1454–1466: Thirteen Years' War
1455–1485: Wars of the Roses
1456: Ottoman Siege of Belgrade
1460–1462: Ottoman-Wallachian War
1467–1477: Ōnin War
1467–1603: Wars of Sengoku Period in Japan
1471: First Swedish-Danish War
1474–1477: Burgundian Wars of Duchy of Burgundy
and the Swiss Confederation
1478: War between the Principality of Moscow
and the Republic of Novgorod
1478–1479: War of the Priests
1480: Ottoman Siege of Rhodes
1482–1484: War of Ferrara
1494–1559: Italian Wars
1494–1498: Charles VIII's Italian War
1499–1500: Louis XII's War with Milan
1496–1499: First Russo-Swedish War
1499: Swabian War
1499–1503: Ottoman-Venetian War
1499–1503: Third Ottoman-Venetian War
1500–1504: Second Italian War
1500–1537: Muscovite-Lithuanian Wars
1508–1516: War of the League of Cambrai

1509: First Portuguese-Turkish War
1509–1512: Ottoman Civil War
1514–1516: Ottoman-Safavid War
1515: Slovenian Peasant Revolt
1516–1517: Ottoman-Mamluk War
1519–1521: Polish-Teutonic War
1520–1521: Spanish Conquest of Mexico
1520–1522: Uprising of the Comuneros in Castile
1521–1526: Italian War
1521–1523: The Swedish War of Liberation
1521–1526: Ottoman-Hungarian War
1522: Ottoman Conquest of Rhodes
1522: The Knights' War
1524–1525: The Peasants' War
1524–1697: Spanish Wars against the Mayas
1526–1528: Hungarian Civil War
1526–1555: Fourth Ottoman-Venetian War
1526–1576: Mughal Conquest of India
1526–1530: War of the League of Cognac
1528–1540: Campaigns of Ahmad ibn Ibrihim al-Ghazi
1529: First War of Kappel
1529: Siege of Vienna
1529–1532: Inca Civil War
1530–1552: Little War in Hungary
1531: Second War of Kappel
1532–1544: Spanish Conquest of Peru
1532–1546: Ottoman-Spanish Habsburg War in the Mediterranean
1532–1555: Ottoman-Persian War
1533–1536: The Counts' War in Denmark
1535–1538: Italian War of 1535
1538–1557: Second Portuguese-Turkish War
1542–1546: Italian War of 1542
1542–1543: Dacke War

1537–1544: Renewed Ottoman-Habsburg War in Hungary
1540: Russo-Kazan War
1546–1547: Schmalkaldic War
1548–1549: Burmo-Siamese War, Invasion of Ayutthaya
1551–1559: Italian War of 1551
1551–1562: Ottoman-Habsburg War in Hungary
1551–1581: Ottoman-Habsburg War in the Mediterranean
1552–1555: Charles V's War with Maurice of Saxony
1552: Conquest of Kazan
1554–1557: Second Russo-Swedish War
1558–1583: Livonian War
1559–1560: Scottish Rebellion against the French
1562–1598: Wars of Religion (aka War of the Three Henries or Huguenot Wars) in France
1562–1563: First War of Religion
1567–1568: Second War of Religion
1568–1570: Third War of Religion
1572–1573: Fourth War of Religion
1575–1576: Fifth War of Religion
1576–1577: Sixth War of Religion
1580: Seventh War of Religion (Lovers' War)
1585–1598: Eighth War of Religion
1589–1598: Franco-Spanish War
1562–1568: Ottoman-Habsburg War in Hungary
1563–1570: Northern Seven Years' War
1568–1571: Morisco Revolt in Spain
1568–1570: Russo-Turkish War
1568–1648: Eighty Years' War
1568–1609: First Phase
1588–1654: Dutch-Portuguese War
1621–1648: Second Phase
1569–1583: Desmond Wars in Munster, Ireland
1570–1573: Fifth Ottoman-Venetian War

1570–1871: Native Revolts against the Spanish Empire in the Philippines
1571: Russo-Crimean War
1573: Croatian and Slovenian Peasant Revolt
1577–1582: Livonian War
1578–1590: Ottoman-Persian War
1580–1583: Portuguese Civil War
1580–1589: Third Portuguese-Turkish War
1585–1604: Anglo-Spanish War
1590–1595: Fourth Russo-Swedish War
1592–1598: Japanese Invasions of Korea and China
1593–1606: "Long War" between the Habsburgs and the Turks
1593–1617: Moldavian Magnate Wars
1594–1603: Nine Years War in Ireland
1596–1597: Cudgel War in Finland
1600–1611: Polish-Swedish War
1603–1618: Ottoman-Safavid War
1605–1618: Russo-Polish War
1609: First Anglo-Powhatan War
1610–1617: Ingrian War
1611–1613: War of Kalmar
1620–1621: Polish-Ottoman War
1617–1629: Polish-Swedish Wars
1618–1648: Thirty Years' War
1618–1625: Bohemian/Palatine Phase
1618–1629: Austro-Transylvanian War
1625–1629: Danish Phase
1625–1630: Anglo-Spanish War
1626–1630: Anglo-French War
1627–1631: War of the Mantuan Succession
1630–1635: Swedish Phase
1635–1648: French Phase
1635–1659: Franco-Spanish War

1643–1645: The "Hannibal War"
1645: Renewed Austro-Transylvanian War
1620–1645: Manchu Conquest of China
1622–1890: Indian Wars
1623–1638: Turkish-Persian War
1625–1629: Huguenot Uprising in France
1627–1636: Manchu Invasion of Korea
1632–1634: Smolensk War
1633–1634: Polish-Turkish War
1634: Polish-Swedish War
1637: Pequot War
1639–1645: Kieft's War
1639–1652: Wars of the Three Kingdoms / British Civil Wars
1639: First Bishops' War
1640: Second Bishops' War
1641–1649: Irish Confederate Wars
1642–1646: First English Civil War
1644–1647: Wars of the Three Kingdoms in Scotland
1648: Second English Civil War
1649–1651: Third English Civil War
1649–1653: Cromwellian Conquest of Ireland
1650–1652: Cromwellian Conquest of Scotland
1651–1786: Three Hundred and Thirty Five Years' War
1640–1656: Catalan Revolt
1640–1668: Portuguese Restoration War
1641–1649: Wars of Castro
1644: Second Anglo-Powhatan War
1644–1674: Mauritanian Thirty Years War
1645–1669: Sixth Turkish-Venetian War Cretan War
1648–1653: The Fronde
1648–1649: First Fronde
1650–1653: Second Fronde
1654–1660: Second Northern War

1655–1656: Swedish-Polish War
1655–1656: Swedish-Brandenburgian War
1656–1658: Russo-Swedish War
1657–1658: Dano-Swedish War
1657–1660: Dutch-Swedish War
1658–1660: Dano-Swedish War
1654–1667: Russo-Polish War
1651–1986: Three Hundred and Thirty Five Years' War
Netherlands vs. Isles of Scilly
1652–1654: First Anglo-Dutch War
1652–1686: Russian-Manchu Border Conflicts
1654–1659: Anglo-Spanish War
1655–1660: Peach Tree War
1657–1662: Turkish-Transylvanian War
1662–1664: Austro-Turkish War
1665–1667: Second Anglo-Dutch War
1667–1668: War of Devolution
1670–1671: Stenka Razin Rebellion
1671–1676: Polish-Turkish War
1672–1678: Franco-Dutch War
1672–1674: Third Anglo-Dutch War
1675–1679: Scanian War
1673–1681: War of the Three Feudatories
1675–1677: King Philip's War
1676–1681: Russo-Turkish War
1681–1707: War of 27 Years between Mughals and the
Maratha Empire
1682–1699: War of the Holy League
1684–1699: Seventh Turkish-Venetian War
1683–1684: War of the Reunions
1685: Monmouth's Rebellion
1686–1700: Russo-Turkish War
1687–1689: Crimean Campaigns

1695–1696: Azov Campaigns

1688–1697: War of the Grand Alliance

1689–1697: King William's War, North American part of the War of the Grand Alliance

1689–1691: Williamite War in Ireland

1689–1691: Jacobite Rising in Scotland

1696: Chinese-Mongolian War

1699–1700: Darién War

1700–1721: Great Northern War

1701–1714: War of Spanish Succession

1702–1713: Queen Anne's War, the North American part of the War of Spanish Succession

1703–1711: Hungarian Revolt

1702–1715: Camisard Rebellion

1707–1709: Astrakhan Rebellion

1710–1711: Pruth Campaign

1711: Tuscarora War

1712–1714: First Fox War

1714–1718: Eighth Turkish-Venetian War

1715–1717: Yamasee War

1715–1716: First Jacobite Rising, "The Fifteen"

1716–1718: Austro-Turkish War

1718–1720: War of the Quadruple Alliance

1722: Dummer's War in Maine

1722–1723: Russo-Persian War

1722–1727: Turco-Persian War

1728–1737: Second Fox War

1730–1736: Turco-Persian War

1733–1738: War of the Polish Succession

1736–1739: Russo-Turkish War

1737–1739: Austro-Turkish War

1740–1748: War of the Austrian Succession

1739–1748: War of Jenkins' Ear

1740–1742: First Silesian War
1741–1743: Hats' Russian War
1744–1748: King George's War
1744–1745: Second Silesian War
1744–1748: First Carnatic War
1745–1746: Second Jacobite Rising, "The Forty-Five"
1740–1779: Revolt of the Comuneros
1743–1747: Turco-Persian War
1748–1754: Second Carnatic War
1756–1763: Seven Years' War
1754–1763: French and Indian War
1756–1763: Third Silesian War
1756–1763: Third Carnatic War
1759–1763: Anglo-Cherokee War
1761–1763: Spanish-Portuguese War
1763–1766: Pontiac's Rebellion
1766–1799: Anglo-Mysore Wars
1766–1769: First Anglo-Mysore War
1780–1784: Second Anglo-Mysore War
1789–1792: Third Anglo-Mysore War
1798–1799: Fourth Anglo-Mysore War
1768: Rebellion of 1768
1768–1774: Russo-Turkish War
1768–1776: War of the Confederation of Bar in Poland
1773–1774: Pugachev's Rebellion
1774–1783: First Anglo-Maratha War
1775–1783: American Revolutionary War or
American War of Independence
1778–1783: Anglo-French War
1779–1783: Anglo-Spanish War
1780–1784: Fourth Anglo-Dutch War
1776–1794: Chickamauga Wars
1776–1777: Second Cherokee War

1777–1779: War of the Bavarian Succession
1779–1879: Cape Frontier Wars
1779: First Cape Frontier War
1793: Second Cape Frontier War
1799–1801: Third Cape Frontier War
1811: Fourth Cape Frontier War
1818–1819: Fifth Cape Frontier War
1834–1836: Sixth Cape Frontier War
1846: Seventh Cape Frontier War
1851–1853: Eighth Cape Frontier War
1877–1878: Ninth Cape Frontier War
1785–1795: Northwest Indian War
1785–1787: Dutch Civil War
1787–1791: Austro-Turkish War
1787–1792: Russo-Turkish War
1788–1790: Gustav III's Russian War
1788: The Lingonberry War between Denmark-Norway and Sweden
1791–1804: Haitian Revolution
1792: War in Defense of the Constitution in Poland
1792–1802: French Revolutionary Wars
1792–1797: War of the First Coalition
1793–1796: Revolt in the Vendée
1798–1801: War of the Second Coalition
1794: Nickajack Expedition
1798–1800: Quasi-War
1794: Kościuszko Uprising in Poland
1795–1804: United Irishmen Revolt, see Irish Rebellion of 1798 against British rule in Ireland
1796: Persian Expedition of Catherine the Great
1810–1819: Colombian War of Independence/Spanish American Wars of Independence
1810–1818: Argentine War of Independence
1810–1811: Anglo-Dutch Java War

1810–1810: US Occupation of West Florida
1810–1817: Merina Conquest of Madagascar
1810–1820: Punjab War
1810–1826: Chilean War of Independence
1810–1818: Amadu's Jihad
1810–1813: Lamu Expansion
1810–1821: Mexican War of Independence
1811–1812: Fourth Xhosa War
1811–1811: Ga-Fante War
1811–1815: Arakanese Uprising
1811 -1811: Banda Oriental Occupation
1811–1812: Cambodian Rebellion Cambodian Usurpation
1811–1812: Korean Revolt
1811–1811: Paraguayan Revolt
1811–1812: Owu-Ife War
1811–1818: Ottoman-Saudi War
1811–1823: Venezuelan War of Independence
1812–1812: French Invasion of Russia / Napoleonic Wars
1812–1814: War of the Sixth Coalition / Napoleonic Wars
1812–1816: Second Barbary War
1813–1814: Creek War
1813–1813: Peoria War
1814–1814: Norwegian-Swedish War / Napoleonic Wars
1814–1816: The Gurkha War
1814–1816: Ashanti-Akim-Akwapim War
1814–1814: Hadži ProDon's Revolt / Serbian Revolution
1815–1817: Second Serbian Uprising / Serbian Revolution
1815–1816: Spanish Reconquest of New Granada
1815–1815: Second Kandyan War
1815–1815: Hundred Days War of the Seventh Coalition
1815–1815: Neapolitan War
1815–1815: Temne-Susu War
1817–1864: Caucasian War

1819–1820: Bolívar's Campaign to liberate New Granada
1819–1820: Ecuadorian War of Independence
1817–1818: Third Anglo-Maratha War
1817–1819: Ndwandwe-Zulu War
1817–1818: First Seminole War
1818–1819: Fifth Xhosa War
1818–1828: Zulu Wars of Conquest
1820–1823: Spanish Civil War
1820–1830: Greek War of Independence
1820–1823: Turko-Persian War
1821–1825: Brazilian War of Independence
1821–1837: Padri War
1822–1844: Haitian Invasion of the Spanish Haiti Republic
1823–1831: First Anglo-Ashanti War
1823–1826: First Anglo-Burmese War
1823–1825: Peruvian War of Independence
1825–1828: Russo-Persian War
1825–1828: Argentina–Brazil War
1825–1830: Java War
1825–1825: Franco-Trarzan War
1827–1827: Winnebago War
1828–1829: Gran Colombia-Peru War
1828–1834: Liberal Wars
1828–1829: Russo-Turkish War
1829–1829: Chilean Civil War
1830–1830: July French Revolution
1830–1831: November Uprising
1830–1831: Belgian Revolution
1830–1847: French Conquest of Algeria
1831–1834: First Siamese-Vietnamese War
1832–1832: Black Hawk War
1832–1833: First Turko-Egyptian War
1833–1840: First Carlist War

1834–1836: Sixth Xhosa War
1835–1836: Toledo War
1835–1836: Texas Revolution
1835–1842: Second Seminole War
1835–1845: War of the Farrapos
1836–1839: War of the Confederation
1837–1838: Lower Canada Rebellion
1838–1839: The Cherokee War
1838–1838: The Zulu-Boer War
1838–1838: Missouri Mormon War
1838–1839: Pastry War
1838–1839: Aroostook War
1839–1839: Honey War
1839–1842: First Anglo-Afghan War
1839–1842: First Opium War
1839–1851: Uruguayan Civil War
1840–1840: Texas-Comanche War
1841–1845: Second Siamese-Vietnamese War
1843–1843: Wairau AffGil
1843–1849: Dominican War of Independence
1844–1844: First Franco-Moroccan War
1845–1846: First Anglo-Sikh War
1845–1846: Flagstaff War
1845–1875: Texas-Indian Wars
1846–1864: Navajo Wars
1846–1846: Hutt Valley Campaign
1846–1847: Seventh Xhosa War
1846–1848: Second Carlist War
1846–1848: Mexican-American War
1847–1855: Cayuse War
1847–1847: Wanganui Campaign
1848–1852: Praieira Revolt
1848–1848: Revolutions of 1848 in the Italian states

1848–1848: Greater Poland Uprising
1848–1848: French Revolution
1848–1848: Revolutions in the German states
1848–1849: Revolutions of 1848 in the Habsburg areas
1848–1848: Wallachian Revolution of 1848
1848–1848: Sicilian Revolution of Independence of 1848
1848–1849: First Italian War of Independence
1848–1849: Second Anglo-Sikh War
1848–1849: Hungarian Revolution of 1848
1848–1851: First Schleswig War
1850–1865: California Indian Wars
1850–1864: Taiping Rebellion
1850–1853: Eighth Xhosa War
1851–1900: Apache Wars
1851–1852: Platine War
1852–1852: Second Burmese War
1853–1856: Crimean War
1854–1854: French Conquest of Senegal
1854–1860: Bleeding Kansas
1855–1858: Yakima War
1855–1856: Rogue River Wars
1855–1855: Battle of Ash Hollow
1855–1856: Puget Sound War
1855–1858: Third Seminole War
1856–1857: The National War in Nicaragua
1856–1860: Second Opium War
1856–1857: Anglo-Persian War
1856–1857: Cheyenne Expedition
1857–1858: Indian Mutiny
1857–1858: Utah War
1933 Caste War of Yucatán
1858–1860: Ecuadorian-Peruvian war
1858–1858: Spokane-Coeur d'Alene-Paloos War

1858–1858: Fraser Canyon War
1859–1859: Second Italian War of Independence
1859–1863: Federal War
1860–1873: Paiute War
1860–1861: First Taranaki War
1861–1883: Occupation of Araucanía
1861–1865: American Civil War
1861–1867: The Franco-Mexican War
1862–1862: Dakota War of 1862
1862–1877: Dungan revolt
1863–1863: Ecuadorian-Colombian War
1863–1865: Dominican Restoration War
1863–1863: Naval Battle of Shimonoseki
1863–1864: Bombardments of Shimonoseki
1863–1863: Bombardment of Kagoshima
1863–1865: January Uprising
1863–1866: Invasion of Waikato
1863–1866: Tauranga Campaign
1863–1865: Colorado War
1863–1864: Second Anglo-Ashanti War
1864–1865: Uruguayan War
1864–1865: Mito Rebellion
1864–1864: Hamaguri Rebellion and First Chōshū Expedition
1864–1864: Second Schleswig War
1864–1864: Tauranga Campaign
1864–1865: Bhutan War
1864–1868: Snake War
1864–1865: Russo-Kokandian War
1864–1870: War of the Triple Alliance
1864–1866: Chincha Islands War
1865–1865: Powder River Expedition of 1865
1865–1865: Morant Bay Rebellion
1865–1870: Hualapai War

1865–1868: Basuto-Boer War

1865–1866: Bukharan-Kokandian War

1865–1868: East Cape War

1865–1868: Russo-Bukharan Wars

1865–1865: Hyōgo Naval Expedition

1866–1866: Second Chōshū Expedition

1866–1866: Austro-Prussian War

1866–1868: Third Italian War of Independence

1866–1868: Red Cloud's War

1866–1866: French Campaign against Korea, 1866

1867–1875: Comanche Campaign

1867–1874: Klang War

1868–1869: Titokowaru's War

1868–1869: Boshin War

1868–1868: Expedition to Abyssinia

1868–1872: War of the Abyssinian Succession

1868–1872: Te Kooti's War

1868–1878: Ten Years' War

1869–1869: Haitian Revolution of 1869

1869–1869: Red River Rebellion

1870–1871: Franco-Prussian War

1872–1873: Modoc War

1873–1904: Aceh War

1873–1874: Third Anglo-Ashanti War

1874–1875: Red River War

1876–1877: Great Sioux War

1877–1877: Nez Perce War

1877–1877: Satsuma Rebellion

1877–1879: Ninth Xhosa War

1877–1878: Russo-Turkish War

1878–1878: Bannock War

1878–1878: Lincoln County War

1878–1879: Cheyenne War

1878–1880: Second Anglo-Afghan War
1879–1880: Little War (Cuba)
1879–1879: Anglo-Zulu War
1879–1884: War of the Pacific
1879–1879: Sheepeater Indian War
1880–1881: Basuto Gun War
1880–1881: First Boer War
1881–1881: French Occupation of Tunisia
1881–1899: Mahdist War
1883–1885: First Madagascar Expedition
1883–1886: Tonkin Campaign
1884–1885: Sino-French War
1885–1885: North-West Rebellion
1885–1885: Serbo-Bulgarian War
1885–1887: Third Anglo-Burmese War
1890–1890: Dog Tax War
1890–1890: First Franco-Dahomean War
1890–1891: Pine Ridge Campaign
1891–1891: Chilean Civil War
1892–1894: Second Franco-Dahomean War
1893–1893: Franco-Siamese War
1893–1894: First Rif War
1893–1894: First Matabele War
1894–1896: Fourth Anglo-Ashanti War
1894–1895: First Sino-Japanese War
1894–1895: Second Madagascar Expedition
1895–1896: First Italo-Ethiopian War
1895–1898: Cuban War of Independence
1895–1895: Japanese invasion of Taiwan
1896–1896: Anglo-Zanzibar War
1896–1898: Philippine Revolution
1896–1897: Second Matabele War
1897–1897: Greco-Turkish War

1897–1898: Anglo-Pathan War
1898–1898: Spanish-American War
1898–1900: Voulet-Chanoine Mission
1899–1901: Boxer Rebellion
1899–1902: Second Boer War
1899–1902: Thousand Days War
1913: Philippine-American War
1900–1900: War of the Golden Stool
1901–1902: Anglo-Aro War
1902–1925: War of Unification of Saudi Arabia
1903–1904: British Expedition to Tibet
1904–1905: Russo-Japanese War
1904–1909: Black Patch War
1905–1905: Russian Revolution
1906–1909: Pig War
1907–1907: Romanian Peasants' Revolt
1908–1909: Moroccan War
1908–1909: Persian Civil War
1909–1910: Second Rif War
1909–1911: Nicaraguan Civil War
1909–1911: Wadai War
1910–1921: Mexican Revolution
1911–1912: Second Franco-Moroccan War
1911–1912: Italo-Turkish War
1912–1913: First Balkan War
1912–1916: Contestado War
1912–1933: United States Occupation of Nicaragua
1913–1913: Second Balkan War
World War I
1914–1914: Tampico Affair
1914–1914: United States Occupation of Veracruz
1915–1934: United States Occupation of Haiti
1916–1924: United States Occupation of the Dominican Republic

1917–1917: Russian Revolution
1917–1923: Russian Civil War
1917–1918: Soviet-Turkish War
1917–1921: Ukrainian War of Independence
1918–1918: Battle of Bear Valley
1918–1918: Finnish Civil War
1918–1918: Georgian-Armenian War
1918–1919: German Revolution
1918–1919: Greater Poland Uprising
1918–1919: Polish-Ukrainian War
1918–1920: Georgian-Ossetian conflict
1918–1920: Armenian-Azerbaijani War
1918–1920: Estonian War of Independence
1918–1920: Latvian War of Independence
1918–1919: Lithuanian-Soviet War
1919–1919: Lithuanian War of Independence
1919–1919: Polish-Czechoslovak War
1919–1919: Hungarian-Romanian War
1919–1923: Turkish War of Independence
1919–1919: Third Anglo-Afghan War
1919–1919: Portuguese Monarchist Civil War
1919–1920: Italo-Yugoslav War
1919–1921: Polish-Soviet War
1919–1919: First Silesian Uprising
1919–1920: Hungarian Revolutionary War
1919–1921: Franco-Syrian War
1919–1921: Irish War of Independence
1919–1922: Greco-Turkish War
1920–1921: Franco-Turkish War
1920–1926: Third Rif War
1920–1920: Polish-Lithuanian War
1920–1920: Second Silesian Uprising
1920–1920: Turkish-Armenian War

1920–1920: Zhili-Anhui War
1920–1921: Guangdong-Guangxi War
1921–1921: Red Army Invasion of Georgia
1921–1921: Third Silesian Uprising
1921–1922: East Karelian Uprising
1922–1922: First Zhili-Fengtian War
1922–1923: Irish Civil War
1924–1924: August Uprising
1924–1924: Second Saud-Sharif War
1924–1924: Second Zhili-Fengtian War
1925–1925: Incident at Petrich
1926–1928: Northern Expedition
1926–1929: Cristero War
1927–1933: Nicaraguan Civil War
1927–1949: Chinese Civil War
1928–1929: Afghan Civil War
1929–1929: Sino-Soviet conflict
1929–1930: Igbo Women's War
1930–1930: Central Plains War
1931–1932: Japanese Invasion of Manchuria
1932–1932: Ecuadorian Civil War
1932–1932: Shanghai War
1932–1935: Chaco War
1932–1933: Colombia-Peru War
1934–1934: Austrian Civil War
1934–1934: Saudi-Yemeni War
1935–1936: Second Italo-Abyssinian War
1936–1939: Spanish Civil War
1937–1945: Second Sino-Japanese War
1938–1938: Changkufeng Incident
1939–1939: Hungarian Invasion of the Carpatho-Ukraine
1939–1939: Slovak-Hungarian War
1939–1939: Italian Invasion of Albania

1939–1939: Soviet-Japanese Border War
1939–1945: World War II
1939–1940: Winter War
1940–1941: Franco-Thai War
1941–1942: Ecuadorian-Peruvian War
1941–1941: Anglo-Iraqi War
1941–1944: Continuation War
1944–1945: Lapland War
1944–1953: Guerilla War in the Baltic States
1945–1949: Indonesian National Revolution
1946–1954: First Indochina War
1946–1949: Greek Civil War
1947–1947: Paraguayan Civil War
1947–1948: Indo-Pakistani War of 1947
1947–1948: Civil War in Mandatory Palestine
1948–1949: Arab-Israeli War
1948–1948: Costa Rican Civil War
1948–present: Internal Conflict in Burma/Myanmar
1948–1960: Malayan Emergency
1948–1948: Operation Polo
1950–1951: Invasion of Tibet
1952–1956: Tunisian War of Independence
1952–1960: Mau Mau Uprising
1953–1959: Cuban Revolution
1953–1975: Laotian Civil War
1954–1962: Algerian War
1955–1972: First Sudanese Civil War
1956–1956: Hungarian Revolution
1956–1957: Suez Crisis
1957–1958: Ifni War
1959–1975: Vietnam War
1959–present: ETA's Campaign of Terror
1964–1967: The War over Water

1965–1965: Dominican Civil War
1965–1966: United States Occupation of the Dominican Republic
1965–1965: Indo-Pakistani War
1965–1979: Civil War in Chad
1966–1989: South African Border War
1966–1988: Namibian War of Independence
1967–1967: Six-Day War
1967–1975: Cambodian Civil War
1967–1970: Nigerian Civil War
1967–1967: Chola Incident
1967–1970: War of Attrition
1968–1989: Communist Insurgency War
1968–1998: The Troubles
1968–1968: Warsaw Pact Invasion of Czechoslovakia
1969–present: Insurgency in the Philippines
1969–1969: Football War
1969–1969: Sino-Soviet border Conflict
1970–1971: Black September in Jordan
1971–1971: Bangladesh Liberation War
1971–1971: Indo-Pakistani War
1973–1973: Yom Kippur War
1973–1991: Western Sahara War
1974–1974: Turkish Invasion of Cyprus
1974–1991: Ethiopian Civil War
1975–2002: Angolan Civil War
1975–1990: Lebanese Civil War
1975–1989: Cambodian-Vietnamese War
1975–1975: Hmong Insurgency
1975–1975: Indonesian invasion of East Timor
1976–1983: Dirty War
1976–2005: Insurgency in Aceh
1977–1992: Mozambican Civil War
1977–1977: Libyan-Egyptian War

1977–1978: Ogaden War
1977–1977: Shaba I
1978–1978: Shaba II
1978–1978: South Lebanon conflict
1978–1979: Uganda-Tanzania War
1978–1987: Chadian-Libyan conflict
1978: Turkey-Kurdistan Workers' Party Conflict
1979–1979: Sino-Vietnamese War
1979–1982: Civil War in Chad
1979–1989: Soviet War in Afghanistan
1980–1992: Salvadoran Civil War
1980–2000: Internal Conflict in Peru
1980–1988: Iran-Iraq War
1981–1981: Paquisha War
1981–1986: Ugandan Bush War
1982–1982: Falklands War
1982–1982: Lebanon War
1982–2000: South Lebanon conflict
1982–1982: Ethiopian-Somali Border War
1983–1983: Invasion of Grenada
1983–2009: Sri Lankan Civil War
1983–2005: Second Sudanese Civil War
1985–1985: Agacher Strip War
1987–1991: First Intifada
1987–1988: Thai-Laotian Border War
1987–2009: Lord's Resistance Army Insurgency
1988–1994: Nagorno-Karabakh War
1989–1991: Mauritania-Senegal Border War
1989–1990: United States Invasion of Panama
1989–1992: Civil War in Afghanistan
1989–1989: Romanian Revolution
1989–1996: First Liberian Civil War
1989: Insurgency in Jammu and Kashmir

1990–1991: Gulf War
1990–1993: Rwandan Civil War
1990–1995: Tuareg Rebellion
1990–2006: Casamance Conflict
1991–1991: Ten-Day War
1991–1992: South Ossetia War
1991–1994: Djiboutian Civil War
1991–1995: Croatian War of Independence
1991–2002: Sierra Leone Civil War
1991–2002: Algerian Civil War
1991–present: Somali Civil War
1992–1996: Civil War in Afghanistan
1992–1992: War in Transnistria
1992–1993: War in Abkhazia
1992–1995: Bosnian War
1992–1997: Civil War in Tajikistan
1993–1993: Lebanon war
1993–2005: Burundi Civil War
1993: Ethnic Conflict in Nagaland
1994–1997: Iraqi-Kurdish Civil War
1994: Zapatista Rebellion
1994–1994: Civil War in Yemen
1994–1996: First Chechen War
1995–1995: Cenepa War
1995–1995: Hanish Islands Conflict
1995–2009: Insurgency in Ogaden
1996–1996: Lebanon War
1996–2006: Nepalese Civil War
1996–2001: Civil War in Afghanistan
1996–1997: First Congo War
1997–1997: Rebellion in Albania
1998–1998: War in Abkhazia
1998–2002: Civil War in Chad

1998–1999: Kosovo War

1998–2000: Eritrean-Ethiopian War

1998–2003: Second Congo War

1998–1998: Bombing of Iraq

1999–1999: Kargil War

1999–2001: Insurgency in the Preševo Valley

1999–2003: Second Liberian Civil War

1999–2007: Ituri Conflict

1999–1999: Invasion of Dagestan

1999–2009: Second Chechen War

2000–2008: Second Intifada

2001–2001: Indian-Bangladeshi border Conflict

2001–2001: Insurgency in the Republic of Macedonia

2001–present: War in Afghanistan

2002–2002: Operation Defensive Shield

2002–2007: Ivorian Civil War

2002–present: Insurgency in the Maghreb

2003–2009: War in Darfur

2003–2003: Invasion of Iraq

2003–present: Iraq War

2004–present: Balochistan Conflict

2004–present: War in North-West Pakistan

2004–2008: Iran-Party for a Free Life in Kurdistan Conflict

2004–2004: Haitian Rebellion

2004–2007: Central African Republic Bush War

2004–2004: Operation Rainbow

2004–2010: Sa'dah Insurgency

2004–present: Conflict in the Niger Delta

2004–present: South Thailand Insurgency

2004–2004: Operation Days of Penitence

2004–2004: French-Ivorian clashes

2004–2009: Kivu Conflict

2005–present: Civil War in Chad

2005–2008: Mount Elgon Insurgency
2006–present: Mexican Drug War
2006–2006: Israel-Gaza Conflict
2006–2006: Lebanon War
2006–2009: War in Somalia
2006–2009: Fatah-Hamas Conflict
2007–2009: Tuareg Rebellion
2007–2007: Lebanon Conflict
2007–present: Civil War in Ingushetia
2007–2008: Kenyan Crisis
2008–2008: Invasion of Anjouan
2008–2008: Conflict in Lebanon
2008–present: Cambodian-Thai Standoff
2008–2008: Djiboutian-Eritrea Conflict
2008–2008: South Ossetia War
2008–2009: Gaza War
2009–present: Sudanese Nomadic Conflicts
2009–present: Insurgency North Caucasus
2009–present: War in Somalia
2009–2009: Nigerian Sectarian Violence
2009–present: South Yemen Insurgency
2010–present: Yemeni Al-Qaeda crackdown

Appendix J

BIBLE VERSES related to miracles:

" . . . and if they drink anything deadly, it will by no means hurt them; they will lay hands on the sick, and they will recover." (Mark 16:15)

"Then He called His twelve disciples together and gave them power and authority over all demons, and to cure diseases." (Luke 9:1)

"And He called the twelve to Him, and began to send them out two by two, and gave them power over unclean spirits . . . And they cast out many demons, and anointed with oil many who were sick, and healed them." (Mark 6:7, 13)

"And when He had called His twelve disciples to Him, He gave them power over unclean spirits, to cast them out, and to heal all kinds of sickness and all kinds of disease." (Matthew 10:1)

"But go rather to the lost sheep of the house of Israel. And as you go, preach saying, 'The kingdom of heaven is at hand.' Heal the sick, cleanse the lepers, raise the dead, cast out demons. Freely you have received, freely give." (Matthew 10:6)

"Now God worked unusual miracles by the hands of Paul, so that even handkerchiefs or aprons were brought from his body to the sick, and the diseases left them and the evil spirits went out of them." (Acts 19:11)

"And it happened that the father of Publius lay sick of a fever and dysentery. Paul went in to him and prayed, and he laid hands on him and healed him." (Acts 28:8)

"And the multitudes with one accord heeded the things spoken by Philip, hearing and seeing the miracles which he did. For unclean spirits, crying with a loud voice, came out of many who were possessed; and many who were paralyzed and lame were healed." (Acts 8:6)

"Therefore they stayed there a long time, speaking boldly in the Lord, who was bearing witness to the word of His grace, granting signs and wonders to be done by their hands." (Acts 14:3)

"And I will give you the keys of the kingdom of heaven, and whatever you bind on earth will be bound in heaven, and whatever you loose on earth will be loosed in heaven." (Matthew 16:19)

"Now there are diversities of gifts, but the same Spirit. There are differences of ministries, but the same Lord. And there are diversities of activities, but it is the same God who works all in all. But the manifestation of the Spirit is given to each one for the profit of all: For to one is given the word of wisdom through the Spirit, to another the word of knowledge through the same Spirit, to another faith by the same Spirit, to another gifts of healings by the same Spirit, to another the working of miracles, to another prophecy, to another discerning of spirits, to another different kinds of tongues, to another the interpretation of tongues. But one and the same Spirit works all these things, distributing to each one individually as He wills." (1 Corinthians 12:4)

Appendix K

RABBINICAL PROCLAMATION Adar 5695
(February 1935)

WE HAVE OBSERVED the conditions prevailing in the general Jewish community, where some youth have left the haven of their faith and have assimilated with non-Jews; in certain cases they have made efforts to marry gentiles, sometimes without any effort to convert them, and other times an effort is made for conversion to our faith. This conversion type is absolutely invalid and worthless in the eyes of the law of our Torah. We have therefore bestirred ourselves to build and establish an iron wall to protect our identity and religious integrity and to bolster the strong foundations of our faith and religious purity which we have maintained for many centuries going back to our country of origin, Syria.

We, the undersigned rabbis, constituting the Religious Court, together with the Executive Committee of the Magen David Congregation and the outstanding laymen of the community, do hereby decree, with the authority of our Holy Torah, that no male or female member of our community has the right to intermarry with non-Jews; this law covers conversions, which we consider to be fictitious and valueless. We further decree that no future rabbinic court of the community should have the right or authority to convert male or female non-Jews who seek to marry into our community. We have followed the example of the community in Argentina, which maintains a rabbinic ban on any of the marital arrangements enumerated above, an edict which has received the wholehearted and unqualified endorsement of the Chief Rabbinate in Israel. This response is discussed in detail in *Devar Sha'ul, Yoreh Deah,* Part II to Part VI. In the event that any member of our community should ignore our ruling and marry, their issue will have to suffer the consequences. Announcements to this effect will be made advising the community not to allow any marriage with children of such converts. We are confident that the Jewish People are a holy people and they will adhere to the decision of their rabbis and will not conceive of doing otherwise.

Chief Rabbi Haim Tawil
Rabbi Jacob Kassin
Rabbi Murad Masalton
Rabbi Moshe Gindi
Rabbi Moshe Dweck Kassab

Appendix L

SUBSEQUENT CLARIFICATION OF THE ORIGINAL PROCLAMATION

ADAR 5706 (February 1946)—On the 9th day of Adar I in the year 5706 corresponding to the 10th day of February, 1946, the rabbis of the community and the Committee of Magen David Congregation once again discussed the question of intermarriage and conversions. The following religious rabbinic decisions were promulgated and accepted:

1. Our community will never accept any converts, male or female, for marriage.
2. The rabbi will not perform any religious ceremonies for such couples, i.e., marriages, circumcisions, bar mitzvahs, etc. In fact, the Congregation's premises will be barred to them for use of any religious or social nature.
3. The Mesadrim of the Congregation will not accord any honors to the convert or one married to a convert, such as offering an Aliyah to the Sefer Torah. In addition, the aforesaid person, male or female, will not be allowed to purchase a seat, permanently (If for the holidays, in our Congregations.)
4. After death of said person, he or she is not to be buried on the cemetery of our community, known as Rodfe Zedek, regardless of financial considerations. Seal of the Beth Din of Magen David Congregation

Chief Rabbi Jacob S. Kassin

REAFFIRMING OUR TRADITION

WHEREAS, throughout the history of our community, our rabbis and lay leaders have always recognized the threat of conversions and the danger of intermarriage and assimilation; and have issued warnings and proclamations concerning these evils in February 1935, February 1946 and in May 1972. NOW, THEREFORE, we assembled rabbis and Presidents of the congregations and organizations of the Syrian and Near Eastern Jewish communities of Greater New York and New Jersey do now and hereby reaffirm these proclamations, and pledge ourselves to uphold, enforce and promulgate these regulations. We further declare that Shabbat Shuvah of each year be designated as a day to urge our people to rededicate themselves to these principles. IN WITNESS WHEREOF, we have caused this document to he prepared and have affixed our signatures thereto, at a special convocation held on this third day of Sivan 5744 corresponding to the 3rd day of June, 1984.

Dr. Jacob S. Kassin, Chief Rabbi

The proclamation was signed by the rabbis and Presidents of every synagogue, yeshiva, and social organization of the Sephardic Jewish communities of New York and New Jersey.

What's True

EVEN THOUGH this book is a work of fiction, many facts are blended in; therefore many sources were referenced. In this book, as is done in creative nonfiction, all the key learning points are true and brought to life by fiction, but it may be helpful to confirm a few things:

- Haym Salomon, a Jew, funded the American Revolutionary War.
- Many Founding Fathers were not proponents of the Bible.
- John P. Holdren serves as advisor to President Barack Obama for Science and Technology, Director of the White House Office of Science and Technology Policy.
- There are indeed over 20,000 denominations of Christianity worldwide.
- The policies of non-intermarriage of Syrian Jews are real and in force today.
- There are now more than 1000 organized racial supremacy movements in the US.
- Easter came into practice hundreds of years after Jesus's death.
- Countries do have the requirement to protect their people under the UN's "R2P."
- The courageous stories of Rudolf Vrba, Araminta Ross, and others are true.
- E. coli is quickly becoming drug resistant.
- Our foods are somewhat toxic and the "tolerable" level is determined by the FDA.

- Dorothy Irvin is exposing through hard work what has been covered up for years about women and their role in the early Christian church.
- Jammu, India appears to be due east of Bethlehem, Israel.
- Churches and synagogues could act as safe houses to slaves under Bible rules.
- The King James Version of the Bible, in print since 1611, has an expired copyright.

What's Not True

- Lists in the book are mostly from Wikipedia; they are *mostly* reliable, but not perfect.
- The revenue figures related to Bible sales are pure fiction and admittedly shoddy math.
- All characters are fictional.

For more topical information, suggested reading lists, in-depth discussions, monthly webinars, and to find out how you can begin to bring change to your own faith community, please visit our website: www.progressplanet.com.

Endnotes

1. A Muslim prayer for peace and religious tolerance. (n.d.). Retrieved from http://www.religioustolerance.org/isl_peac.htm
2. Odinism - WikiPagan. (n.d.). Retrieved from http://pagan.wikia.com/wiki/Odinism
3. White supremacism: Reference (The Full Wiki). (n.d.). Retrieved from http://www.thefullwiki.org/White_supremacism
4. Stand Strong Against Racism / Change.org. (n.d.). Retrieved from http://www.change.org/petitions/view/stand_strong_against_racism
5. See Appendix B
6. BERA: Issue 3/4 The Sports Industry: Soccer (Business ... (n.d.). Retrieved from http://www.loc.gov/rr/business/BERA/issue3/soccer.html
7. Genocide in biblical and recent times. (n.d.). Retrieved from http://www.religioustolerance.org/god_cana.htm
8. Religiously motivated genocides, in biblical times and recently. (n.d.). Retrieved from http://www.religioustolerance.org/god_cana0.htm
9. Religiously motivated genocides, in biblical times and recently. (n.d.). Retrieved from http://www.religioustolerance.org/god_cana0.htm
10. Ideas and research attributed to Raymund Schwager, author, biblical expert, researcher, and contributor to the website www.religioustolerance.org

11. Hurricane Katrina - Wikipedia, the free encyclopedia. (n.d.). Retrieved from http://en.wikipedia.org/wiki/Hurricane_Katrina
12. Family Tree DNA - Geneographic Project. (n.d.). Retrieved from http://www.familytreedna.com/genographic-project.aspx
13. Retrieved from http://www.womenpriests.org/wow/chittist.asp
14. See Appendix C
15. http://zombietime.com/john_holdren/
16. http://zombietime.com/john_holdren/
17. See Appendix E
18. UK Eugenicists Demand We need a global initiative for... (n.d.). Retrieved from http://www.roguegovernment.com/index.php?news_id=21672
19. The Futurequake Radio blog: Our science czar wants to kill us... (n.d.). Retrieved from http://futurequakeradio.blogspot.com/2009/07/our-science-czar-wants-to-kill-userr-at.html
20. PolitiFact | Glenn Beck claims science czar John Holdren... (n.d.). Retrieved from http://politifact.com/truth-o-meter/statements/2009/jul/29/glenn-beck/glenn-beck-claims-science-czar-john-holdren-propos/
21. From The John Holdren Book "Mass sterilization of humans... (n.d.). Retrieved from http://aconservativeedge.com/2009/07/16/from-the-john-holdren-book-mass-sterilization-of-humans-though-drugs-in-the-water-supply-is-ok-as-long-as-it-doesn%E2%80%99t-harm-livestock-oh-and-it-gets-much-much-worse-in-the-new-obamanation/
22. What the New Testament says about slavery. (n.d.). Retrieved from http://www.religioustolerance.org/sla_bibl2.htm
23. King James Bible (KJV) - Ephesians 6. (n.d.). Retrieved from http://www.godrules.net/library/kjv/kjveph6.htm
24. What the New Testament says about slavery. (n.d.). Retrieved from http://www.religioustolerance.org/sla_bibl2.htm

25. MLA: "oremus Bible Browser." N.p., n.d. Web. 6 July 2010 <http://bible.oremus.org/?ql=102056690>
26. The Underground Railroad :: The National Underground Railroad... (n.d.). Retrieved from http://freedomcenter.org/underground-railroad/
27. Slavery Today: Human Traficking :: National Underground... (n.d.). Retrieved from http://www.freedomcenter.org/slavery-today/
28. Trokosi: Opportunity to Abuse... | Feature Article 2008-02-23. (n.d.). Retrieved from http://www.ghanaweb.com/GhanaHomePage/features/artikel.php?ID=139525
29. Trokosi: Opportunity to Abuse... | Feature Article 2008-02-23. (n.d.). Retrieved from http://www.ghanaweb.com/GhanaHomePage/features/artikel.php?ID=139525
30. See Appendix D
31. The English translation of the Hebrew proclamations of 1935 and 1946, as well as the text of the 1984 proclamation.
32. See Appendix K
33. See Appendix L
34. Amazon associate brings together books on Christianity and... (n.d.). Retrieved from http://jesuslivedinindia.com/
35. Indian Jews - Wikipedia, the free encyclopedia. (n.d.). Retrieved from http://en.wikipedia.org/wiki/Indian_Jews
36. http://www.infidels.org/library/modern/jim_meritt/bible-contradictions.html
37. http://www.bringyou.to/apologetics/bible.htm
38. http://www.islamway.com/english/images/library/contradictions.htm
39. http://www.christiananswers.net/menu-at1.html
40. Raid on Deerfield - Wikipedia, the free encyclopedia. (n.d.). Retrieved from http://en.wikipedia.org/wiki/Raid_on_Deerfield

41. Fishermen's Voice Monthly Newspaper, Gouldsboro Maine. (n.d.). Retrieved from http://www.fishermensvoice.com/archives/witchindians.html

42. See Appendix A

43. http://pewforum.org/Faith-in-Flux.aspx

44. http://www.mfa.gov.il/MFA/Archive/Speeches/FM PERES IN THE KNESSET ON ASSIMILATION AND ISRAEL

45. http://www.nytimes.com/2009/07/15/books/15ebooks.html

46. See Appendix F

47. Ten translations of the Bible are available completely free of charge in their current forms from the site www.e-sword.net.

48. http://www.biblegateway.com/versions/New-International-Version-NIV-Bible/

49. See Appendix G

50. http://www.answers.com/topic/bible

51. http://en.wikipedia.org/wiki/Religious_war

52. http://en.wikipedia.org/wiki/Religious_war

53. See Appendix H

54. See Appendix I

55. See Appendix J

56. APA: Constantine I and Christianity - Wikipedia, the free encyclopedia. (n.d.). Retrieved from http://en.wikipedia.org/wiki/Constantine_I_and_Christianity

57. http://www.ekklesia.co.uk/node/11704